Buffy the Vampire Slayer™

The Script Book
Season One, Volume One

POCKET BOOKS
New York   London   Toronto   Sydney   Singapore

Historian's Note: These teleplays represent the original shooting scripts for each episode; thus we have preserved all typos and mis-attributions. The scripts may include dialogue or even full scenes that were not in the final broadcast version of the show because they were cut due to length. Also, there may be elements in the broadcast that were added at a later date.

An *Original* Publication of POCKET BOOKS

 POCKET BOOKS, a division of Simon & Schuster, Inc.
1230 Avenue of the Americas, New York, NY 10020

™ and © 1997, 2000 by Twentieth Century Fox Film Corporation. All rights reserved.

ISBN:0-7434-1934-0

First Pocket Books trade paperback printing December 2000

10 9 8 7 6 5 4

POCKET and colophon are registered trademarks of Simon & Schuster, Inc.

Printed in the U.S.A.

For orders other than by individual consumers, Pocket Books grants a discount on the purchase of **10 or more** copies of single titles for special markets or premium use. For further details, please write to the Vice President of Special Markets, Pocket Books, 1230 Avenue of the Americas, 9th Floor, New York, NY 10020-1586.

For information on how individual consumers can place orders, please write to Mail Order Department, Simon & Schuster, Inc., 100 Front Street, Riverside, NJ 08075.

<u>BUFFY THE VAMPIRE SLAYER</u>

"Welcome to the Hellmouth"

Written by

Joss Whedon

Directed by

Charles Martin Smith

<u>SHOOTING SCRIPT</u>

August 26, 1996
September 4, 1996 - BLUE
September 5, 1996 - PINK
September 5, 1996 - GREEN
September 6, 1996 - YELLOW
September 10, 1996 - GOLDENROD
January 17, 1997 - SALMON

BUFFY THE VAMPIRE SLAYER

"Welcome to the Hellmouth"

CAST LIST

BUFFY SUMMERS............................	Sarah Michelle Gellar
XANDER...................................	Nicholas Brendon
GILES....................................	Anthony S. Head
WILLOW...................................	Alyson Hannigan
CORDELIA.................................	Charisma Carpenter
MR. FLUTIE...............................	*Ken Lerner
JESSE....................................	*Eric Balfour
THE MASTER...............................	*Mark Metcalf
ANGEL....................................	*David Boreanaz
LUKE.....................................	*Brian Thompson
VAMPIRE BOY..............................	*Patrick Lawlor
DARLA....................................	*Julie Benz
JOYCE SUMMERS............................	*Kristine Sutherland
BOY......................................	*Carmine D. Giovinazzo
TEACHER..................................	*Natalie Strauss
GIRL #1..................................	*Amy Chance
GIRL #2..................................	
GIRL #3..................................	*Persia White
THE BAND.................................	Sprung Monkey

BUFFY THE VAMPIRE SLAYER

"Welcome to the Hellmouth"

<u>SET LIST</u>

<u>INTERIORS</u>

SUNNYDALE HIGH SCHOOL
      HALL
      CLASSROOM
      BOB FLUTIE'S OFFICE
      HISTORY CLASS
      THE LIBRARY
      WOMEN'S LOCKER ROOM
      HALLWAY OUTSIDE LOCKER ROOM
BUFFY'S BEDROOM
THE CHURCH
      DARK PLACE
THE BRONZE
      BACKSTAGE
MAUSOLEUM

<u>EXTERIORS</u>

SUNNYDALE HIGH SCHOOL
      FOUNTAIN QUAD
      SIDE OF GYM
AN ALLEY
STREET
ANOTHER STREET
THE BRONZE
STREET BY WOODED GLADE
GRAVEYARD
MAUSOLEUM
THE FOREST

BUFFY THE VAMPIRE SLAYER

"Welcome to the Hellmouth"

TEASER

FADE IN:

1   EXT.   SUNNYDALE HIGH SCHOOL - NIGHT   1

The front of the affluent Southern California school gleams
darkly in the moonlight.

                                                    CUT TO:

2   INT.   HALL - CONTINUOUS   2

TRACK through the hall. Nothing.

                                                    CUT TO:

3   INT.   CLASSROOM - CONTINUOUS   3

Silent.

We track along the wall, past the maps and drawings tacked
up on it, past the window, which SHATTERS in our faces!

It's just a single pane, knocked-in by someone's hand. It
unlocks the window and slides it up.

The intruder is a college age BOY, a timid GIRL beside him.
She looks about nervously.

                         GIRL
                Are you sure this is a good idea?

                         BOY
                It's a great idea! Come on.

As they climb in.   *

                                                    CUT TO: *

4   INT.   HALL - A MOMENT LATER   4*

He leads her out here. It's even darker than the classroom.

                         GIRL
                You go to school here?

                         BOY
                Used to.   *

4 CONTINUED: 4

                                                                            *

                                                                            *

                                                                            *

                          BOY
               On top of the gym, it's so cool --
               you can see the whole town.

                          GIRL
               I don't want to go up there.

                          BOY
               Oh, you can't wait, huh?

He moves to kiss her.

                          GIRL
               We're just gonna get in trouble.

                          BOY
               Count on it.

He kisses her, but she turns suddenly, real fear crossing
her face.

                          GIRL
               What was that?

                          BOY
               What was what?

                          GIRL
               I heard a noise.

                          BOY
               It's nothing.

                          GIRL
               Maybe it's something...

                          BOY
               Maybe it's some **Thing**...

                          GIRL
               That's not funny.

He looks about them. The place is dark, shadowy. She
cowers behind him.

                                              (CONTINUED)

4   CONTINUED: 2   4

                         BOY
              Hello...?
Silence.

                         BOY
              There's nobody here.

                         GIRL
              Are you sure?

                         BOY
              I'm sure.

                         GIRL
              Okay...

She bares HORRIBLE FANGS and BURIES them in his neck.

BLACKOUT.

                    END OF TEASER

CREDITS.

ACT ONE

5   INT. MASTER'S LAIR (THE DREAM)   5*

    ANGLE: BUFFY   *

    walks through the lair, looking around. Confused, lost.   *

5A OMITTED   5A*

5B OMITTED   5B*

5C ANGLE: A GIRL IN BED   5C

    tossing and turning, as the camera moves down to reveal the
    shadow of someone -- something -- approaching her -- and we
    hear an impossibly low voice.

                        VOICE (O.S.)
              I'll take you... like a cancer...
              I'll get inside you and eat my way
              out..

5D INT. MASTER'S LAIR   5D*

    CLOSE-UP of The Master   *

    as he rises up behind Buffy, ROARING.   *

                                                    CUT TO:

6   INT. BUFFY'S BEDROOM - MORNING   6

Her eyes snap open. Despite the morning light, we recognize
the girl -- and the bed -- from the dream. A moment, as she
gets her bearings, shaking off the immediacy of the dream.

                    BUFFY'S MOM (O.S.)   *
          Buffy...

                    BUFFY
          I'm up, mom.

                    BUFFY'S MOM (O.S.)
          Don't want to be late for your
          first day.

                    BUFFY
               (to herself)
          No... wouldn't want that...

Her voice betrays her uncertainty. She sits up. A wider
angle on her room reveals that it's only half decorated:
there are still boxes as yet unpacked in the corner.

                                        CUT TO:

7   EXT. SUNNYDALE HIGH SCHOOL - MORNING   7

A day as bright and colorful as the night was black and
eerie. Students pour in before first bell, talking,
laughing. They could be from anywhere in America, but for
the extremity of their dress and the esoteric mania of their
slang. This is definitely So Cal.

ANGLE: A CAR

pulls up outside the school. Buffy's mom, JOYCE, is   *
driving. Buffy gets out the passenger side.

                    JOYCE
          Now, you have a good time. I know
          you'll make friends right away.
          Think positive. And honey... try   *
          not to get kicked out.

                    BUFFY
          I promise.

The girl turns, looks at the school. She starts in as her
mother drives away.

ANGLE: A SKATEBOARD

Weaving along the road. On it is XANDER, dressed with the
shaggy indifference common to skateboarders.

                                        (CONTINUED)

7   CONTINUED: 7

He is bright, funny, and will one day be suave and handsome.
Till that day arrives, he'll do the best he can with bright
and funny.

He weaves through a thickening mass of students toward the
school.

                        XANDER
              Coming through... Coming through...
                   (as the crowd increases)
              Not certain how to stop...

But he's doing okay until he passes Buffy -- intrigued by
the new face, he cranes to look at her, and nearly takes a
header. He saves himself from falling, however, coming to a
stop just in front of:

WILLOW. She is shy, bookish, and very possibly dressed by
her mother. The intelligence in her eyes and the sweetness
of her smile belie a genuine charm that is lost on the
unsubtle high school mind. It's certainly lost on Xander,
though he brightens considerably to see her. The new face
forgotten, at least for now.

                        XANDER
              Willow! You're so very much the
              person I wanted to see.

Her excitement at the sentiment is sweetly pathetic, and
typically unnoticed.

                        WILLOW
              Really?

                        XANDER
              Yeah. You know, I kind of had a
              problem with the math.

                        WILLOW
                   (hiding disappointment)
              Which part?

                        XANDER
              The math. Can you help me tonight?
              Please? Be my study buddy?

                        WILLOW
              Well, what's in it for me?

                        XANDER
              A shiny nickel...   *

                                                                    *

7   CONTINUED: 2   7

                         WILLOW
              Okay. Do you have "Theories in
              Trig?" You should check it out.

                         XANDER
              Check it out?

                         WILLOW
              From the library. Where the books
              live.

                         XANDER
              Right. I'm there. See, I **want**
              to change.

8   INT. SCHOOL HALL - CONTINUOUS   8

They are approached by JESSE, their bud. He is a little
more awkward than Xander, a little less likely to become a
lady killer in his later years.

                         JESSE
              Hey.

                         XANDER
              Jesse! What's what.

                         JESSE
              New girl!

                         XANDER
              That's right, I saw her. She's
              pretty much a hotty.

                         WILLOW
              I heard someone was transferring
              here.

                         XANDER
              So. Tell.

                         JESSE
              Tell what?

                         XANDER
              What's the sitch? What do you know
              about her?

                         JESSE
                ("that's all")   *
              New girl.

                         XANDER
              Well, you're certainly a font of   *
              nothing.

                              11

*

*

*

*

*

*

                                        CUT TO:

9   INT.   BOB FLUTIE'S OFFICE - CONTINUOUS   9

Buffy sits before principal FLUTIE. He is middle aged, a
tad officious. Caught between the old school of strict
discipline and the new school of sensitivity.

He pulls her transcript from a folder. He looks at it,
looks at her.

                    MR. FLUTIE
          Buffy Summers. Sophomore, late of
          Hemery High in Los Angeles.
          Interesting record. Quite a
          career.

He smiles, and carefully tears her transcript up into four
pieces.

                    MR. FLUTIE
          Welcome to Sunnydale. A clean
          slate, Buffy, that's what you get
          here. What's past is past. We're
          not interested in what it says on a
          piece of paper.
                    (MORE)

                                        (CONTINUED)

                    MR. FLUTIE (CONT'D)
          Even if it says
                (looks down at a piece,
                 reacts:)
          -- whoa. At Sunnydale we nurture
          the whole student. The inner
          student.

He is taking the pieces of the transcript as he talks and
carefully placing them together again.

                    MR. FLUTIE
          Other schools might look at the
          incredible decline in grade point
          average -- we look at the
          struggling young **woman** with the
          incredible decline in grade point
          average. Other schools might look
          at the reports of gang fights --

                    BUFFY
          Mr. Flutie --

                    MR. FLUTIE
          All the kids here are free to call
          me Bob --

                    BUFFY
          Bob --

                    MR. FLUTIE
          -- but they don't.

He pulls out a piece of tape, starts taping the transcript back
together.

                    BUFFY
          Mr. Flutie. I know my transcripts
          are a little colorful --

                    MR. FLUTIE
          Hey, we're not caring about that!
          Do you think "colorful" is the
          word? Not "dismal"? Just off
          hand, I'd go with "dismal."

                    BUFFY
          It wasn't that bad.

                    MR. FLUTIE
          You burned down the gym.

                                        (CONTINUED)

9   CONTINUED: 2   9

                         BUFFY
               I did. I really did. But you
               gotta see the big picture. I mean
               the gym was full of vamp... uh,
               asbestos.

                         MR. FLUTIE
               Buffy. Don't worry. Any other
               school, they might say "watch your
               step", or, "we'll be watching you"
               or, "get within a hundred yards of
               the gym with a book of matches and
               you'll grow up in juvie hall" but
               that's just not the way here. We
               want to service your needs, and
               help you to respect our needs. And
               if your needs and our needs don't
               mesh...

Still smiling blandly, he slips the taped up transcript back in
her folder.

                                                    CUT TO:

10   INT. HALL - A MOMENT LATER   10

Buffy exits the office, looking a bit depressed. She starts
rummaging through her bag and a student runs by, bumps into
her. Her books and stuff spill out. Frustrated, she kneels
down, starts scooping it back in.

Xander sees this, goes up to her, kneeling.

                         XANDER
               Can I have you? Dyeh -- can I help
               you?

                         BUFFY
               Oh, thanks...

He starts picking things up, handing them to her.

                         XANDER
               I don't know you, do I?

                         BUFFY
               I'm new. I'm Buffy.

                         XANDER
               Xander. Is me. Hi.

                         BUFFY
               Thanks.

                                                    (CONTINUED)

10 CONTINUED: 10

                         XANDER
                    Maybe I'll see you around. Maybe
                    at school, since we both... go
                    there...

                         BUFFY
                    Great. Nice to meet you.

He gives her the rest of her books. She stuffs it all in
her bag and hurries away.

                         XANDER
                    "We both go to school..." Very suave. Very not
                    pathetic.

He notices something on the floor, bends down to get it. Calls
after her:

                         XANDER
                    Oh, hey, you forgot your...
                         (looks at the thing in
                          his hand)
                    ...stake...

But she's too far off to hear. He looks at the wooden
stake, puzzled.

                                                       CUT TO:

11 INT. HISTORY CLASS - MORNING   11

THE TEACHER is in front, lecturing. We hear her mostly in
voice over as we see Buffy near the back, earnestly taking
notes. Trying to keep up.

                         TEACHER
                    It's estimated that about 25
                    million people died in that one
                    four year span. But the fun part
                    of the Black Plague is that it
                    originated in Europe how? As an
                    early form of germ warfare. The
                    plague was first found in Asia, and
                    a Kipchak army actually catapulted
                    plague-infested corpses into a
                    Genoese trading post. Ingenious.
                    If you look at the map on page 63
                    you can trace the spread of the
                    disease...

Buffy looks about as kids open their books -- She hasn't got
one. The girl next to her, CORDELIA, leans over. She is
pretty, self assured. Killer outfit.

                                                       (CONTINUED)

11 CONTINUED: 11

                              CORDELIA
                    Here.

She moves her book over so Buffy can read off it as well.

                              BUFFY
                    Thanks.

                              TEACHER
                    And this popular plague led to what
                    social changes?

                                                      CUT TO:

12 INT.   SAME - END OF CLASS   12

    Kids are piling up their books and leaving as the bell
    RINGS. Cordelia introduces herself:

                              CORDELIA
                    Hi, I'm Cordelia.

                              BUFFY
                    I'm Buffy.

                              CORDELIA
                    If you're looking for a textbook of
                    your very own, there's probably a
                    few in the Library.

                              BUFFY
                    Oh, great. Thanks. Where would
                    that be?

                              CORDELIA
                    I'll show you.

                                                                  *

                                                                  *

    As the girls walk through the crowded hall.

                              CORDELIA
                    You transferred from Hemery, right?
                    In L.A.?

                              BUFFY
                    Yeah.

                                                      (CONTINUED)

12 CONTINUED: 12

                           CORDELIA
               Oh! I would kill to live in L.A.
               Being that close to that many
               shoes... Why'd you come here?
                                                                    *

                           BUFFY
               Because my Mom moved, is the
               reason. I mean we both moved. But
               my Mom wanted to.

                                            CUT TO: *

13 INT. HALL - CONTINUOUS   13*

                           CORDELIA
               Well, you'll be okay here. If you
               hang with me and mine you'll be
               accepted in no time. Of course we
               do have to test your coolness
               factor. You're from L.A., so you
               can skip the written, but, let's
               see... Vamp nail polish.

                           BUFFY
                    (tentatively)
               Over?

                           CORDELIA
               SO over. James Spader.

                           BUFFY
               He **needs** to call me.

                           CORDELIA
               Frappachinos?

                           BUFFY
               Trendy but tasty.

                           CORDELIA
               John Tesh.

                           BUFFY
               The Devil?

                           CORDELIA
               Well, that was pretty much a gimme,
               but you passed.

                           BUFFY
               Oh, good.

They stop at the water fountain, which is being used by:

                                            (CONTINUED)

13 CONTINUED: 13

                              CORDELIA
                    Willow! Nice dress.
                         (off Willow's smile)
                    Good to know you've seen the softer
                    side of Sears.

That hurt. Buffy says nothing, surprised by Cordelia's
sudden viciousness. Willow says, almost apologetically:

                              WILLOW
                    Well my Mom picked it out.

                              CORDELIA
                         (witheringly)
                    No wonder you're such a guy-magnet.
                    Are you done?

                              WILLOW
                    Oh.

She vacates the fountain. Cordy steps up to it, looking at
Buffy.

                              CORDELIA
                    You wanna fit in here, the first
                    rule is "know your losers". Once
                    you can identify them all by sight,
                    they're a lot easier to avoid.

She bends down to drink. Buffy looks at the departing Willow,
unhappily.

                                                   CUT TO:

14 INT. ANOTHER HALL - A MINUTE LATER   14

    As Buffy and Cordelia walk toward the library.

                              CORDELIA
                    --and if you're not too swamped
                    with catching up you should come
                    out to the Bronze tonight.

                              BUFFY
                    The who?

                              CORDELIA
                    The Bronze. It's the only club
                    worth going to around here. They
                    let anybody in but it's still the
                    scene. It's in the bad part of
                    town.

                                                   (CONTINUED)

14 CONTINUED: 14

                         BUFFY
               Where's that?

                         CORDELIA
               About half a block from the good
               part of town. We don't have a
               whole lot of town. You should
               show.

They arrive at the entrance to the Library.

                         BUFFY
               Well, I'll try, thanks.

                         CORDELIA
               Good. I'll see you at gym and you
               can tell me absolutely everything
               there is to know about yourself.

She goes off.

                         BUFFY
                    (thrown by the notion)
               That sounds like fun...

                                        CUT TO:

15 INT. THE LIBRARY - CONTINUOUS   15

Buffy enters, looking about her. It's elegant, full of dark
wood, streaming sunlight, and (duhh) books. It's also
empty. Buffy steps in, looking around. She looks down at
the check-out counter to see:

ANGLE: A NEWSPAPER

Folded, with an article on the first page circled in red.
The headline reads: LOCAL BOYS STILL MISSING, with a blurry
picture of three brothers.

Buffy wanders further in. She peers around a bookcase --

                         BUFFY
               Hello... Is anybody here?

And someone touches her from behind. Startled, she spins.

                         GILES
               Can I help you?

He is British, of middle age, with a quiet intensity.

                                        (CONTINUED)

15 CONTINUED: 15

                              BUFFY
                    I was looking for some, well,
                    books. I'm new.

                              GILES
                    Miss Summers.

                              BUFFY
                    Good call. I guess I'm the only
                    new kid.

                              GILES
                    I'm Mr. Giles, the librarian.   *

                              BUFFY
                    Great. So you have, uh, --

                              GILES
                    I know what you're after.

He leads her to the check-out desk by the door. His office can
be seen behind it.

He pulls a book out and slides it toward Buffy. Huge, leather
bound, with a single word set in gild in the cover.

"VAMPYR"

Real concern floods Buffy's face, along with understanding. She
steps back from the desk, eyes on the librarian.

                              BUFFY
                    That's not what I'm looking for.

                              GILES
                    Are you sure?

                              BUFFY
                    I'm way sure.

                              GILES
                    My mistake.

He replaces the book under the counter.

                              GILES
                    So, what is it you said --

But she's gone.

                                                    CUT TO:

16   INT. WOMEN'S LOCKER ROOM - AFTERNOON   16

Two GIRLS approach their lockers, talking. They begin
undressing (just shoes and coats and stuff. Get your mind
out of the gutter.)

>   GIRL #1
>   The new kid? She seems kind of
>   weird to me. And what kind of name
>   is Buffy?

>   GIRL #2
>   Hey, Aphrodesia.

>   GIRL #1
>   Hey.

>   GIRL #3
>   Well, the chatter in the caf is
>   that she got kicked out and that's
>   why her mom had to get a new job.

>   GIRL #1
>   Neg.

>   GIRL #3
>   Pos. She was starting fights.

>   GIRL #1
>   (opening her locker)
>   Negly!

>   GIRL #3
>   (opening hers)
>   Well, I heard it from Blue, and she saw the
>   transcripts --

Something **FLIES OUT** of the locker at her! She SCREAMS as
the dead body of the boy from the opening collapses on her,
eyes horribly wide.

ANGLE: FROM ABOVE

The body sprawls out on the floor as the girl steps back,
screaming for all she's worth.

>   BLACK OUT.

                        END OF ACT ONE

<u>ACT TWO</u>

17 EXT. FOUNTAIN QUAD - DAY   17

    Willow is carefully taking out her packed lunch (and how
    healthy it **is**). Buffy approaches her.

                         BUFFY
              Uh, hi. Willow, right?

                         WILLOW
              Why? I mean Hi. Did you want me
              to move?

                         BUFFY
              Why don't we start with "hi I'm
              Buffy."
                   (sits by her)
              And then let's segue directly into
              me asking you for a favor. It
              doesn't involve moving, but it does
              involve you hanging out with me for
              a while.

                         WILLOW
              But aren't you... hanging with
              Cordelia?

                         BUFFY
              I can't do both?

                         WILLOW
              Not legally.

                         BUFFY
              Look, I really want to get by here.
              New school... Cordelia's been
              really nice -- to me, anyway -- but
              I have this burning desire not to
              flunk all my classes, and I heard a
              rumor that you were the person to
              talk to if I wanted to get caught
              up.

                         WILLOW
              Oh, I could totally help you out!
              If you have sixth period free we
              could meet in the library --

                                              (CONTINUED)

17 CONTINUED: 17

                         BUFFY
          --or not. Or, you know, we could
          meet somewhere quieter. Louder.
          That place kind of gives me a
          wiggins.

                         WILLOW
          It has that effect on most kids. I
          love it, though. It's a great
          collection, and the new librarian's
          really cool.

                         BUFFY
          He's new?

                         WILLOW
          Yeah, he just started. He was a
          curator of some British Museum. Or
          the British Museum, I'm not sure..
          But he knows everything and he
          brought all these historical
          volumes and biographies and am I
          the single dullest person alive?

                         BUFFY
          Not at all!

                         XANDER
               (entering with Jesse)
          Hey. Are you guys busy? Can we   *
          interrupt? We're interrupting.   *

                         BUFFY
          Hey.

                         JESSE.
          Hey there.

                         WILLOW
          Buffy, this is Jesse, and that's   *
          Xander.   *

                         XANDER
          Oh, me and Buffy go way back. Old
          friends, very close. Then there
          was that period of estrangement, I
          think we were both changing as
          people, but here we are and it's
          like old times, I'm quite moved.

                                              (CONTINUED)

BUFFY THE VAMPIRE SLAYER "Welcome to the Hellmouth" Rev. 9/4/96   20.

17 CONTINUED: 2   17

                         JESSE
          Is it me, or are you turning into a
          bibbling idiot?

                         XANDER
                (a little embarrassed)
          It's not you.

                         BUFFY
          It's nice to meet you guys... I
          think.

                         JESSE
          Well, we wanted to welcome you,
          make you feel at home. Unless you
          have a scary home.

                         XANDER
          And to return this.

He produces the stake.

                         XANDER
          The only thing I can figure is that
          you're building a really little
          fence.

                         BUFFY
          Oh. No. That was for self
          defense. Everyone has them in L.A.
          Pepper spray is so passe.

                         XANDER
          So. What do you like, what do you
          do for fun, what do you look for in
          a man... Let's hear it.

                         JESSE
          If you have any dark, painful
          secrets that we could publish...

                         BUFFY
          Gee, everybody wants to know about
          me. How keen.

                         XANDER
          Well, not a lot happens in a
          one-Starbucks town like Sunnydale.
          You're big news.

                         BUFFY
          I'm not. Really.

                                        (CONTINUED)

BUFFY THE VAMPIRE SLAYER "Welcome to the Hellmouth" Rev. 9/4/96 21.

17 CONTINUED: 3   17

                    CORDELIA
          Are these people bothering you?

She has appeared behind Jesse, all disdain on her face.

                    BUFFY
          Oh! No.
                    WILLOW
               (covering for her)
          She's not hanging out with us.

                    JESSE
               (smitten)
          Hey, Cordelia.

                    CORDELIA
          Oh, please.
               (to Buffy)
          I don't want to interrupt your
          downward mobility. I just thought
          I'd tell you that you won't be
          meeting Coach Foster, the woman
          with chest hair, because gym has
          been canceled due to the extreme
          dead guy in the locker.

                    BUFFY
          What?

                    WILLOW
          What are you talking about?

                    CORDELIA
          Some guy was stuffed in Aura's
          locker.

                    BUFFY
          Dead.

                    CORDELIA
          Way dead.

                    XANDER
          So not just a little dead then.

                    CORDELIA
          Don't you have an elsewhere to be?

                    JESSE
               (to Cordelia)
          If you need a shoulder to cry on,
          or just to nibble on --

                                        (CONTINUED)

17 CONTINUED: 4   17

                         BUFFY
                    How did he die?

                         CORDELIA
                    I don't know...

                         BUFFY
                    Well, were there any marks?

                         CORDELIA
                    Morbid much? I didn't ask!

                         BUFFY
                    Uh, look, I gotta book. I'll see
                    you guys later.

          She takes off, the others watching her.

                         CORDELIA
                    What's her deal?

18 INT.   HALLWAY OUTSIDE LOCKER ROOM - CONTINUOUS   18

          Mr. Flutie closes the door quietly. He turns to see Buffy
          before him.

                         MR. FLUTIE
                    Oh! Buffy! Uh, what do you want?

                         BUFFY
                    Um, is there a guy in there that's
                    dead?

                         MR. FLUTIE
                    Where did you hear that? Okay. Yes.
                    But he's not a student! Not currently.

                         BUFFY
                    Do you know how he died?

                         MR. FLUTIE
                    What?

                         BUFFY
                    I mean -- how could this have
                    happened?

                         MR. FLUTIE
                    Well, that's for the police to
                    determine when they get here. But
                    this structure is safe, we have
                    inspections, and I think there's no
                    grounds for a lawsuit.

                                                              (CONTINUED)

18 CONTINUED: 18

                         BUFFY
               Was there a lot of blood? Was
               there any blood?

                         MR. FLUTIE
               I would think you wouldn't want to
               involve yourself in this kind of
               thing.

                         BUFFY
               I don't. Could I just take a peek?

                         MR. FLUTIE
               Unless you already **are**
               involved...

                         BUFFY
               Never mind.

                         MR. FLUTIE
                    (being nicer)
               Buffy, I understand this is
               confusing. You're probably feeling
               a lot right now. You should share
               those feelings. With someone else.

Buffy smiles wanly, backs off.

                                              CUT TO:
19 EXT. SIDE OF GYM - CONTINUOUS   19

    Buffy comes around the side of the gym. There is a door to   *
    the locker room and she tries it. It's locked.   *

    She looks around to make sure she's alone, and then <u>PULLS</u>   *
    the door open with a quick tug, splintering the lock. One   *
    last look around and she slips inside.   *

                                              CUT TO:

20 INT. WOMEN'S LOCKER ROOM - CONTINUOUS   20

    Buffy approaches the body laid out under a blanket.   *

    She hesitates, sure she's not going to like what she sees.
    Pulls the blanket from his head and shoulders.

                                              (CONTINUED)

20 CONTINUED: 20

ANGLE: HIS NECK

Has two big ol' bite marks in it.

What floods onto Buffy's face is not horror, but grim
frustration. She stares down at the body, nearly seething.

                    BUFFY
          Oh, **great**!

                                          CUT TO:

21 INT. LIBRARY - MOMENTS LATER   21

Buffy strides back in, attitude high.

                    BUFFY
          Okay? What's the sitch?

She spies Giles and starts up toward him.

                    GILES
          Sorry?

                    BUFFY
          You heard about the dead guy,
          right? The dead guy in the locker?

                    GILES
          Yes.

                    BUFFY
          Well, it's the weirdest thing.
          He's got two little holes in his
          neck and all his blood's been
          drained. Isn't that bizarre?
          Aren't you just going, "Ooooh...."

                    GILES
          I was afraid of this.

                    BUFFY
          Well, I wasn't! It's my first day.
          I was afraid that I'd be behind in
          all the classes, that I wouldn't
          make any friends, that I'd have
          last month's hair. I didn't think
          there would be vampires on campus.
          And I don't care.

                    GILES
          Then why are you here?   *

                                          (CONTINUED)

She's stopped for a moment.

> BUFFY
> To tell you that I don't care.
> Which I don't, and... have now told
> you. So bye.

She starts out, maybe a little unsatisfied with her exit.

> GILES
> Will he rise again?

> BUFFY
> Who?

> GILES
> The boy.

> BUFFY
> No, he's just dead.

> GILES
> Can you be sure?

> BUFFY
> To make you a vampire, they have to
> suck your blood and then you have
> to suck their blood, it's a whole
> big sucking thing. Mostly they'll
> just take all your blood and then
> you just die -- why am I still
> talking to you?

> GILES
> You have no idea what's going   *
> on, do you? Do you think it's   *
> coincidence, your coming here?
> That boy was just the beginning.

> BUFFY
>   (turning)
> Oh, why can't you leave me alone?

> GILES
> Because you are the Slayer.

She stops. No comeback just now. He starts down after her,
solemnly intoning:

> GILES
> Into every generation, a Slayer is
> born. One girl, in all the world,
> a Chosen One. One born with the --

                                        (CONTINUED)

BUFFY THE VAMPIRE SLAYER "Welcome to the Hellmouth" Rev.9/6/96 26.

21 CONTINUED: 2   21

She finishes along with him:

> BUFFY & GILES
> -- the strength and skill to hunt
> the vampires --

> BUFFY
> To stop the spread of their evil
> blah blah I've **heard** it, okay?

> GILES
> I don't understand this attitude.
> You've accepted your duty, you've
> slain vampires before --

> BUFFY
> Well, I have both been there and
> done that. And I am moving on.

> GILES
> What do you know about this town?

> BUFFY
> It's two hours on the freeway from
> Neiman Marcus.

> GILES
> Dig a bit in the history of this
> place and you'll find there've been
> a steady stream of fairly odd
> occurrences. I believe this area
> is a center of mystical energy.
> Things gravitate toward it that you
> might not find elsewhere.

> BUFFY
> Like Vampires.

She tries to move past him and he pulls a book off the
shelf, hands it to her. It resembles the vampire book he
showed her earlier. He continues to pull more off, piling
them up in her arms.

> GILES
> Like werewolves. Zombies.   *
> Succubi, incubi... Everything you   *
> ever dreaded under your bed and
> told yourself couldn't be by the
> light of day.

> BUFFY
> What, did you send away for the   *
> Time Life series?   *
>   *

(CONTINUED)

21 CONTINUED: 3   21

                              GILES
                    Uh, yes.

                              BUFFY
                    Did you get the free phone?

                              GILES
                    The calendar.

                              BUFFY
                    Cool.
                         (remembering her agenda)
                    Okay, first of all, I'm a **vampire**
                    slayer. And secondly I'm retired.
                    Hey, I know! Why don't you kill
                    them?

                              GILES
                    I'm a Watcher. I haven't the
                    skill.

                              BUFFY
                    Oh, come on. Stake through the
                    heart, a little sunlight -- it's
                    like falling off a log.

                              GILES
                    The Slayer slays. The Watcher --

                              BUFFY
                    Watches?

                              GILES
                    Yes. No! He -- he -- trains her,
                    he prepares her --

                              BUFFY
                    Prepares me for what? For getting
                    kicked out of school? Losing all   *
                    my friends? Having to spend all
                    my time fighting for my life and   *
                    never getting to tell anyone
                    because it might 'endanger' them?
                    Go ahead. Prepare me.

A beat, and she leaves. Giles heads out after her.

ANGLE: IN THE STACKS

A shadowy figure moves about back there, emerges into the
light. It's Xander, excitement, amusement and disbelief
dancing in his face. "Theories in Trig" in his hands.

                                                    (CONTINUED)

21 CONTINUED: 4   21

He tries for a long time to form a word. When he does, it
is merely:

                         XANDER
             WHAT?

                                                    CUT TO:

22 INT. HALL - CONTINUOUS   22

Giles comes out of the library, calls out to Buffy.

                         GILES
             It's getting worse.

She stops, turns. There are people about, so they are
forced to whisper.

                         BUFFY
             What's getting worse?

                         GILES
             The influx of the undead, the
             supernatural occurrences. It's
             been building for years and now...
             There's a reason why you're here,
             and there's a reason why it's now.

                                             (CONTINUED)

22 CONTINUED: 22

                         BUFFY
               Because **now** is the time my mom
               moved **here**.

                         GILES
               Something is coming. Something is
               going to happen here soon.

                         BUFFY
               Gee, can you vague that up for
               me...?

                         GILES
               As far as I can tell, the signs   *
               point to a crucial mystical   *
               upheaval very soon -- days,
               possibly less.

                         BUFFY
               Come on. This is Sunnydale. How
               bad an evil can there be here?

                                             CUT TO:

23 INT.   DARK PLACE - NIGHT   23

The camera TRACKS silently through a dark and eerie place.
We see candles, broken statuary. A few figures bent in
supplication. An ominous CHANTING fills the chamber.

As we move up, we see a single figure kneeling, well ahead
of the rest. He is large, powerful, appears to be in his
late twenties. In fact, LUKE is much older than that. His
dress speaks of many eras, but definitively of none.

The CHANTING increases in intensity as the camera continues
to move about the place, passing over Luke and we see what
he is kneeling before for the first time.

A pool of blood.

                         LUKE
               The sleeper will awaken.

As he speaks, we see his face clearly. Vampire. Not
pretty.

                         LUKE
               The sleeper will awaken. And the
               world will bleed.

He dips his finger in the blood.

                                             (CONTINUED)

23 CONTINUED: 23

                                   LUKE
                    Amen.

And now we see:

WIDER ANGLE: THE CHURCH

It's a bizarre ruin we're in, buried beneath the ground.
The stanchions and arches stand at haphazard angles, sheeted
rock pushing in at all sides. The pool of blood is on what
would be the altar.

The CHANTING fills the vast room as we

                                              BLACK OUT.

                    END OF ACT TWO

ACT THREE

24 INT.   BUFFY'S BEDROOM - NIGHT   24

She is in the agony of outfit choosage, getting ready to go
out. She has two, one scanty, the other somewhat plain. She
holds them alternately in front of her, looking in the
mirror.

                    BUFFY
               (holding up one)
          Hi! I'm an enormous slut!
               (the other)
          Hi! Would you like a copy of the
          Watchtower?
               (throws them both down)
          I used to be so good at this...

Joyce enters, watches her.

                    JOYCE
          Are you going out tonight, honey?

                    BUFFY
          Yeah, Mom. I'm going to a club.

                    JOYCE
          Will there be boys there?

                    BUFFY
          No, Mom; it's a nun club.

                    JOYCE
          Well, just be careful.

                    BUFFY
          I will.   *

As the conversation segues into serious territory, both
women become somewhat uncomfortable with each other.

                    JOYCE
          I think we can make it work here.
          I've got my positive energy
          flowing. I'm gonna get the gallery
          on its feet -- We may already have
          found a space.

                                              (CONTINUED)

24 CONTINUED: 24

                              BUFFY
                    Great.

                              JOYCE
                    And that school is a very nurturing
                    environment, which is what you
                    need.

                              BUFFY
                    Mom...

                              JOYCE
                    Oh, not too nurturing. I know.
                    You're sixteen, I read all about
                    the dangers of overnurturing.
                         (honestly)
                    It's hard. New town, and all. For
                    me, too. I'm trying to make it
                    work.
                         (correcting herself)
                    I'm **going** to make it work.

                              BUFFY
                    I know.

                              JOYCE
                    You're a good girl, Buffy. You
                    just fell in with the wrong crowd.
                    But that's all behind us now.   *

                              BUFFY
                    It is. From now on, I'm only
                    hanging out with the living. I --
                    I mean, the lively... people.

                              JOYCE
                    Okay. You have fun.

                                                      CUT TO:

25 EXT STREET - NIGHT   25

     Buffy makes her way on foot to the Bronze. She leaves the
     suburban area the house is in for the deserted city streets
     on the edge of town.

     She turns a corner, walks down the street, lost in
     thought -- until she HEARS FOOTSTEPS behind her.

                                                      (CONTINUED)

25 CONTINUED: 25

   She stops, turns slowly.

   A figure stands in the dark behind her. Far enough away
   that she doesn't feel right saying anything to it. It
   doesn't move -- she can't see its face but it seems to be
   looking at her.

   Buffy turns to go.

   The figure follows.

                                                    CUT TO:

26 EXT. ANOTHER STREET - A MOMENT LATER   26

   Buffy turns the corner, somewhat worried -- moving faster.

   The figure follows, always at a discreet distance.

                                                    CUT TO:

27 EXT. AN ALLEY - A MOMENT LATER   27

Buffy turns in. She looks about her. A pipe runs across
the narrow alley some ten feet above her. Garbage cans
cluster at the other end.

ANGLE: BUFFY   *

doing a handstand on a pipe overhead.   *

The figure turns into the now-empty alley, starts down it.   *

Buffy suddenly DROPS down on him, legs locked over his neck.
She throws herself back, tipping him over, rolling herself
and SLAMMING his body onto the ground.

He's on his feet quickly, but she grabs him and throws him
up against the wall. She closes in, but he makes no move to
attack. Puts up his hands.

                    ANGEL
          Is there a problem, ma'am?

He seems faintly amused. Buffy eyes him suspiciously,
getting her first good look at him.

ANGEL is strikingly handsome, with intelligence and a kind
of distance in his eyes. Moves with a fighter's grace.

                    BUFFY
          There's a problem. Why are you
          following me?

                    ANGEL
          I know what you're thinking, but
          don't worry. I don't bite.

She backs off a bit, perplexed.

                    ANGEL
          Truth is, I thought you'd be taller.
          Or bigger, muscles and all
          that. You're pretty spry, though.

                    BUFFY
          What do you want?

                    ANGEL
          Same thing you do.

                    BUFFY
          Okay, what do I want?

The amusement leaves his face.

                                              (CONTINUED)

27 CONTINUED: 27
                            ANGEL
               To kill 'em. To kill 'em all.

                                                        (CONTINUED)

27 CONTINUED: 27

                              BUFFY
                        (game show:)
                    Sorry! That's incorrect but you do
                    get this lovely watch and a year's
                    supply of Turtle Wax what I
                    want... is to be left alone.

                              ANGEL
                    You really think that's an option
                    anymore? You're standing at the
                    mouth of Hell. And it's about to
                    open.

He reaches into his coat for something. It's a jewelry   *
box. He throws it to her.

                              ANGEL
                    Don't turn your back on this.
                    You've got to be ready.

                              BUFFY
                    What for?

                              ANGEL
                    For the Harvest.

He starts out.

                              BUFFY
                    Who are you?

                              ANGEL
                    Let's just say I'm a friend.

                              BUFFY
                        (exasperated)
                    Well, maybe I don't want a friend.

                              ANGEL
                    I didn't say I was **yours**...

He goes. Buffy watches him go, then opens the box.

ANGLE: IN THE BOX

is a cross. Small, antique, on a gold chain.

WIDER ANGLE: BUFFY ALONE IN THE ALLEY

Buffy looks at the cross, at the departing figure of the
mysterious man.

And as she walks slowly away, the camera TRACKS past the
corner, past another group of garbage cans.

                                            (CONTINUED)

27 CONTINUED: 2   27

    In front of them, right before us but unseen by Buffy, are
    two figures. The poor man we saw in her dream, and a
    vampire. The beast has its face burrowing in his neck, as
    the last of his life shudders out.

                                                    CUT TO:

28 EXT. THE BRONZE - NIGHT   28

    A decent crowd mills aimlessly around the joint, high school
    students and older. The place has an appealingly dive-y
    earthiness; no waiting in line for the bouncer to decide
    whether you're cool or not. Those that are in line wait
    only to pay the four bucks and get their hands stamped if
    they're old enough to drink.

    Buffy moves her way up the line, scanning about for a
    familiar face. She doesn't find one. As she is let in we
    FOLLOW HER INTO:

29 INT. THE BRONZE - CONTINUOUS   29

    It's dark, crowded and noisy. A fairly thrashsome band
    holds forth on stage, blasting the kind of music that would
    cause major moshing in a rowdier crowd. Coffee bar in the
    back, and a balcony above with tables for two.

    Buffy makes her way through, still looking about. A good   *
    looking GUY spies her and waves, smiling.

    Buffy smiles vaguely, waving back. A moment before she
    realizes he's waving to a guy right behind her. She
    attempts to turn her wave into fixing her hair, looking
    embarrassed.

29A ANGLE: WILLOW   29A*

    is getting a soda at the bar. She turns back to look at   *
    the band just as Buffy comes up to her.

                        BUFFY
                Hi!

                        WILLOW
                Oh, hi! Hi.

                        BUFFY
                Are you here with someone?

                                                    (CONTINUED)

9A CONTINUED: 29A

                         WILLOW
          No, I'm just here. I thought
          Xander was gonna show up...

                         BUFFY
          Oh, are you guys going out?

                         WILLOW
          No. We're just friends. We used   *
          to go out, but we broke up.

                         BUFFY
          How come?

                         WILLOW
          He stole my Barbie.
               (off Buffy's look)
          We were five.

                         BUFFY
          Oh.

                         WILLOW
          I don't actually date a whole
          lot... lately.

                         BUFFY
          Why not?

                         WILLOW
          Well, when I'm with a boy I like,
          it's hard for me to say anything
          cool, or witty, or at all... I can
          usually make a few vowel sounds,
          and then I have to go away.

                         BUFFY
               (laughing)
          It's not that bad.

                         WILLOW
          It is. I think boys are more
          interested in a girl who can talk.

                         BUFFY
          You really **haven't** been dating
          lately.

                         WILLOW
          It's probably easy for you.

                         BUFFY
               (a little forlornly)
          Oh, yeah. Real easy.

                                              (CONTINUED)

BUFFY THE VAMPIRE SLAYER "Welcome to the Hellmouth" Rev. 9/4/96 36.

29A CONTINUED: 2   29A

                          WILLOW
          I mean, you don't seem too shy.

                          BUFFY
          Well, my philosophy is -- do you
          wanna hear my philosophy?

                          WILLOW
          I do.

                          BUFFY
          Life is short.

                          WILLOW
          Life is short.

                          BUFFY
          Not original, I'll grant you. But
          it's true. Why waste time being
          all shy? Why worry about some guy
          and if he's gonna laugh at you?
          You know? Seize the moment.
          'Cause tomorrow you might be dead.

                          WILLOW
          Oh... That's nice...

Buffy sees somebody moving about on the balcony. Her brow
furrows.

                          BUFFY
          Uh, I'll be back in a minute.

                          WILLOW
          That's okay. You don't have to
          come back.

                          BUFFY
                    (smiling at her
                     self-effacing attitude)
          I'll be back in a minute.

She takes off, leaving Willow at the bar.

                          WILLOW
                    (to herself)
          Seize the moment...

29B ANGLE: ATOP THE BALCONY   29B*

Buffy comes up, makes her way to the railing overlooking the
stage. She leans on it, and we see that Giles is standing
beside her. He doesn't even look at her.

                                              (CONTINUED)

                                    BUFFY
                    So, you like to party with the
                    students? Isn't that kind of
                    skanky?

                                    GILES
                            (witheringly)
                    Right. This is me having fun.
                            (looking out on stage)
                    Watching clown-hair prance about is
                    hardly my idea of a party. I'd
                    much prefer to be home with a cup
                    of bovril and a good book.

                                    BUFFY
                    You need a personality, **STAT.**

                                    GILES
                    This is a perfect breeding ground
                    for Vampire activity. Dark,
                    crowded... Besides, I knew you were
                    likely to show up. And I have to
                    make you understand --

                                    BUFFY
                    That the Harvest is coming, I know,
                    your friend told me.

                                    GILES
                            (thrown)
                    What did you say?

                                    BUFFY
                    The... Harvest. That means
                    something to you? 'Cause I'm
                    drawing a blank.

                                    GILES
                    I'm not sure... Who told you this?

                                    BUFFY
                    This guy. Dark, gorgeous in an
                    annoying sort of way. I figured
                    you were buds.

                                    GILES
                    No... The Harvest... Did he say
                    anything else?

                                    BUFFY
                    Something about the mouth of Hell.
                    I really didn't like him.

                                                (CONTINUED)

They both look down at the floor a moment, at the dancing
kids.

                    GILES
          Look at them. Throwing themselves
          about.... Completely unaware of the
          danger that surrounds them.

                    BUFFY
          Lucky them...

                    GILES
          or perhaps you're right, Perhaps
          there is no trouble coming. The
          signs could be wrong. It's not as
          though you're having the
          nightmares...

And we MOVE IN on Buffy's face, clouding over. She says
nothing, just looks down at the dancing kids.

29C ANGLE: THE FLOOR   29C*

Kids writhe about to the music with healthy abandon.

We find Cordelia off to the side, watching with her friends.

                    CORDELIA
          My mom doesn't even get out of bed
          anymore. The doctor says it's
          Epstein Barr, I'm like, "**please,**
          it's chronic hepatitis or at
          least Chronic Fatigue Syndrome."
          I mean nobody cool has Epstein Barr
          anymore.

Jesse approaches her, smiling.

                    JESSE
          Cordelia!

                    CORDELIA
          Oh, yay, it's my stalker.

                    JESSE
          Hey, you look great.

                    CORDELIA
          Well, I'm glad we had this chat --

                    JESSE
          Listen, I, um, do you wanna dance?

                                        (CONTINUED)

BUFFY THE VAMPIRE SLAYER "Welcome to the Hellmouth" Rev.9/6/96 39.

29C CONTINUED: 2   29C

                         CORDELIA
                      (witheringly)
                 With you?

                         JESSE
                 Well, uh, yeah.

                         CORDELIA
                 Well, uh, no.

She takes off, posse in tow. Jesse just soaks up the pain.

                         JESSE
                 Fine. Plenty of other fish in the
                 sea. Oh yeah. I'm on the prowl.
                 Witness me prowling.

He looks around at the throng, officially beginning his
prowl.

29D ANGLE: BUFFY AND GILES   29D

In mid-conversation. Shaken by the dreams thing, Buffy is
giving ground.

                         BUFFY
                 I didn't say I'd never slay another
                 vampire. I'm just not gonna get   *
                 way extracurricular with it. If I
                 run into one, sure...

                         GILES
                 But will you be ready? There's so
                 much you don't know, about them and
                 about your own powers. A vampire
                 appears to be a normal person,
                 until the feed is upon them. Only
                 then do they reveal their true
                 demonic visage.

                         BUFFY
                 You're like a textbook with arms!
                 I know this!   *

                         GILES
                 The point is, a Slayer should be
                 able to see them anyway. Without
                 looking, without thinking. Can you
                 tell me if there's a vampire in
                 this building?

                                             (CONTINUED)

29D CONTINUED: 29D

                         BUFFY
               Maybe?

                         GILES
               You should know! Even through this
               mass and this din you should be
               able to sense them. Try. Reach
               out with your mind.

She looks down at the mass of kids on the floor. Furrows
her brow.

                         GILES
               You have to hone your senses, focus
               until the energy washes over you,
               till you can feel every particle
               of--

                         BUFFY
               There's one.

Giles stops, nonplused.

                         GILES
               What? Where?

                         BUFFY
                    (pointing)
               Down there. Talking to that girl.

ANGLE: THEIR POV

In the corner stands a good-looking young man, talking to a
girl we can't really see.

                         GILES
               But you don't know --

                         BUFFY
               Oh, please. Look at his jacket.
               He's got the sleeves rolled up.
               And the shirt... Deal with that   *
               outfit for a moment.

                         GILES
               It's dated?

                         BUFFY
               It's carbon dated! Trust me:
               only someone who's been living
               underground for ten years would
               think that was the look.

                                              (CONTINUED)

                            47

29D CONTINUED: 2   29D

> GILES
> But ... you didn't **hone**...

> BUFFY
> (noticing something)
> Oh, no...

ANGLE: THE VAMPIRE

Is still chatting with the girl. He motions for her to come
with him, and she comes into view.

It's Willow.

> GILES
> Isn't that --

> BUFFY
> Willow.

> GILES
> What is she doing?

> BUFFY
> Seizing the moment.

She starts toward the stairs.

29E ANGLE: WILLOW AND THE VAMPIRE BOY   29E*

Head out the back door by the stage.

Buffy fights her way down the stairs. She looks toward
where they were and sees they're gone. She looks about a
moment, and then, guessing correctly, heads for the
backstage door as well.

But it's a struggle: the closer she gets to the stage, the
more crowded it gets. She finally pushes to the door.
>   CUT TO:

30 INT. BACKSTAGE - CONTINUOUS   30

It's dark here, and somewhat labyrinthian. Buffy moves
slowly, cautiously. There is no one about.

She finds an old chair, snaps the leg off, a makeshift   *
stake.

There is no one about. Buffy heads for the exit door.
Sticks her head out it but there's no one in the alley
either.

>   (CONTINUED)

30 CONTINUED: 2   30

Slowly, perturbed, she starts back for the main door.

She turns the corner and he's **ON HER!** She grabs him,
throws him up against the wall, holding him two feet off the
ground --

Well, holding **her**, actually. Holding Cordelia, who has
the same dumbfounded gape that the other girls coming out of
the bathroom have.

                         BUFFY
              Cordelia!

                         CORDELIA
              Excuse me... could you be any
              weirder? Is there a more weirdness
              that you could have?

Buffy lets her down, lowering the stake.

                         CORDELIA
              God, what is your childhood trauma?

                         BUFFY
                    (trying to be chipper)
              Did you guys see Willow? Did she
              come by here?

                         CORDELIA
              Why? Did you need to attack her
              with a stick?   *

Buffy gives up. Face red, she retreats back the way she
came.

Cordy and the others are still agape. After a moment, Cordy
regains her composure.

                         CORDELIA
              Excuse me. I have to call everyone
              that I've ever met right now.

                                                CUT TO:

31 INT. THE BRONZE - CONTINUOUS   31

Buffy comes back out, finds Giles at the bottom of the   *
stairs. She looks around as he says: *

                    GILES   *
          That was fast. Well done. I'd   *
          best go to the library. This   *
          "Harvest" is --   *

                    BUFFY   *
          I didn't find them.   *

                    GILES   *
          The vampire's not dead?   *

                                        (CONTINUED)

31 CONTINUED: 2   31

                          BUFFY   *
             No, but my social life is on the   *
             critical list.   *

                          GILES   *
             What do we do?   *

                          BUFFY   *
             You go on. I'll take care of it.   *

                          GILES   *
             I should come with you, no?   *

                          BUFFY
                       (heading out)
             Don't worry. One vampire I can
             handle.

As she exits, she brushes past Jesse. The camera STAYS on
him, as we see he is chatting up a girl.

                          JESSE
             What did you say your name was?

And the camera comes around to show the girl he's talking
to: it's the **vampire** from the opening. Needless to say,
she has her normal face on. And she'll be known from now on
as:

                          DARLA
             Darla.

                          JESSE
             Darla. I haven't seen you before.
             Are you from around here?

                          DARLA
             No, but I've got family here.

                          JESSE
             Have I met them?

                          DARLA
             You probably will.
                                              CUT TO:

32 INT. THE CHURCH - CONTINUOUS   32

The CHANTING we heard earlier continues, peaking in
intensity. By the altar, Luke suddenly looks up.

                                              (CONTINUED)

32   CONTINUED: 32

He starts moving slowly back, eyes wide with religious
fervor. All the figures in the church start moving back,
almost as one.

ANGLE: THE POOL OF BLOOD

We are low, right above the surface, as Luke prays before
it. Suddenly **a HEAD shoots up** from in the blood. Luke
starts, looks at it. He moves back, away from the pool.

Something breaks the surface of the liquid. Something
rises.

It is THE MASTER, the most powerful of vampires. Born
Heinrich Joseph Nest (some six hundred years ago,) he wears
a vaguely SS-like outfit.

What he does not wear is anything resembling a human face.
He is as much demon as man. As powerful as Luke is, it's
clear that this man is much more so, both from his bearing
and from the reverence with which Luke looks upon him.

He steps forward, holds out his hand. Luke grasps it
reverently.

                         LUKE
                Master...

                                             BLACK OUT.
                    END OF ACT THREE

ACT FOUR

33   INT.   THE CHURCH - MOMENTS LATER   33

The Master steps forward, his face still in relative darkness. Luke steps back reverentially. The Master looks about him a moment.

                    THE MASTER
          Luke.

                    LUKE
          Master...

                    THE MASTER
          I am weak.

                    LUKE
          Come the Harvest, you'll be
          restored.

                    THE MASTER
          The Harvest...

                    LUKE
          We're almost there. Soon you'll be
          free.

The Master takes another step forward, past Luke. He reaches his hand out slowly. As he does, the air in front of him starts to ripple slightly -- a kind of mystical wall. He pulls his hand back.

                    THE MASTER
          I must be ready. I need my
          strength.

                    LUKE
          I've sent your servants to bring
          you some food.

                    THE MASTER
          Good.

Luke starts out.

                    THE MASTER
          Luke...

                                        (CONTINUED)

33 CONTINUED: 33

                              LUKE
                         (stopping)
                    Yes?

                              THE MASTER
                    Bring me something... young.

                                                        CUT TO:

34 EXT.   STREET BY WOODED GLADE - NIGHT   34

    Willow and the Vampire Boy walk along, alone in the dark.
    She is clearly nervous, though not for the reason she should
    be.

                              WILLOW
                    Sure is dark...

                              VAMPIRE BOY
                    It's night.

                              WILLOW
                    That's a dark time. Night.
                    Traditionally.

    They walk a bit more.

                              WILLOW
                    I still can't believe I've never
                    seen you at school. Do you have
                    Mr. Chomsky for History?

    He doesn't answer. Stops.

                              WILLOW
                    The ice cream bar's down this
                    way -- it's past Hamilton street.

    He takes her hand.

                              VAMPIRE BOY
                    I know a shortcut.

    He leads her into the dark of the wood.

                                                        CUT TO:

35 EXT. OUTSIDE THE BRONZE - NIGHT   35

    Buffy comes from around the back, looking around. Xander   *
    comes up to her, carrying his skateboard.   *

                                                        (CONTINUED)

35 CONTINUED: 35

                              XANDER
               You're leaving already?

                              BUFFY
               Xander, have you seen Willow?

                              XANDER
               Not tonight.

                              BUFFY
               I need to find her. She left with
               a guy.

                              XANDER
               We are talking about Willow, right?
                    (impressed)
               Scoring at the Bronze. Work it,
               girlfriend.

                              BUFFY
                    (looking around)
               Where would they go?

                              XANDER
               Why, you know something about Mr.
               Goodbar that she doesn't? Oh!
               Hey. I hope he's not a **vampire**.
               'Cause then you'd have to **slay**
               him.

          She turns back to him, surprised and miffed.

                              BUFFY
               Was there a school bulletin? Was
               it in the news? Is there anybody
               in this town who **doesn't** know I'm
               a slayer?

                              XANDER

               I only know that you **think** you're
               a slayer, and I only know that
               'cause I was in the library today.

                              BUFFY
               Whatever. Just tell me where
               Willow would go.

                              XANDER
               You're serious.

                              BUFFY
               We don't find her, there's gonna be
               another dead body in the morning.

                                        (CONTINUED)

35 CONTINUED: 2   35

A beat, as he looks at her. Sees she isn't kidding. Isn't
wrong.

                         XANDER
              Come on.

As they head off.

                                                    CUT TO:

36 EXT. GRAVEYARD - CONTINUOUS   36

Willow is still walking with Vampire Boy, but getting
increasingly creeped out.

                         WILLOW
              Okay, this is nice and... scary...   *
              Are you sure this is faster?

He says nothing. She keeps walking beside him, uncertain.

He stops at a small mausoleum. The entrance is a well of
black.

                         VAMPIRE BOY
              Hey. You ever been in one of
              these?

                         WILLOW
              No thank you.

He moves in close, holding her intimately.

                         VAMPIRE BOY
              Come on. What are you afraid of?

He pulls her into the blackness of the entrance.
                                                    CUT TO:

37 INT. MAUSOLEUM - CONTINUOUS   37

Willow stumbles in., She looks about her frightenedly,
adjusting to the increased dark.

                                                    (CONTINUED)

37 CONTINUED: 37

The place is small, with carved stone walls. A large tomb
takes up much of the middle, the stone figure of a man lying
atop it. Behind her is the doorway she came in, ahead, a
much smaller, iron door, locked shut.

She spins all the way round to see the boy filling the
entrance.

                    WILLOW
          That wasn't funny.

No response. He steps closer, his face in shadow. She
circles away from him, moving closer to the doorway.

                    WILLOW
          I think I'm gonna go.

                    VAMPIRE BOY
          Is that what you think?

All the playfulness has drained out of his voice. She takes
a step back, another, turns and moves WHAM -- right into
DARLA.

Emitting something between a scream and a squeak, Willow
steps back. Darla looks at her, at the boy.

                    DARLA
              (to him; re: her)
          Is this the best you could do?

                    VAMPIRE BOY
          She's fresh.

                    DARLA
          Hardly enough to share.   *
                                                             *

                    VAMPIRE BOY
          Why didn't you bring your own?   *

                    DARLA
          I did.

She indicates the doorway behind her, as Jesse stumbles
dazed from the darkness.

                                              (CONTINUED)

BUFFY THE VAMPIRE SLAYER "Welcome to the Hellmouth" Rev. 9/4/96 50.

37 CONTINUED: 2   37

                         JESSE
              Hey, wait up...

                         WILLOW
              Jesse!

She goes over to him, relieved. He is clutching his neck.

                         JESSE
                    (to Darla)
              I think you gave me a hickey...

He takes his hand away. There is blood on it, on his neck.
Willow looks over at the other two, eyes wide.

                                                                    *

                         DARLA
                    (off the boy's look)   *
              I got hungry on the way.

                         WILLOW
              Jesse, let's get out of here.

                                                                    *

                                                                    *

                                                                    *

                         DARLA
              You're not going anywhere.

                         WILLOW
              Leave us alone.

                         DARLA
                    (in Willow's face)
              You're not going anywhere until
              we've **FED!**

And on the last word she brings her face right up to
Willow's and it CHANGES, snaps right before our eyes into
the grotesque demon-face we saw before.

Willow SCREAMS, takes a stumbling step back and falls.

The boy laughs, circling, and we see that he has changed as
well.

                         BUFFY
              Well, this is nice.

                                                  (CONTINUED)

BUFFY THE VAMPIRE SLAYER "Welcome to the Hellmouth" Rev. 9/4/96 51.

37 CONTINUED: 3   37

She steps in, Xander following her. Everybody stops.

                    BUFFY
          A little bare, but a dash of paint,
          a few throw pillows -- call it
          home.

                    DARLA
          Who the hell are you?

                    BUFFY
          Wow, you mean there's actually
          somebody around here who doesn't
          know already? That's a relief.
          I'm telling you, having a secret
          identity in this town is a job of
          work.

He is moving between the two Vampires, who loosen their grip
on their respective victims.

                                                              *

                    XANDER
          Buffy, we bail now, right?   *

                    VAMPIRE BOY
          Not yet.   *

                    BUFFY
          Okay, first of all, what's with
          this outfit? Live in the now,
          okay? You look like DeBarge.
               (turning to Darla)
          Now, we can do this the hard way,
          or... well, actually, there's just
          the hard way.

                    DARLA
          Fine with me.

                    BUFFY
          You sure? It's not gonna be
          pretty. We're talking violence,
          strong language, adult content.

                                        (CONTINUED)

                                                             *

                                                             *

                                                             *

                                                             *

As she speaks, the Boy Vampire RUSHES her from behind, charging at her with incredible speed and momentum --

Buffy whips a stake out from her jacket and in one graceful motion sticks it out behind her, letting the boy impale himself on it. He stops, eyes wide, and falls back.

Buffy never even faces him.

ANGLE: THE BOY VAMPIRE

As he hits the ground, his body crumbles to dust.

> BUFFY
> (to Darla)
> See, what happens when you
> roughhouse?

Xander and Willow are speechless, staring at the ground where a body used to be.

Darla is wide eyed, exceedingly wary. But not cowed. She moves slowly around, preparing to fight herself.

> DARLA
> He was young. And stupid.

> BUFFY
> Xander, go.

> DARLA
> Don't go far.

She lunges at Buffy, who parries her blows with marital arts precision.

Xander herds the others out.

                                                CUT TO:

38   EXT.   GRAVEYARD - CONTINUOUS   38

The three kids run out of the mausoleum, Willow and Xander
supporting Jesse. All three are totally freaked -- Jesse
the least so, since he's still weak and dazed.

                                                 CUT TO:

39   INT.   MAUSOLEUM - CONTINUOUS   39

Darla hits the ground with a painful thud.

Buffy stands over her. She's a bit out of breath, and the
humor is gone from her visage.

                         BUFFY
                You know, I just wanted to start
                over. Be like everybody else.
                Have some friends, maybe a dog...
                But no. You had to come here. You
                couldn't go suck on some other
                town.

                         DARLA
                Who are you?

                         BUFFY
                Don't you know?

HANDS suddenly GRAB Buffy by the throat, lift her bodily
from the ground.

                         LUKE
                I don't care.

He steps out of the shadows from behind her -- his bulk
dwarfing her -- and throws her a good fifteen feet. She
hits the wall face first, landing badly.

Luke turns on Darla, who is getting up.

                         LUKE
                You were supposed to be bringing an
                offering for the Master. We're
                almost at Harvest and you dally
                with this child?

                         DARLA
                We had someone. But she came
                and... she killed Thomas... Luke,
                she's strong.

                                            (CONTINUED)

39 CONTINUED: 39

                         LUKE
                    (contemptuously)
               You go. I'll see if I can handle
               the little girl.

ANGLE: BUFFY

She lifts herself off the floor just as Luke suddenly closes
on her, grabs her. She's ready this time, though, and she
knocks his arms away, kicks him in the face. It sends him
back a bit but he recovers in a second, landing a solid
punch to her jaw.

                         LUKE
               You **are** strong.

He **slams** her back to the ground.

                         LUKE
               I'm stronger.

                                              CUT TO:

40 EXT. THE FOREST - CONTINUOUS   40

The three kids are making pretty good time, despite having
to support Jesse.

                         WILLOW
               We'll get the police -- it's just a
               few blocks up --

They stop. They stare, despair creeping onto their faces.

Three Vampires stand waiting for them.   *

                                              CUT TO:

41 INT. THE MAUSOLEUM - CONTINUOUS   41

Buffy looks like she's been kicked around a bit. She
circles around the tomb, keeping it between her and Luke.

                         LUKE
               You're wasting my time.

                         BUFFY
               Hey, I had other plans, too, okay?

He SHOVES the top of the tomb with all his might, sends it
flying at her.

                                              (CONTINUED)

41 CONTINUED: 41

    She LEAPS over it -- jumps up onto the tomb, leaps off it,
    flipping, and **WHAM** -- plants both feet solidly in Luke's
    chest.

    He falls back, as does she -- she gets up first and pulls
    out her stake, drives it toward his chest -- but he grabs it
    just before it reaches.

                LUKE
        You think you can stop me? Stop
        us?

    He squeezes -- and the stake **splinters** in his powerful
    grip. He PUNCHES Buffy, knocks her back.

                LUKE
        You have no idea what you're
        dealing with.

    He stands, triumphant, over her. Begins intoning the sacred
    text:

                LUKE
        And like a plague of boils, the
        race of Man covered the earth. But,
        on the third day of the newest
        light will come the Harvest...

                              CUT TO:

42 INT. LIBRARY - CONTINUOUS   42

    Giles has his ancient texts out, is studying them in growing
    consternation.

                LUKE (V.O.)
        ...when the blood of men will flow
        as wine...

    ANGLE: GILES'S BOOK

    Shows a Dore-like engraving: a massacre. People writhing.
    blood everywhere -- in the center of them all, a Demon with
    a three-pointed star on his forehead, feeding off a woman.

                              CUT TO:

43 INT. THE CHURCH - CONTINUOUS   43

    We TRACK IN on the Master sitting, his face in darkness.

                          (CONTINUED)

43 CONTINUED: 43

                         LUKE (V.O.)
                    ... when the Master will walk among
                    them once more...

                                                        CUT TO:

44 EXT. FOREST - CONTINUOUS   44

       Xander, Willow and Jesse back away from the vampires --

                         LUKE (V.O.)
                    ... the world will belong to the
                    Old Ones...

       -- to find Darla right behind them!

                                                        CUT TO:

45 INT. MAUSOLEUM - CONTINUOUS   45

       Buffy is getting up, keeping her eyes on Luke --

                         LUKE
                    ... and Hell itself will come to
                    town.

       She tries to move to the side, to get away -- he backhands
       Buffy with all the force he has. She flies back -- right
       into the tomb!

       ANGLE: IN THE TOMB

       Buffy falls and lands HARD on her back, the wind knocked out
       of her. She looks beside her -- and sees the **withered
       corpse** of the tomb's owner.

       She's hurt pretty bad. She looks up but no Luke. Only the
       walls of the tomb. He could be anywhere.

       Slowly, achingly slowly, she lifts her head. Truly scared.
       Looks over one side of the tomb -- nothing. Looks over the
       other.

       Luke **FILLS THE FRAME**, roaring, jumping into the crypt on
       top of her.

       She tries to fight him off but she's well pinned. He
       contemplates her a moment with gleeful animal hunger. Teeth
       dripping.

                                                     (CONTINUED)

45 CONTINUED: 45

                              LUKE
                    Amen.

He bears down.

BLACKOUT.

TO BE CONTINUED

BUFFY THE VAMPIRE SLAYER "Welcome to the Hellmouth" Rev. 9/4/96 57.

65

BUFFY THE VAMPIRE SLAYER

"The Harvest"

Written by

Joss Whedon

Directed by

John Kretchmer

<u>SHOOTING SCRIPT</u>

September 11, 1996
September 13, 1996 - BLUE
September 30, 1996 - PINK
October 21, 1996 - GREEN
October 22, 1996 - YELLOW
October 28, 1996 - GOLDENROD
January 21, 1997 - SALMON

BUFFY THE VAMPIRE SLAYER

"The Harvest"

<u>CAST LIST</u>

BUFFY SUMMERS........................... Sarah Michelle Gellar
XANDER.................................. Nicholas Brendon
GILES.................................. Anthony S. Head
WILLOW................................. Alyson Hannigan
CORDELIA............................... Charisma Carpenter

MR. FLUTIE............................. Ken Lerner
JESSE.................................. Eric Balfour
THE MASTER............................. Mark Metcalf
ANGEL.................................. David Boreanaz
LUKE................................... Brian Thompson
DARLA.................................. Julie Benz
JOYCE SUMMERS.......................... Kristine Sutherland
HARMONY................................ Mercedes McNab
GUY....................................
BOUNCER................................
GIRL...................................

BUFFY THE VAMPIRE SLAYER

"The Harvest"

SET LIST

INTERIORS

SUNNYDALE HIGH SCHOOL
      THE LIBRARY
      COMPUTER CLASSROOM
MAUSOLEUM
TUNNELS
      A JUNCTION OF TUNNELS
      A SUBTERRANEAN ROOM
THE CHURCH
AIR VENT
THE BRONZE
      BACKSTAGE
BUFFY'S BEDROOM

EXTERIORS

SUNNYDALE HIGH SCHOOL
      SCHOOL GROUNDS
      FOUNTAIN QUAD
THE BRONZE
      OUTSIDE THE BRONZE
      BEHIND THE BRONZE
GRAVEYARD
STREET

BUFFY THE VAMPIRE SLAYER

"The Harvest"

<u>TEASER</u>

NOTE: THIS EPISODE WILL OPEN WITH A <u>RECAP</u> OF THE LAST, ENDING WITH LUKE PINNING BUFFY IN THE TOMB.

FADE IN:

1   INT. MAUSOLEUM - NIGHT   1

LUKE bears down on BUFFY, fangs bared. She struggles, but he's got her pinned. He rips open her shirt a bit to get at her throat. Grabs her -- and SCREAMS.

He jumps back, SMOKE curling out of his hand.

ANGLE: BUFFY'S NECK

The cross Angel gave her has slipped out of an inside pocket.

Buffy takes the moment and KICKS with both legs, sends Luke flying back out of the tomb. She jumps up herself and before he can recover, she RUNS out of there.

                                                    CUT TO:

2   EXT. GRAVEYARD - CONTINUOUS   2

As fast as she can -- stumbling a bit and breathing hard from the beating she took -- Buffy books through the graveyard. As she reaches the trees on the edge of it, she looks back at the Mausoleum.

Nobody's coming.

She hears WILLOW SCREAM.

                        WILLOW
            No! Nooo! Get -- off --

Buffy runs to the sound of the voice -- comes to find:

ANGLE: WILLOW

on the ground, struggling with a vampire.

The vampire has Willow pinned, is going in for the neck -- then he looks up, hearing something.

                                                    (CONTINUED)

Buffy's foot **whips** into his face, sending him flying way back.

He lands hard on his back and scrambles away, holding his nose.

Buffy is all business now, looking around her in quiet fury. Her senses alert.

She hears a CRACK, some SCUFFING on the ground. Takes off, leaving Willow wide-eyed and freaked. After a moment, she rises and follows.

ANGLE: XANDER

is unconscious, being dragged away by two other vampires. They hear something behind them, turn slowly around.

It's Willow, stumbling out from behind a tree. She looks extremely unthreatening.

They turn back and Buffy is right in front of them. She takes them both out with one punch. They fly back, then scramble to their feet.

Buffy grabs a branch, snaps it off the tree. She comes at them with this makeshift stake -- nails one in the chest.

The other flees.

Willow runs up to XANDER, cradles his head. He is just coming to.

> WILLOW
> Xander, are you okay?

> XANDER
> Man... something hit me...

Buffy is still looking around, unsatisfied.

> BUFFY
> Where's Jesse?

> WILLOW
> I don't know -- they surrounded
> us -- he was really weak...

> XANDER
> That girl grabbed him. Took off.

> BUFFY
> Which way?

(CONTINUED)

>   XANDER
>   I don't know.

Buffy looks into the night. The camera CIRCLES her as she
looks around. There is nothing to see.

>   BUFFY
>   (quietly)
>   Jesse ....

>   BLACK OUT.
>   <u>END OF TEASER</u>

ACT ONE

3   INT. THE LIBRARY - MORNING   3

We open on a Globe. As we hear GILES begin to SPEAK, we PAN
over to Xander and Willow, sitting in the middle of the
library. Neither of them appears to have slept since last
night.

                    GILES (O.S.)
              This world is older than any of you
              know, and contrary to popular
              mythology, it did not begin as a
              paradise. For untold eons, Demons
              walked the earth; made it their
              home... their Hell.

Still we PAN, to find Giles on the upper level, standing at
the railing. His expression is as grave as theirs.

                    GILES
              In time they lost their purchase on
              this reality, and the way was made
              for the mortal animals. For Man.
              What remains of the Old Ones are
              vestiges: Certain magicks, certain
              creatures...

                    BUFFY
              And vampires.

She emerges from Giles' office, wrapping a bandage around
her forearm. Xander rises, agitated.

                    XANDER
              Okay, this is where I have a
              problem, see, because we're now
              talking about vampires. We're
              having a talk with vampires in it.

                    WILLOW
              Isn't that what we saw last night?

                    BUFFY
              No, those weren't vampires. Those
              were just some guys in thundering
              need of a facial. Or maybe they
              had rabies -- coulda been rabies.
              And that guy turning to dust ...
              just a trick of the light.
                        (MORE)

                                              (CONTINUED)

3   CONTINUED: 3

                          BUFFY (cont'd)
                        (to Xander)
                    That's exactly what I said the
                    first time I saw a vampire. I
                    mean, when I was done with the
                    screaming part.

                          WILLOW
                    Oooh... I need to sit down.

                          BUFFY
                    You are sitting down.

                          WILLOW
                    Oh. Good for me.

                          XANDER
                    So vampires are demons?

                          GILES
                    The books tell that the last Demon
                    to leave this reality fed off a
                    human, mixed their blood. He was a
                    human form possessed -- infected --
                    by the Demon's soul. He bit
                    another, and another... and so they
                    walk the earth, feeding. Killing
                    some, mixing their blood with
                    others to make more of their kind.
                    Waiting for the animals to die out,
                    and the Old Ones to return.

                                          CUT TO:

4   INT. A TUNNEL - MORNING   4

Not that you could see whether it was morning or night in
this place -- it remains as dark and humid as the earth that
swallowed it.

JESSE is being dragged through the tunnel by Luke, DARLA by
his side. Jesse is still staggering into consciousness, and
the more he awakens, the less he likes it.

He looks about in fear at the two inhuman faces, at the end
of the tunnel they are dragging him through. It seems to be
an old cracked pipe, and it ends at:

5   INT. THE CHURCH - CONTINUOUS   5

Coming out of the Pipe, the threesome makes its way down a
pile of rocks to the floor of the wrecked church.

                                          (CONTINUED)

5   CONTINUED: 5

Jesse looks about, wonder tingeing the edges of his fear.
He is stood before the altar, before the pool of blood.

From the darkness, something moves. Emerges.

THE MASTER regards his servants, his total authority obvious
to all. He looks at Jesse.

                    THE MASTER
               Is this for me?

                    LUKE
               An offering, Master.

                    DARLA
               He's a good one. His blood is
               pure.

                    THE MASTER   *
                    (quietly -- almost
                    innocuously)
               You've tasted it.

Darla starts back a step, afraid.

                    THE MASTER   *
                    (smiling)   *
               I'm your faithful dog. You bring   *
               me scraps.   *

                    DARLA   *
               I didn't mean to --   *

                    THE MASTER   *
               I have waited. For three score   *
               years I have waited. While you   *
               come and go I have been stuck here,   *
                    (voice rising)   *
               here, in a house of **worship**. My   *
               ascension is almost at hand. Pray   *
               that when it comes ... I'm in a   *
               better mood.   *

                    DARLA   *
               Master, forgive me. We had more   *
               offerings but there was trouble. A   *
               girl.   *

                                                                 *

                                                                 *

                                              (CONTINUED)

> LUKE
> There **was** a girl. She fought
> well, and she knew of our breed.
> It's possible that she may be...

The Master turns to him.

> THE MASTER
> A Slayer?

SMASH CUT TO:

6   INT.   THE LIBRARY - CONTINUOUS   6

> XANDER
> And that would be a what?

> GILES
> As long as there have been
> vampires, there has been the
> Slayer. One girl in all the
> world --

> BUFFY
> He loves doing this part.

> GILES
> (speeding up)
> All right: They hunt vampires, one
> Slayer dies, the next is called,
> Buffy is the Slayer, don't tell
> anyone. I think that's all the
> vampire information you need.

> XANDER
> Except for one thing. How do you
> kill them?

> BUFFY
> You don't. I do.

> XANDER
> Well, Jesse --

(CONTINUED)

6   CONTINUED: 6

                         BUFFY
              Jesse's my responsibility. I let
              him get taken.

                         XANDER
              That's not true.

                         WILLOW
              If you hadn't showed up, they would
              have... taken us too... Does
              anybody mind if I pass out?

                         BUFFY
              Breathe...

                         WILLOW
              Breathe.

                         BUFFY
              Breathe.
                   (to Giles)
              This big guy, Luke, he talked about
              an offering to the Master. I don't
              know who or what, but if they
              weren't just feeding, Jesse may
              still be alive. I'm gonna find
              him.

                         WILLOW
              This is probably the dumb question,
              but shouldn't we call the police?

                         GILES
              Do you think they'd believe us?

                         WILLOW
              We don't have to say vampires. We
              could say there was... a bad man.

                         BUFFY
              They couldn't handle it if they did
              come. They'd only show up with
              guns.

                         GILES
                   (to Buffy)
              You've no idea where they took
              Jesse?

                                        (CONTINUED)

                         BUFFY
               I looked around, but ... soon as
               they got clear of the woods they
               could have just
                    (indicating flight)
               -- whoom.

                         XANDER
               They can **fly**?

                         BUFFY
               They can drive.

                         XANDER
               Oh.

                         WILLOW
               I don't remember hearing a car...

                         GILES
               Well, let's take an enormous
               intuitive leap and say they went
               underground.

                         BUFFY
               Vampires really jam on sewer
               systems. You can get anywhere in
               town without catching any rays. I
               didn't see any access around there,
               though.

                         XANDER
               Well, there's electrical tunnels.
               They run under the whole town.

                         GILES
               If we had a diagnostic of the
               tunnel system, it might indicate a
               meeting place. I suppose we could
               go to the building commission --

                         BUFFY
               We **so** don't have time.

                         WILLOW
               Uh, guys? There may be another
               way.

                                        CUT TO:

7   INT. THE CHURCH - CONTINUOUS   7

                        THE MASTER
              A Slayer... Have you any proof?

                        LUKE
              Only that she fought me and yet
              lives.

                        THE MASTER
              Very nearly proof enough. I can't
              remember the last time that
              happened.

                        LUKE
              1843, in Madrid. And the bastard
              caught me sleeping.

                        THE MASTER
              She mustn't be allowed to interfere
              with the Harvest.

                        LUKE
              I would never let that happen.

                        THE MASTER
              You needn't worry. I believe
              she'll come to us. We have
              something that she wants. If she
              is a Slayer, and this boy lives,
              she'll try to save him.

Luke goes up to Jesse, smiling.

                        LUKE
              I thought you nothing more than a
              meal, boy. Congratulations.
              You've just been upgraded to
              "bait".

                                              CUT TO:

8   INT. THE LIBRARY - CONTINUOUS   8

ANGLE: A MAP OF THE ELECTRICAL TUNNELS

On a computer screen.

                        BUFFY (O.S.)
              There it is.

WIDER ANGLE:

Willow sits at the computer, everyone else gathered around
her.

                                         (CONTINUED)

                         WILLOW
          This runs under the graveyard.

                         XANDER
          I don't see any access.

                         GILES
          So all the city plans are just open
          to the public?

                         WILLOW
          Uh, well, in a way. I sort of
          stumbled onto them when I
          accidentally... decrypted the city
          council's security system.

                         XANDER
               (still focused on the
                screen)
          Someone's been naughty...

                         BUFFY
          There's nothing here. This is
          useless!

                         GILES
          I think you should ease up on
          yourself.

                         BUFFY
          You're the one who told me I wasn't
          prepared enough. Understatement.
          I thought I was on top of it, and
          then that Monster Luke came out of
          nowhere --

          She stops. Pauses.

                         XANDER
          What?

                         BUFFY
               (working it out)
          He didn't come out of nowhere. He
          came from behind me. I was facing
          the entrance. He came from behind
          me and he didn't follow me out.
               (looks at them)
          The access to the tunnels is in the
          mausoleum.

                         GILES
          Are you sure?

                                              (CONTINUED)

                        BUFFY
The girl must have doubled back
with Jesse after I got out. God,
I'm so mentally challenged!

                        XANDER
So, what's the plan? We saddle up,
right?

                        BUFFY
There's no 'we'. Okay? I'm the
Slayer, and you're not.

                        XANDER
I knew you were gonna throw that in
my face.

                        BUFFY
Xander, this is deeply dangerous.

                        XANDER
I'm inadequate. That's fine. I'm
less than a man.

                        WILLOW
Buffy, I'm not anxious to go into a
dark place full of monsters, but I
do want to help. I need to.

                        GILES
Then help me. I've been
researching this Harvest affair.
Seems to be some sort of
pre-ordained massacre. Rivers of
blood, Hell on earth... Quite
charmless. I am fuzzy on the
details, however, and it may be
that you can wrest some information
from that dread machine.
            (off their
             uncomprehending looks)
That was a bit British, wasn't it?

                        BUFFY
Welcome to the new world.

                        GILES
            (translates to Willow)
I want you to go on the Net.

                        WILLOW
Oh! Yeah. Sure. I can do that.

                                        (CONTINUED)

8   CONTINUED: 3   8

                              BUFFY
                    Then I'm out of here.
                         (to Xander and Willow)
                    If Jesse's alive, I'll bring him
                    back.

                              GILES
                    Do I have to tell you to be
                    careful?

Buffy looks at him a moment. Then she's out.

                                                           CUT TO:

9   EXT.   SCHOOL GROUNDS - DAY   9

Buffy heads toward a gate that stands open. She is about to
go through it when FLUTIE appears right behind her.

                              MR. FLUTIE
                    And where do we think we're going?

                              BUFFY
                    We? I? Me?

                              MR. FLUTIE
                    We're not leaving school grounds,
                    are we?

                              BUFFY
                    No! I'm just ... admiring the
                    fence. This is quality fencework.

                              MR. FLUTIE
                    Because if we were leaving school
                    grounds on our second day at a new
                    school after being kicked out of
                    our old school for delinquent
                    behavior -- do you see where I'm
                    going with this?

                              BUFFY
                         (it comes to her:)
                    Mr. Giles!

                              MR. FLUTIE
                    What?

                              BUFFY
                    He asked me to get a book for him.
                    From the store 'cause I have a free
                    period and I'm a big reader did it
                    mention that on my transcripts?

                                                      (CONTINUED)

9   CONTINUED: 9

                         MR. FLUTIE
               Mr. Giles.

                         BUFFY
               Ask him.

Mr. Flutie shuts and locks the gate, saying:

                         MR. FLUTIE
               Well, maybe that's how they do
               things in Britain, they've got that
               royal family and all kinds of
               problems. But here at Sunnydale
               nobody leaves campus while school's
               in session. Are we clear?

                         BUFFY
               We're clear.

                         MR. FLUTIE
               That's the Buffy Summers I want in
               my school. The sensible girl, with
               her feet on the ground.

He smiles, leaves.

ANGLE: BUFFY'S FEET

Standing before the fence. After a bit they jump up, leave
the frame. A moment later we see her land on the other
side, take off running.

                                        CUT TO:

A9   INT. HALL.   A9*

Willow and Xander enter the hall from the library. Students   *
are filing into classes.   *

                         WILLOW   *
                    (listing)   *
               Murder, Death, Disaster -- what   *
               else?   *

                         XANDER   *
               Paranormal, Unexplained -- you got   *
               Natural Disasters?   *

                         WILLOW   *
                    (nodding)   *
               Earthquake, flood...   *

                                        (CONTINUED)

A9 CONTINUED: A9

                          XANDER   *
          Rain of toads.   *

                          WILLOW   *
          Right.   *

                          XANDER   *
               (it's unbelievable)   *
          Rain of toads. Are they really   *
          gonna have anything like that in   *
          the paper?   *

                          WILLOW   *
          I'll put it on the search. If it's   *
          in there it'll turn up. Anything   *
          that'll lead us to vampires.   *

                          XANDER   *
          And I meanwhile will help by   *
          standing around like an idiot.   *

                          WILLOW   *
          Not like an idiot. Just standing.   *
          Buffy doesn't want you getting   *
          hurt.   *
               (smaller voice)   *
          I don't want you getting hurt.   *

     They arrive at Willow's class, stand by the door.   *

                          XANDER   *
          This is just too much. Yesterday   *
          my life-is like, "Oh no. Pop   *
          Quiz." Today -- Rain of toads.   *

                          WILLOW   *
          I know.   *
               (looking at other   *
                students)   *
          And everyone else thinks it's just   *
          a normal day.   *

                          XANDER   *
          Nobody knows. It's like we've got   *
          this big secret.   *

                          WILLOW   *
          We do. That's what a secret is: *
          when you know something other guys   *
          don't.   *

                                              (CONTINUED)

A9 CONTINUED: 2   A9

                              XANDER   *
                        (somewhat distracted)   *
                   Right. Well, you better get to   *
                   class.   *

                              WILLOW   *
                   You mean "we." "We" should get to   *
                   class.   *

                              XANDER   *
                   Yeah.   *

                              WILLOW   *
                   Buffy will be okay. Whatever's   *
                   down there, I think she can handle   *
                   it.   *

                              XANDER   *
                        (not believing it)   *
                   Yeah, I do too.   *

                              WILLOW   *
                        (not believing it)   *
                   So do I.   *

                                                       CUT TO: *

10 EXT. GRAVEYARD - DAY   10

     Buffy makes her way to the Mausoleum. Enters.

                                                       CUT TO:

11 INT. MAUSOLEUM - CONTINUOUS   11

     But for the light from the doorway, it's just as dark in
     here as it was last night. Buffy makes her way cautiously,
     looking about her. She senses a lurking presence, but the
     shadows give up nothing.

     She reaches the iron door on the other side. Tries it.
     It's locked. She stops, letting out a long breath.

                                                       (CONTINUED)

11 CONTINUED: 11

                         BUFFY
                  (not looking around)
            I don't suppose you've got a key on
            you?

ANGEL steps from the shadows, a smile in his eyes.

                         ANGEL
            They really don't like me dropping
            in.

                         BUFFY
            Why not?

                         ANGEL
            They really don't like me.

                         BUFFY
                  (sarcastically)
            How could that possibly be?

                         ANGEL
            I knew you'd figure out this
            entryway sooner or later.
            Actually, I thought it was gonna be
            a little sooner.

                         BUFFY
            I'm sorry you had to wait. Look,
            if you're gonna be popping up with
            this cryptic wise man act on a
            regular basis, can you at least
            tell me your name?

                         ANGEL
            Angel.

                         BUFFY
            Angel.
                  (offhand)
            It's a pretty name.

                         ANGEL
            Don't go down there.

                         BUFFY
            Deal with my going.

                         ANGEL
            You shouldn't be putting yourself
            at risk. Tonight is the Harvest.
            Unless you can prevent it, the
            Master walks.

                                        (CONTINUED)

                              BUFFY
                    If this Harvest thing is such a
                    suckfest, why don't **you** stop it?

                              ANGEL
                    Because I'm afraid.

The unashamed openness of the statement catches her a bit
off guard. She looks at him a moment.

She KICKS the door open.

                              ANGEL
                    They'll be expecting you.

                              BUFFY
                    I've got a friend down there -- or,
                    a potential friend.
                         (joking)
                    Do you know what it's like to have
                    a friend?

He doesn't answer.

                              BUFFY
                         (gently)
                    That wasn't supposed to be a
                    stumper.

                              ANGEL
                    When you hit the tunnels, head
                    east, toward the school. That's
                    where you're likely to find them.

                              BUFFY
                    You gonna wish me luck?

He says nothing. She looks at him a moment more, then heads
into the darkness.

He stands there, not moving. Quiet concern on his face.

                              ANGEL
                         (softly)
                    Good luck.

                                             BLACK OUT.

                         <u>END OF ACT ONE</u>

ACT TWO

12 INT. TUNNELS - DAY   12

They are dark, forbidding, and they run in all directions.

Buffy climbs down a ladder, drops into them. She looks
about her, taking it in.

ANGLE: A RAT

Scurries by her foot.

Buffy doesn't flinch. She starts down a tunnel, moving
slowly. The dark enveloping her.

She turns a corner, slowly. Nothing. Starts down it.

She hears something and spins, sneaks up and looks down
another tunnel.

ANGLE: DOWN THE OTHER TUNNEL

Shadows. Noise. Nothing solid.

She pulls her head back and he's **right behind her!**

                    XANDER
          Did you see anything?

                    BUFFY
          Xander! What are you doing here?

                    XANDER
          Something stupid. I followed you.
          I couldn't just sit around not
          doing anything.

                    BUFFY
          I understand. Now go away.

                    XANDER
          Jesse's my bud, okay? If I can
          help him, then that's what I gotta
          do.

A beat, as she accepts this.

                    XANDER
          Besides, it's this or Chem class.

                                        (CONTINUED)

12   CONTINUED: 12

    They make their way through the dark.

                                                            CUT TO:

13   INT.   THE LIBRARY - DAY   13

    Giles has his arcane volumes out, is consulting them. After
    some digging, he finds something interesting. He looks
    closely at one passage, translating to himself from the
    Latin.

                        GILES
                "For they will gather, and be
                gathered. All that is theirs shall
                be his... From the Vessel pours
                life." Pours life...

    ANGLE: AN ENGRAVING

    A bestial fellow holds his hand out, commanding a throng of
    villagers, all of whom are bleeding. Below, in what might
    be Hell, a demon glows with power.

    Upon the bestial one's forehead, a crude symbol has been
    drawn, a star with three points.

    He looks over at another passage.

                        GILES
                    (reads)
                "On the night of the crescent moon,
                the first past the solstice, it
                will come." Of course.
                    (he looks up)
                Tonight.

                                                            CUT TO:

14   INT.   COMPUTER CLASS - DAY   14

    Everyone is working, alone and in groups, devising programs.
    CORDELIA and HARMONY struggle mightily with theirs.

                        CORDELIA
                No! It's supposed to find the
                syntax and match it. Or, wait...

                        HARMONY
                    (typing slowly)
                Are we going to the Bronze tonight?

                                                        (CONTINUED)

14   CONTINUED: 14

                              CORDELIA
                    No, we're going to the other cool
                    place in Sunnydale.

Harmony looks at her inquisitively.

                              CORDELIA
                    Of course we're going to the
                    Bronze! Friday night, no cover.
                    But you should have been there last
                    night.

                              HARMONY
                         (re: program)
                    I think we did this part wrong.

                              CORDELIA
                    Why do we have to devise these
                    programs? Isn't that what nerds
                    are for?
                         (quietly)
                    What did **she** do?

Harmony cranes over to look at:

ANGLE: WILLOW

Sitting next to them, but in her own world. She is bringing
things up on the Net, typing intently, scrolling,
searching...

                              HARMONY
                    Uh, she's doing something else.

                                                      CUT TO:

15   INT. TUNNELS - LATER   15

Buffy and Xander turn a corner, ready for anything.

Nothing. They keep walking, alert. Xander picks up the
conversation they were in:

                              XANDER
                    Okay, so: crosses, garlic, stake
                    through the heart.

                              BUFFY
                    That'll get it done.

                              XANDER
                    Cool. of course, I don't actually
                    have any of those things.

                                                   (CONTINUED)

                              BUFFY
                         (hands him a cross)
                    Good thinking.

                              XANDER
                    Well, the part of my brain that
                    would tell me to bring that stuff
                    is still busy telling me not to
                    come down here. I brought this,
                    though.

He produces a flashlight, turns it on.

                              BUFFY
                    Turn that off!

                              XANDER
                         (he does)
                    Okay, okay. So, what else?

                              BUFFY
                    What else what?

                              XANDER
                    For Vampire Slayage.

                              BUFFY
                    Fire, beheading, sunlight, holy
                    water... the usual.

                              XANDER
                         (a little weakly)
                    So you've done some beheading in
                    your time?

                              BUFFY
                    Oh, yeah. There was this one time,
                    I was pinned down by this vampire,
                    he played left tackle for the
                    varsity -- I mean, before he was...
                    well anyway he's got one of those
                    really thick necks and all I've got
                    is a little Exacto knife --
                         (off Xander's gape)
                    You're not loving this story.

                              XANDER
                    Actually, I find it oddly
                    comforting.

                                             CUT TO:

16 INT.   COMPUTER CLASS - DAY   16

Willow is busily bringing up relevant data from the Net, her brow furrowed in concentration. At the next terminal, Cordelia is struggling with a program while holding court.

                    CORDELIA
          Okay, and then "Pattern Run",
          right? Or "Go To End". That's it.

                    HARMONY
          Maybe... I think...

                    CORDELIA
          Well, what does the book say?
               (as Harmony looks it up)
          So anyway, I come out of the
          bathroom and she comes running at
          me with a stick, screaming, "I'm
          gonna kill you! I'm gonna kill
          you!" I swear.

                    GUY
               (leaning in)
          Who?

                    CORDELIA
          Buffy.

                    HARMONY
          The new girl.

                    GUY
          What's her deal?

                    CORDELIA
          She's crazed!

                    HARMONY
          Did you hear about her old school?
          Booted.

                    CORDELIA
          I exhibit no surprise.

                    GUY
          Why was she kicked out?

                    CORDELIA
          'Cause she's a psycho-loony.

                    WILLOW
          No, she's not.

Silence, as Cordelia registers the concept that Willow just contradicted her.

                                        (CONTINUED)

16 CONTINUED: 16

                         CORDELIA
              What?

                         WILLOW
              She's not a psycho. You don't even
              know her.

                         CORDELIA
              Excuse me? Who gave you permission
              to exist? Do I horn in on your
              private discussions? No. Why?
              Because you're boring.

Willow looks down, hurt. She stands and takes some pages
that have come up on the printer. The girls turn back to
their project.

                         HARMONY
              There. I think the program's done.

                         CORDELIA
              Finally, the nightmare ends. Now
              how do we save it?

                         WILLOW
                  (as she exits)
              "Deliver."

                         CORDELIA
                  (staring at the screen)
              Deliver -- where is that -- Oh!

ANGLE: A KEY

Marked "DEL". Cordelia hits it.

Long pause, the two girls staring at the screen, their
smiles about to melt into perplexity as we

                                                        CUT TO:

17   INT. TUNNELS - LATER   17

Buffy and Xander are still making their way through the
dark. The banter quotient has plummeted -- they're both
fairly tense.

Buffy looks around, brow furrowed.

                         BUFFY
              They're close.

                                                      (CONTINUED)

                          XANDER
                How can you tell?

                          BUFFY
                No rats.

Xander doesn't love that information, but he says nothing.
Still they progress, until:

                          XANDER
                Over there. What's that?

He indicates a small, dark side-chamber. Nothing can be
seen past the first few inches.

They come up to it. Xander pulls out his flashlight, shines
it.

ANGLE: IN THE CHAMBER

A beam of light finds a body, lying face down. It looks
like

                          XANDER
                Jesse!

                          BUFFY
                Oh, no...

She starts forward, Xander keeping the light on her. Goes
over to the body, reaches out --

and Jesse JUMPS UP, brandishing a pipe. He's about to slam
her with it when Xander calls out:

                          XANDER
                Jesse!

                          JESSE
                  (stops, amazed)
                Xander?

He drops the pipe and the two friends hug. Xander pulls
away, looking him over.

                          XANDER
                Jesse, man, are you okay?

                          JESSE
                I'm not okay on an epic scale. We
                gotta get out of here!

He indicates his leg -- he's been chained to the wall.

                                              (CONTINUED)

                              XANDER
                It's cool! Buffy's a superhero!

The superhero frowns at the chain, feels it.

                              BUFFY
                          (to Jesse)
                Hold on.

She takes the pipe he dropped and SMASHES the lock on his
shackles. It's not a quiet operation.

                              XANDER
                You think anybody heard that?

ANGLE: A TUNNEL - CONTINUOUS

A few black shapes move in the shadows, hearing it.

ANGLE: BUFFY AND THE OTHERS

They start out.

                              JESSE
                They knew you were gonna come.
                They said that I -- I was the
                bait...

                              XANDER
                Oh, now you tell us.

                              JESSE
                I've seen their leader.

The look in his eyes describes their leader in detail.

Buffy leads the two boys back through the tunnel. She
stops.

Shadows move at the other end.

                              BUFFY
                Oops.

                              JESSE
                Oh, no, no...

                              BUFFY
                Do you know another way out?

                              JESSE
                I don't, uh, maybe?

                                              (CONTINUED)

17 CONTINUED: 3   17

                         XANDER
              Come on.

They truck out the other way.

                                             CUT TO:

18 INT. A JUNCTION OF TUNNELS - A SECOND LATER   18

    They come into this one, moving at a good clip. Try one
    avenue --

    Eyes gleam in the dark. Whispered LAUGHS drift at us.

    They turn back, pause at a fork.

                         JESSE
              Wait, wait. They brought me
              through here! There's a way up. I
              hope.

    They take off.

                                             CUT TO:

19 INT. A SUBTERRANEAN ROOM - MOMENTS LATER   19

    The run in, vampires approaching slowly behind them. Look
    around, horror growing on their faces.

    There is no door. There is no exit. Buffy and Xander look
    about them, frantically.

                         BUFFY
              I don't think this is the way out.

    She goes back to the doorway they came in, listens for the
    approaching vampires.

                         XANDER
              We can't fight our way back through
              those things... what do we do?

                         JESSE
              I've got an idea...

    And the CAMERA PANS over to Jesse standing right behind
    Xander. His visage grotesque, his smile icy. He's a
    vampire.

                                             (CONTINUED)

19 CONTINUED:

                          JESSE
          You can die.

                                        BLACK OUT.

                    END OF ACT TWO

ACT THREE

20   INT. A SUBTERRANEAN ROOM - TWO SECONDS LATER   20

Xander backs away from Jesse. Buffy looks from him to the
entrance, not sure what to do.

ANGLE: THE ENTRANCE

We HEAR approaching vampires, see shadows begin to move,
thrown on the outer wall by figures down the hall.

                    XANDER
          Jesse... Man, I'm sorry...

                    JESSE
          Sorry? I feel good, Xander. I
          feel strong.

Buffy grabs the door, tries to close it. But it's thick
metal, rusted open.

                    JESSE
          I'm connected, man. To everything.
          I can hear the worms in the earth.

                    XANDER
          Well, that's a plus.

                    JESSE
          I know what the Master wants. I'll
          serve his purpose. That means you
          die. And I feed.

                    BUFFY
          Xander! The cross!

Xander holds it up -- and Jesse stops coming toward him.
The smile leaves his face.

Buffy continues trying to shut the door -- it's beginning to
budge. But coming down the hall are:

ANGLE: THE VAMPIRES

Making their way down the hall to the door. They move
slowly, grinning -- sure of victory.

                    XANDER
          Jesse. Man, we're buds. Can't you
          remember?

                                        (CONTINUED)

20 CONTINUED: 20

                              JESSE
                You're like a shadow to me now.

Xander moves forward, cross in hand.

                              XANDER
                Then get out of my face.

Jesse stumbles back, pissed. Xander backs him toward the
door.

Buffy continues to strain. The vampires approach.

Jesse lashes out, knocks the cross from Xander's grasp. He
grins -- and then Buffy grabs him from behind and HURLS him
out of the room, knocking vampires over like bowling pins.

                              BUFFY
                Help me!

Xander snaps out of his shock and comes to the door with
her. With both their backs to it, they slam it shut --

-- an arm SHOOTS in, grasping for them. Buffy opens the
door slightly and slams it again till the arm withdraws.
She bolts the door, breathing heavily.

                              XANDER
                I can't believe it ... we were too
                late.

A resounding THUD shudders the door. The vampires are gonna
break it down.

                              BUFFY
                We need to get out of here.

                              XANDER
                There is no out of here!

Another THUD and the door begins to buckle on its hinges.
Buffy looks around -- there is some junk lying around. She
throws it out of the way to see if there is a doorway behind
it. No joy.

Xander also looks around. He spies:

ANGLE: AN AIR VENT

We can see just a hint of an air vent's grating behind a
metal sheet. It's high up in the shadows.

                              XANDER
                What's that?

                                                    (CONTINUED)

20 CONTINUED: 2   20

Buffy sees it too. She throws a box down, steps on it to
reach the vent. Pulls away the metal sheet, revealing the
grate. It's big enough to climb through.

She begins trying to pry the grate open with her bare hands.

Another THUD. Xander looks from Buffy to the door.

Buffy pulls, bending a corner.

The door comes off its hinges enough for a vampire to put
his fingers through, grip it.

Buffy RIPS the grating loose, throws it aside.

                    BUFFY
          Come on!

And a vampire SHOOTS out of the air vent at her, grabbing
her head.

The door comes out enough for a vampire to get its face in.

Buffy pulls the vampire all the way out of the vent, throws
it to the floor. Jumps down on top of it.

                    BUFFY
                 (to Xander)
          Go!

He runs by, climbs on the box as Buffy sinks a stake into
the vampire's back. He sticks the flashlight in:

ANGLE: IN THE AIR VENT

Nothing. Clear.

He crawls in, starts worming his way down it.

ANGLE: THE DOOR.

Breaks down. Vampires pile in.

Buffy jumps up and pulls herself into the air vent.

                                            CUT TO:

21 INT. AIR VENT - CONTINUOUS   21

The two of them crawl along in the dark, the vampires at
their heels.

                                            (CONTINUED)

21   CONTINUED: 21

They come to a wider space, with a ladder going up.
Sunlight can be seen through the grating at the very top.

                    XANDER
          Up?

                    BUFFY
          UP!

He starts climbing, Buffy right behind him.

He gets to the top and opens the grating, climbs out into:

                                                        CUT TO:

22   EXT.   STREET - AFTERNOON   22

It's deserted as Xander rolls out, reaches in to help Buffy
up. She is almost out when

ANGLE: A HAND

grabs her ankle, starts pulling her back down.

She pulls up, bringing the hand up into the sunlight. It
begins to SMOKE -- we hear a SHRIEK and it is withdrawn.

Buffy rolls out, slams the grating shut.

For a moment both of them just lie there, catching their
breath.

                                                        CUT TO:

A23 INT. THE CHURCH - LATER   A23*

The Master rises from his chair. He looks less than   *
pleased. A few vampires stand before him, only one of whom   *
has his face visible.   *

                    THE MASTER   *
          She escaped. She walks free when I   *
          should be drinking her heart's   *
          blood right now. Careless.   *

                    VAMPIRE   *
          Master, we had her trapped.   *

                                                   (CONTINUED)

A23 CONTINUED: A23

                         THE MASTER   *
          Are you going to make excuses? You   *
          are all weak. It's been too long   *
          since you faced a Slayer. But it's   *
          no matter to me. She'll not stop   *
          the Harvest. It just means there   *
          will be someone worth killing when   *
          I reach the surface.   *
                    (to the Vampire)   *
          Is Luke ready?   *

                         VAMPIRE   *
          He waits.   *

                         THE MASTER   *
                    (to another)   *
          It's time. Bring him to me.   *
                    (to the first)   *
          And, Lucien, You failed me.   *
                    (with gentle menace)   *
          Tell me you're sorry.   *

                         VAMPIRE   *
          I'm sorry...   *

                         THE MASTER   *
          There now. That wasn't so hard.   *
          Oh, hold on --   *

     He JABS his finger viciously out of frame. We hear a GASP.   *

                         THE MASTER (cont'd)   *
          -- you've got something in your   *
          eye.   *

23 INT. THE LIBRARY - DAY   23

     Giles is sill pouring over his notes when Willow enters.
     He looks up, hoping to see

                         GILES
          Buffy?

                         WILLOW
          It's just me. So there's no word?

                         GILES
          Not as yet.

                         WILLOW
          Well, I'm sure they're... great.

                                              (CONTINUED)

23 CONTINUED: 23

                          GILES
              Did you find anything of interest?

She sits, shows him copied articles as she talks.

                          WILLOW
              I think maybe. I looked through
              the old papers, around the time of
              that big earthquake back in '37.
              And for several months before it,
              there was a rash of murders.

                          GILES
              Great! I mean, not great in a good
              way... Go on.

                          WILLOW
              They sound like the kind you were
              looking for. Throats, blood.
              Months, and not even a clue.

                          GILES
              It's all coming together. I rather
              wish it weren't.

                                              CUT TO:

24 INT. THE CHURCH - CONTINUOUS   24

We see a candle being lit, the last of a row. Darla steps
back from it, the taper in her hand glowing softly.

As she does, another vampire does the same on the opposite
wall. They are at the back of the church, staring ahead.
The rows of candles run up to the altar, where the Master
stands waiting.

CHANTING can be heard, a low, primal whisper.

Luke steps forward, pulling off his shirt. He steps
forward, kneels before the Master. The Master holds out his
hand. Luke leans forward and kisses it. The Master turns
his open palm up and Luke kisses that as well. Gently, Luke
takes the Master's wrist in his hand, brings his lips to
that as well.

And bites it.

The Master winces, shuts his eyes. Luke feeds for a few
moments, then rears his head back with holy pain.

                                              (CONTINUED)

24 CONTINUED: 24

                         THE MASTER
               My blood runs with yours. My soul
               is your province.

                         LUKE
               My body is your instrument.

The Master takes a drop of blood from his wrist, dabs it on
Luke's forehead, **painting the three-pointed star**. He
speaks to the assembled:

                         THE MASTER
               On this most hallowed night, we are
               as one. Luke is the Vessel. Every
               soul he takes shall feed me. Their
               souls will grant me the power to
               free myself. Tonight I will walk
               the Earth... and the stars
               themselves will hide.

                                        CUT TO:

25   INT. THE LIBRARY - CONTINUOUS   25

Buffy and Xander enter, somewhat the worse for their
adventure. Willow takes one look at their faces and doesn't
have to ask. She does anyway.

                         WILLOW
               Did you find Jesse?

                         XANDER
               Yeah.

                         WILLOW
               Was he dead?

                         BUFFY
               Worse.

She sits heavily.

                         BUFFY
               I'm sorry, Willow. We were too
               late. And they were waiting for
               us.

                         WILLOW
               At least you two are okay.

Xander kicks a trash bin in frustration.

                                        (CONTINUED)

                    XANDER
          I don't like vampires. I'm gonna
          take a stand and say they're not
          good.

                    BUFFY
          So, Giles, you got anything that
          can make this day worse?

                    GILES
          How about the end of the world?

                    BUFFY
          I knew I could count on you.

                    GILES
          This is what we know. Some sixty
          years ago a very old, very powerful
          vampire came to this shore, and not
          just to feed.

                    BUFFY
          He came 'cause this town is a
          mystical whoosit?

                    GILES
          Yes. The Spanish who first settled
          here called it Boca Del Infierno --
          roughly translated: Hellmouth. A
          sort of portal from this reality to
          the next. This vampire hoped to
          open it.

                    BUFFY
          Bring the demons back.

                    XANDER
          End of the world.

                    WILLOW
          But he blew it. Or, I mean, there
          was an earthquake that swallowed
          about half the town. And him
          too -- or at least there were no
          more vampire-type killings after.

                    GILES
          Opening dimensional portals is
          tricky business. Odds are he got
          himself stuck. Like a cork in a
          bottle.

                                        (CONTINUED)

25 CONTINUED: 2   25

                    XANDER
          And this Harvest thing is to get
          him out?

                    GILES
          It comes once in a century, on this
          night. A Master can draw power
          from one of his minions while it
          feeds. Enough power to break free,
          and to open the portal. The minion
          is called the Vessel, and he bears
          this symbol.

He shows them a sketch of the three-pointed star.

                    BUFFY
          So, I dust anyone sporting this
          look, and no Harvest.

                    GILES
          Simply put, yes.

                    BUFFY
          Any clue where this little
          get-together is being held?

                    GILES
          Well, there are a number of
          possibilities --

                    XANDER
          They're going to the Bronze.

                    WILLOW
          Are you sure?

                    XANDER
          Come on, tasty young morsels all
          over the place. Anyway, that's
          where Jesse's gonna be. Trust me.

                    GILES
          Then we need to get there. The sun
          will be down before long.

They head out toward the door.

                    BUFFY
          I gotta make a stop. Won't take
          long.

                    GILES
          What for?

                                         (CONTINUED)

25   CONTINUED: 3   25

                              BUFFY
                    Supplies.

                                                   CUT TO:

26   ANGLE: THE SUN   26

      Big and red, sinking low.

27   INT. BUFFY'S BEDROOM - DUSK   27

      The last rays are streaming in as Buffy enters, starts going
      through her closet.

                              JOYCE (O.S.)
                    Buffy?

      Buffy's mom, JOYCE SUMMERS, enters. Buffy keeps going
      through her clothes, picking out a good slaying outfit.

                              JOYCE
                    You're going out?

                              BUFFY
                    I have to.

                              JOYCE
                    I didn't hear you come in last
                    night.

                              BUFFY
                    I was quiet.

                              JOYCE
                    It's happening again, isn't it?

      Buffy stops, looks at her.

                              JOYCE
                    I got a call from your new
                    principal. Says you missed some
                    classes today.

                              BUFFY
                    I was... running an errand.

      She pulls an old trunk out of her closet. She opens it,
      starts going through it.

                                                   (CONTINUED)

                         JOYCE
          We haven't finished unpacking and
          I'm getting calls from your
          principal.

                         BUFFY
          Mom, I promise you, it's not gonna
          be like before. But I have to go.

                         JOYCE
          No.

                         BUFFY
          Mom...

Buffy looks at the window, at the growing dark.

                         JOYCE
          The tapes all say I should get used
          to saying it. No.

                         BUFFY
          This is important.

                         JOYCE
          I know. You have to go out or
          it'll be the end of the world.
          Everything is life or death when
          you're a sixteen year old girl.

                         BUFFY
          Mom, I don't have time to talk
          about it --

                         JOYCE
          You've got all night, Buffy.
          You're not going anywhere. Now you
          can stay up here and sulk if you
          want. I won't hold it against you.
          But if you want to come down, I'll
          make us some dinner.

Joyce leaves, closing the door quietly but firmly behind
her. After a moment, Buffy reaches into the trunk.

ANGLE: IN THE TRUNK

Girl stuff, memorabilia, Teen Beat magazines.

Buffy reaches in and lifts out the inside -- the trunk has a
false bottom. Below it stakes, crosses, host, garlic, and a
widemouthed jar of holy water.

                                        (CONTINUED)

27 CONTINUED: 2   27

Buffy takes out a particularly deadly looking stake. It
fits in her hand like it's part of it. She stuffs it into a
bag, along with a few other items.

She stands, goes to the door. Listens by it.

She goes to the window, opens it. Starts crawling out.

                                                    CUT TO:

28 ANGLE: THE HORIZON   28

The sun is gone. The sky a deepening blue.

                                                    CUT TO: *

A29 INT. THE BRONZE - NIGHT   A29*

From the balcony, we look down on a pool game in progress.   *
Tilt up to see Cordelia holding court at a table.   *

                         CORDELIA   *
             Senior boys are the only way to go.   *
             They're just a better class of   *
             person. The boys in our grade?   *
             Forget about it. They're children.   *
             Like Jesse -- did you see him last   *
             night? The way he follows me   *
             around... He's like a little puppy   *
             dog: you just want to put him to   *
             sleep. Senior boys have mystery,   *
             they have ... what's the word I'm   *
             searching for? Cars.   *

A Cordette starts to speak. Cordelia interrupts: *

                         CORDELIA   *
             I'm just not the type to settle.   *
             If I go into a clothing store, I   *
             always have to have the most   *
             expensive thing not because it's   *
             expensive, but because it **costs**   *
             more.   *

A Cordette starts to speak.   *

                         CORDELIA   *
             Hello! Miss Motormouth -- can I   *
             get a sentence finished? Oh! I   *
             love this song!   *

She gets up, friends in tow, and heads to the balcony.   *

                                                    CUT TO:

29 INT. THE BRONZE - CONTINUOUS   29

    TILT UP on Cordelia, dancing away in the middle of the
    crowd. She looks great.

    ANGLE: AT THE DOOR

    Jesse walks in, a new man. A cool, subtle swagger in his
    step. His eyes go right to Cordelia. He smiles.

                                                      CUT TO:

30 EXT. OUTSIDE THE BRONZE - CONTINUOUS   30

    There are a few people lounging around outside, but not much
    activity. Then, a ways off, we see them coming, walking
    slowly into the half-light.

    Eight vampires, Luke in the middle.

    None of them saying a word.

                                                      BLACK OUT.

                         END OF ACT THREE

<u>ACT FOUR</u>

31 INT. THE BRONZE - MOMENTS LATER   31

Cordelia is still dancing with her friends, having a good
time.

Jesse makes his way slowly through the crowd, not towards
but around her, his eyes never leaving her. She sees him
too -- and for the first time, doesn't look away in disgust.
There's something different about him.

A SLOW SONG starts playing, and Cordelia stops dancing,
heads off the floor.

He's suddenly standing in her way. Smiling that distant
smile.

                         CORDELIA
                   What do you want?

It's the old attitude, but she's not fooling anyone.

He takes her hand, starts leading her onto the floor.

                         CORDELIA
                   Hey! Hello, caveman-brain! What
                   do you think you're doing?

He turns back to her, smiles winningly.

                         JESSE
                   Shut up.

Brings her to the middle of the floor and starts dancing
with her. He holds her, hardly touching her, moving slowly.

                         CORDELIA
                   Just this one dance...

She moves closer to him.

                                                       CUT TO:

32 EXT. THE BRONZE - CONTINUOUS   32

ANGLE: THE DOOR.

The BOUNCER is suddenly confronted with the vampire group.
Their faces are mostly in shadow.

                                                   (CONTINUED)

32 CONTINUED: 32

                         BOUNCER
              I need ID.
                   (as they start past him)
              Hey! Nobody goes inside until I
              see --

Luke stands over him. His face inches from the Bouncer's.

                         LUKE
              Get inside.

The Bouncer complies instantly.

                                             CUT TO:

33 INT. THE BRONZE - A MOMENT LATER   33

Once inside, the vampires spread out, each heading for an
exit. Two of them stay behind and close off the front.

Darla heads for the door by the stage that leads backstage.
Goes in.

One goes to the bar -- swings over it and stands in front of
the door.

One heads upstairs.

And Luke climbs up on stage.

                                             CUT TO:

34 INT. BACKSTAGE - CONTINUOUS   34

Darla checks that the exit door is secure. Then she goes
over to the fuse box, flips a switch.

                                             CUT TO:

35 INT. THE BRONZE - CONTINUOUS   35

The main lights and the music go off. There are GASPS,
MURMURS. A voice from the stage calls out:

                         LUKE
              Ladies and gentlemen, there's no
              cause for alarm.

On stage, a single spot continues to shine. Luke steps into
the light. His face is rivetingly awful.

                                             (CONTINUED)

                              LUKE
                    Actually, there is cause for alarm.
                    It just won't do any good.

Major GASPS and MURMURS at the sight of him.

ANGLE: THE FRONT DOOR

A couple tries to get out. The vampire standing guard --
his normal face gone -- shakes his head no.

They shrink back from him.

ANGLE: CORDELIA

She stares at the stage, Jesse's hands still on her.

                              CORDELIA
                    I thought there wasn't any band
                    tonight.

She looks at Jesse to see his face has changed as well.
Starts to struggle but he holds her, pulls her back into the
dark under the stairs.

ANGLE: DARLA

re-emerges from backstage. Looks up at Luke on stage.

                              LUKE
                    This is a glorious night. It's
                    also the last one any of you shall
                    ever see.
                         (beat)
                    Bring me the first!

One of the vampires pushes the Bouncer up on stage.

                              BOUNCER
                    What do you guys want, you want
                    money? Man, what's wrong with your
                    faces?

Luke grabs him by the scruff of the neck, squeezing any further
conversation out of him.

                              LUKE
                    Watch me, people!
                         (to the Bouncer)
                    Their fear is elixir. It's almost
                    like blood.

As he brings the Bouncer to him and **bites his neck,**
sucking the life out of him in huge gulps.

                                        QUICK DISSOLVE TO:

36 INT. THE CHURCH - CONTINUOUS   36

The Master stands, power coursing through him -- visibly.
It lights him up.

                                          QUICK DISSOLVE TO:

37 INT. THE BRONZE - CONTINUOUS   37

Luke continues feeding. After a bit he pulls his head back,
throws the Bouncer's dead body from him.

                         LUKE
              Next!

                                                CUT TO:

38 EXT. OUTSIDE THE BRONZE - CONTINUOUS   38

Buffy and the others run up to the front door. She tries it
-- it's locked.

                         BUFFY
              It's locked.

                         GILES
              We're too late.

                         BUFFY
              Well, I didn't know I was gonna get
              grounded!

                         XANDER
                    (re: door)
              Can you break it down?

                         BUFFY
              Not this thing. You guys try the
              back entrance. I'll find my own
              way.

                         GILES
              Right
                    (to Xander and Willow)
              Come on.

                         BUFFY
              Guys!

They stop. Buffy hands them her bag of tricks.

                                                (CONTINUED)

42.

38 CONTINUED: 38

> BUFFY
> You get the exit cleared and you
> get people out. That's all. Don't
> go Wild Bunch on me.

> GILES
> See you on the inside.

They take off, as Buffy starts circling in the other
direction, looking up.

                                                        CUT TO:

39 EXT. BEHIND THE BRONZE   39

As Giles and others come around. Xander tries the door,
it's locked. They look around for something to open it
with.

> XANDER
> Damn. We've got to get in there
> before Jesse does something
> stupider than usual.

> GILES
> Xander. Jesse is dead. You have
> to remember that if you see him.
> You're not looking at your friend.
> You're looking at the thing that
> killed him.

                                                        CUT TO:

40 INT. THE CHURCH - CONTINUOUS   40

The Master is even more powerful now. He truly glows.

He steps over to the mystical wall that traps him, pushes at
it. It begins to disintegrate slightly at his touch.

> THE MASTER
> Almost free.
>   (shuts his eyes)
> Yes! Give me more!

                                                        CUT TO:

41 INT. THE BRONZE - CONTINUOUS   41

Luke triumphantly drops another body. He's flush with
power, looking about him at his hostages.

                                                     (CONTINUED)

116

41 CONTINUED: 41

They are really scared now, seeing corpses (two now) lying
before them. There is some screaming, some whimpering.

ANGLE: CORNER UNDER THE STAIRS

Darla is having a face off with Jesse, who holds Cordelia.

                         JESSE
               This one's mine.

                         DARLA
               They are all for the Master.

                         JESSE
               I don't get one?

ANGLE: UPSTAIRS WINDOW BY THE BALCONY

The window opens slowly, an oblivious vampire before it.
Buffy slips in.

She looks down at the stage, at Luke.

                         LUKE
               I feel him rising! I need another!

She sees the three-pointed star on his head.

                         BUFFY
                    (to herself)
               The Vessel...

The vampire turns, hearing this. He grabs Buffy, dragging
her up to the middle of the balcony to present her to Luke.

                         LUKE
               Tonight is his ascension. Tonight
               will be History at its end! Yours
               is a glorious sacrifice.
               Degradation most holy.
                    (looking around)
               What, no volunteers?

Darla emerges, holding Cordelia.

                         DARLA
               Here's a pretty one.

                         CORDELIA
               Noooo...

Darla drags her toward the stage, hands her over to Luke.

                                              (CONTINUED)

ANGLE: BUFFY

slips out of the vampire's grasp and THROWS him off the
balcony. He lands **WHAM** on his back right in front of
the stage.

Silence.

>   BUFFY
>   Oh, I'm sorry. Were you in the
>   middle of something?

>   LUKE
>   YOU!

>   BUFFY
>   You didn't think I'd miss this, did
>   you?

>   LUKE
>   (smiles)
>   I hoped you'd come.

                                              CUT TO:

42 INT. BACKSTAGE - CONTINUOUS   42

The exit door bursts open, a metal pipe-wielding Giles
behind it. He starts in, the other two behind him.

                                              CUT TO:

43 INT. THE BRONZE - CONTINUOUS   43

A vampire comes at Buffy from the side and she grabs him,
THROWS him into the hookah pit.

He scrambles back up and she **FLIPS herself over backwards,**
goes through the hole and lands on top of the pool table. A
cue is lying on the table -- she does a hand spring and
lands on the floor holding the cue.

A vampire rushes her from the side --

ANGLE: BUFFY

without looking, she JAMS the cue end into his heart. We
don't see him -- we just hear the PLUNGE. And when Buffy
lets go, the cue stays right where it is.

>   BUFFY
>   Okay, Vessel-boy. You want blood?

                                          (CONTINUED)

She steps forward just as the cue rises like the arm of a
guard gate and we hear the vampire's body THUD to the floor.

                         LUKE
              I want yours. Only yours.

                         BUFFY
              Then come and get it.

Cordelia, seeing her chance, tries to break free of Luke's
grasp. He throws her to one side --

-- and Buffy runs, LEAPS at him, slams her fist into his
face. This one really hurts, and he stumbles back in pain.

He comes back at her but she ducks, comes back up with a
roundhouse kick to the face. Another score.

She whips out her stake, comes at him -- but he blocks.
Nails her in the face, and she skids into the corner, badly
hurt. The stake falls at his feet.

ANGLE: DOOR TO BACKSTAGE

It bursts open, Xander nearly falling out.

He looks about him -- no vampires in the immediate
vicinity -- and begins herding people out.

                         XANDER
              Come on!

                                             CUT TO:

44   INT. BACKSTAGE - CONTINUOUS   44

The people rush past Willow and Giles, who push them towards
the exit.

                                             CUT TO:

45   INT. THE BRONZE - CONTINUOUS   45

Buffy kicks Luke in the chest. He flies back, landing hard.
She's about to go in for the kill when she sees

ANGLE: A VAMPIRE

going for Xander, who's too busy shepherding people out to
notice.

                                             (CONTINUED)

Buffy turns to the drum kit and kicks the cymbal right off the stand. She catches it in mid air --

-- the vampire reaches Xander, grabs him --

-- Buffy HURLS the cymbal, frisbee style --

-- the vampire turns, eyes wide, and **the cymbal flies straight at his neck** --

ANGLE: XANDER

As he hears the SLICE, his eyes follow the trajectory of the liberated head.

                         XANDER
                      (softly)
                 Heads ups...

ANGLE: BUFFY

barely has time to turn before Luke GRABS her from behind, lifting her up in a crushing bear hug.

ANGLE: XANDER

He is going to help Buffy when he hears a SHRIEK, turns and sees:

ANGLE: CORDELIA

is being dragged off into the area below the stairs by Jesse.

He throws her to the ground, kneeling above her. Pinning her.

                         JESSE
                 Hold still! You're not helping.

Xander appears behind Jesse, holding a stake. He could plunge it right through the back into the heart, but he hesitates.

                         XANDER
                 Jesse, man... don't make me do it.

Jesse looks around, grinning inhumanly.

                         JESSE
                 Buddy...

                                                        (CONTINUED)

45   CONTINUED: 2   45

ANGLE: BUFFY

Is failing to get out of Luke's grasp. He squeezes even
harder and she begins to lose consciousness.

                        LUKE
              I've always wanted to kill a
              Slayer...

We hear something in her begin to CRACK.

                                                   CUT TO:

46   INT. BACKSTAGE - CONTINUOUS   46

People are still rushing out.

                        GILES
              Come on! We've got to open the
              front as well!

He heads for the door to the main room and **Darla JUMPS on
him,** digging for his throat. His stake is knocked out of
his hand as he topples to the ground.

                                                   CUT TO:

47   INT. THE BRONZE - CONTINUOUS   47

Xander takes a step back as Jesse rises, faces him.

                        XANDER
              Jesse, I know there's still a part
              of you in there.

                        JESSE
                   (exasperated)
              Okay, let's deal with this. Jesse
              was an excruciating loser who
              couldn't get a date with anyone in
              the sighted community! Look at me
              now! I'm a new man!

He grabs Xander and HURLS him against the wall. Xander
falls in a heap to the cowering Cordelia.

                        JESSE
              See, the old Jesse would have
              reasoned with you.

                                                   CUT TO:

48 INT. BACKSTAGE - CONTINUOUS   48

Willow frantically digs through Buffy's bag, looking for a
weapon. She pulls out the jar of holy water.

Darla continues to struggle with Giles -- has him pinned on
the ground.

                    WILLOW (O.S.)   *
          Get off him!   *

Darla turns to face Willow and is <u>DOUSED</u> with holy water   *
right in the face.   *

SCREAMING, she brings her hands to her face, smoke pouring   *
out from between her fingers.   *

Giles pushes her off him, getting up to face her. But   *
Darla is already stumbling out the exit in smoking agony.   *

                                              CUT TO:

49 INT. THE BRONZE - CONTINUOUS   49

Buffy is limp in Luke's grasp. Head dangling forward.

                    LUKE
          Master, taste of this and be free.

He opens wide, leans in -- and Buffy HEADBUTTS him with the
back of her head, sends him staggering back.

                    BUFFY
          How'd it taste?

She is weak, despite her bravado. She grabs the cymbal
stand, holds it as a weapon. Looks around her -- and sees:

ANGLE: THE WINDOW

at the back of the stage. It's painted black, one huge
pane.

Buffy looks at it, at Luke.

ANGLE: XANDER

Jesse picks him up again, fury etching his demon face.

                                              (CONTINUED)

> JESSE
> I'm sick of you getting in the way,
> you know? Cordelia, she's gonna
> live forever. You're not.

Xander holds the stake up to Jesse's chest, determined but
scared.

> JESSE
> Oh, right! Put me out of my
> misery! You don't have the g--

And a fleeing woman SLAMS into Jesse from behind, driving
him onto the stake. He drags himself on a stunned Xander,
dying.

And then he's dust. Xander barely has time to react before
two more vampires **grab** him.

ANGLE: BUFFY

She swings the cymbal stand at an approaching Luke. He
smiles.

> LUKE
> You forget. Metal can't hurt me.

> BUFFY
> There's something you forgot about,
> too.

He hesitates, doubt clouding his face.

> BUFFY
> Sunrise.

And she takes the stand and **HURLS it right through the
plate glass window** at the back of the stage -- **SHATTERING**
the entire thing.

ANGLE: LUKE

As the warm light STREAMS IN on him, he SCREAMS, raises his
hands --

-- and stops. Puzzled.

Buffy DRIVES the stake in through his back. He arches
forward, in real agony this time.

> BUFFY
> It's in about nine hours, moron.

                                                    (CONTINUED)

49   CONTINUED: 2   49

     ANGLE: THE BROKEN WINDOW

     And Luke realizes the light from the window is merely a
     streetlight, shining in the darkness.

     Luke stumbles forward --

                                              QUICK DISSOLVE TO:

50   INT. THE CHURCH - CONTINUOUS   50

     And the Master stumbles forward in the exact same position,
     the bright energy beginning to fade from him. He reaches
     out, nearly doubled over --

                                              QUICK DISSOLVE TO:

51   INT. THE BRONZE - CONTINUOUS   51

     -- as does Luke. After a moment he falls, and is dust.
     Buffy stands over him, breathing hard.

                                              CUT TO:

52   INT. THE CHURCH - CONTINUOUS   52

     The last of the energy fades from the Master.

                         THE MASTER
                          (weakly)
                    Nooooo....

     He falls to his knees, reaches out blindly for support.

     What he touches is the wall, once again too strong for him
     to bend. Fury and despair cross his face as he looks up at
     it. A scream wells up inside him, and right before it
     bellows out, we

                                              CUT TO:

53   INT. THE BRONZE - CONTINUOUS   53

     Xander struggles with the remaining vampires, who hold him,
     their attention on the stage.

     Buffy looks down at the spot where Luke's body was. After a
     moment, she turns her gaze slowly toward the vampires.

                                              (CONTINUED)

53 CONTINUED: 53

They look at the expression on her face for about 1/8th of a
second, then they drop Xander and bolt out the front door.

ANGLE: THE BACKSTAGE DOOR

Giles and Willow come slowly out, meet Buffy and Xander in
the middle of the dance floor.

                          GILES
               I take it it's over.

                          WILLOW
               Did we win?

A moment, as they look about at the carnage that surrounds
them. Most of the patrons have fled, though some remain,
stunned and silent.

                          BUFFY
               Well, we averted the apocalypse.
               You gotta give us points for that.

ANGLE: CORDELIA

Sitting right where Jesse left her. Not a word.

                          XANDER
               One thing's for sure. Nothing is
               ever going to be the same.

                                            CUT TO:

A54 EXT. THE BRONZE - CONTINUOUS   A54*

The Vampires run out in a panic. As they bolt down the   *
street, we see Angel step out of the shadows. He looks at   *
them, looks back at the entrance of The Bronze. He smiles.   *

                          ANGEL   *
               She did it. I'll be damned.   *

54 EXT. FOUNTAIN QUAD - DAY   54

Everything is exactly the same. We see kids milling about,
talking, laughing in the bright sunshine. Pick up Cordelia,
walking by with her friends.

                                            (CONTINUED)

54 CONTINUED: 54

                         CORDELIA
              Well, I heard it was rival gangs.
              Anyway, Buffy totally knew these
              guys which is too weird. I can't
              remember anything too well, but I'm
              telling you, it was a freak show.

                         GIRL
              Oh, I wish I'd been there.

And we leave them, picking up Buffy and the others nearby,
crossing the other way. Xander has a look of disbelief on
his face.

                                        (CONTINUED)

                              BUFFY
          Well, what exactly were you
          expecting?

                              XANDER
          I don't know! Something. The dead
          rose! We should've at least had an
          assembly.

                              GILES
          People have a tendency to
          rationalize what they can, and
          forget what they can't.

                              BUFFY
          Believe me, I've seen it happen.

                              WILLOW
          Well, I'll never forget it. None
          of it.

                              GILES
          Good. Next time you'll be
          prepared.

                              XANDER
          Next time?

                              WILLOW
          Next time is why?

                              GILES
          We stopped the Master from freeing
          himself and opening the mouth of
          Hell. Doesn't mean he'll stop
          trying. I'd say the fun is just
          beginning.

                              WILLOW
          More vampires?

                              GILES
          Not just vampires. The next
          creature we face may be something
          quite different.

                              BUFFY
          I can hardly wait.

                              GILES
          We're at a center of mystical
          convergence here. We may in fact
          stand between the earth and total
          destruction.

                                              (CONTINUED)

                         XANDER
              Buffy, this isn't good.

                          BUFFY
              Well, I gotta look on the bright
              side. Maybe I can still get kicked
              out of school.

She smiles at Giles and starts off, the other two keeping up
with her.

                         XANDER
              Hey that's a plan. 'Cause a lot
              of schools aren't **on** Hellmouths.

                         WILLOW
              Maybe you could blow something up.
              They're really strict about that.

                          BUFFY
              I was aiming for a subtle approach,
              like excessive not studying.

Giles watches them go, an uneasy smile plastered on his
lips.

                          GILES
              The earth is doomed.

                                             BLACK OUT.

                         END OF SHOW

BUFFY THE VAMPIRE SLAYER

"Witch"

Written by

Dana Reston

Directed by

Stephen Cragg

<u>SHOOTING SCRIPT</u>

September 25, 1996
September 27, 1996 - BLUE
September 30, 1996 - PINK
September 30, 1996 - GREEN
October 1, 1996 - YELLOW

BUFFY THE VAMPIRE SLAYER

"Witch"

CAST LIST

BUFFY SUMMERS........................... Sarah Michelle Gellar
XANDER HARRIS........................... Nicholas Brendon
*RUPERT GILES........................... Anthony S. Head
WILLOW ROSENBERG........................ Alyson Hannigan
*CORDELIA CHASE......................... Charisma Carpenter

*JOYCE SUMMERS.......................... Kristine Sutherland
*AMY................................... Elizabeth Anne Allen
*CATHERINE............................. Robin Riker
*SENIOR CHEERLEADER..................... Amanda Wilmshurst
*LISHANNE.............................. Nicole Prescott
*MR. POLE.............................. Jim Doughan
*DR. GREGORY........................... William Monaghan
*

BUFFY THE VAMPIRE SLAYER

"Witch"

SET LIST

INTERIORS

SUNNYDALE HIGH SCHOOL
    THE LIBRARY
    THE GYM
    GYM FOYER
    GIRL'S LOCKER ROOM
    HALL
    SCIENCE LAB
    HALL OUTSIDE SCIENCE LAB
    HALL BY THE GYM
BUFFY'S HOUSE
    BUFFY'S BEDROOM
    BUFFY'S KITCHEN
AMY'S HOUSE
    AMY'S ATTIC
    AMY'S LIVING ROOM
DRIVER'S ED CAR

EXTERIORS

SUNNYDALE HIGH SCHOOL
    QUAD
    QUAD - BULLETIN BOARD
    CAMPUS
    DRIVER'S ED
AMY'S HOUSE
STREET

BUFFY THE VAMPIRE SLAYER

"Witch"

<u>TEASER</u>

FADE IN:

1   EXT. SUNNYDALE HIGH - DAY - ESTABLISHING   1

                    GILES (V.O.)
          This is madness.

2   INT. THE LIBRARY - DAY   2

GILES, deeply concerned, is staring at someone we can't see.

                    GILES
          What can you have been thinking?
          You are the Slayer, lives depend
          upon you. I make allowances for
          your youth but I expect a certain
          amount of responsibility. Instead
          you enslave yourself to this...
          this cult!

WIDEN TO REVEAL BUFFY, in cute CHEERLEADING OUTFIT.

                    BUFFY
          You don't like the color.

                    GILES
          I what? I don't -- Buffy, do you
          ignore everything I say? As a
          rule?

                    BUFFY
          No, I believe that's your trick. I
          told you I'm going out for the
          cheerleading squad.

                    GILES   *
          You have a sacred birthright,   *
          Buffy. You have been chosen to   *
          destroy Vampires, not wave pom-poms   *
          at people. As the Watcher, I   *
          forbid it.   *

                    BUFFY   *
          And you'll be stopping me how?   *

                                        (CONTINUED)

2   CONTINUED: 2

                          GILES   *
               Dyeh, uh, well -- by appealling to   *
               your common sense, if such a   *
               creature exists.   *

                          BUFFY
               I'll still have time to fight the
               forces of evil, okay? But I want
               to have a life. I want to do
               something normal. Something safe.

                                                   CUT TO:

3   INT. ATTIC - DAY   3

The windows have been boarded and taped over -- tiny
pinpricks of sunlight stream in to this otherwise dark
place. Whatever this place is, it's not safe.

A figure moves about before us in a black, hooded robe. It
pauses before a bubbling cauldron, then crosses to a shelf.

On the shelf is a doll in a cheerleading outfit. Her hands
have been wrapped with bits of cloth.

The figure reaches out and takes the doll. We HOLD on the
empty shelf.

                                                    CUT TO:

4   INT. THE GYM - DAY   4

CHEERLEADER TRYOUTS reads a sign on the wall. Big banner
showing the FIGHTING SUNNYDALE RAZORBACKS hangs next to it.

PRETTY GIRLS, in short skirts, twirl and warm up.

Buffy enters with WILLOW and XANDER.

                         WILLOW
              Giles didn't approve, huh?

                         BUFFY
              He totally lost his water. We
              haven't even seen a vampire in a
              week. I'd say he should get a
              girlfriend if he wasn't so old.

                         WILLOW
              Well, we're behind you.

                         XANDER
              People scoff at things like school
              spirit -- but when you see these
              young women giving their all like
              this...

AMBER, an attractive, agile girl, her feet on two chairs,
slides down into an extra low split.

                         XANDER
                       (mesmerized)
              ...Oooh, stretchy. Where was I?

                                              (CONTINUED)

4   CONTINUED: 4

                         WILLOW
              You were pretending that seeing
              scantily-clad girls in revealing
              postures was a spiritual
              experience.

                         XANDER
              What do you mean, pretending?

Xander pulls out an I.D. bracelet.

                         XANDER
              Oh, hey. Here's a little good luck
              thing for the tryouts...

                         BUFFY
                    (charmed)
              What is this?

                         WILLOW
                    (less charmed)
              What is that?

Buffy takes the bracelet, puts it on.

                         BUFFY
              This is so sweet!
                    (reads on bracelet:)
              "Yours always..."

                         XANDER
              That was on there when I got it.
              Really. They all said that.

CORDELIA, in cheerleader outfit, moves up, watches Amber
stand on one leg and hold the other straight up in the air.

                         CORDELIA
              Just look at Amber. Who does she
              think she is, a Laker Girl?

                         WILLOW
              I heard she turned them down.

A SENIOR CHEERLEADER (Cordelia two years hence) moves to the
judge's table with two other SENIOR CHEERLEADERS.

                         SENIOR CHEERLEADER
              Let's begin with...
                    (reads from list)
              Amber Grove. If you're not
              auditioning move off the floor.

                                        (CONTINUED)

4   CONTINUED: 2

Xander, Willow, Buffy, Cordelia move back. Willow spots AMY
MADISON (in cheerleader outfit), nice girl, a little tightly
wound today.

                         WILLOW
              Hi Amy.

                          AMY
              Hi.

                         WILLOW
              I didn't know you wanted to be a
              cheerleader. You lost a lot of
              weight.

                          AMY
              Had to.

                         WILLOW
              Do you know Buffy?

                          AMY
              Hi.
                   (to Buffy)
              Oh how I hate this, let me count
              the ways.

Buffy smiles, warming to Amy's honesty.

They watch Amber's routine -- she's really good.

                          AMY
              She trained with Benson -- he's the
              best coach money can buy.

                         BUFFY
              They have cheerleading coaches?

                          AMY
              Oh yeah. You don't have...? I train
              with my mom, three hours in the
              morning, three at night.

                         BUFFY
              That kind of quality time with my
              mom would probably lead to some
              quality matricide.

                          AMY
                   (smiles)
              I know it's kinda hokey... but
              she's really great.

                                        (CONTINUED)

4   CONTINUED: 3   4

Cordelia, standing nearby, feigns boredom with Amber's
performance, turns her back.

Everyone else watches Amber as SMOKE BEGINS TO EMANATE from
her pom-poms.

                        BUFFY
              What the ... ?

                        WILLOW
              That girl's on fire.

                        CORDELIA
                  (back still turned)
              Enough with the hyperbole.

Amber stops, drops the pom-poms. The smoke is coming from
her - and her hands and forearms suddenly burst into FLAMES!
Amber SCREAMS! (as do other girls.) Buffy vaults to the
large RAZORBACKS BANNER, rips it down and tackles Amber,
wrapping her tightly in it and smothering the flames.

                        BUFFY
                  (to Amber)
              It's okay, you're gonna be okay...

Off Buffy,

                                                        BLACK OUT.

                        END OF TEASER

<u>ACT ONE</u>

5   INT. THE LIBRARY - DAY   5

The foursome are gathered.

                    BUFFY
          I've been slaying Vampires for more
          than a year now. I've seen some
          pretty cringeworthy stuff, but
          nobody's hands ever got toasted.

                    GILES
          I imagine not.

                    BUFFY
          So this is not a vampire problem.

                    GILES
          No.

                    BUFFY
          But it is **funky,** right? Not of
          the norm?

                    GILES
          Quite. Spontaneous human
          combustion is rare, and
          scientifically unexplainable. But
          there've been cases reported for
          hundreds of years. Usually all
          that's left is a pile of ashes.

                    WILLOW
          That's all that would have been
          left of Amber if it hadn't been for
          Buffy.

                    XANDER
          So we have no idea what caused
          this? That's a comfort.

                    GILES
          Well, that is the thrill of living
          on a hellmouth -- one has a
          veritable cornucopia of fiends,
          devils and ghouls to engage --
          (off their looks)
          Pardon me for finding the glass
          half full.

                    BUFFY
          Any common denominator in cases of
          spontaneous combustion?

                              (CONTINUED)

5   CONTINUED: 5

                              GILES
                    Rage. In most cases the person who
                    combusted was terribly angry or
                    upset.

                              XANDER
                    So maybe Amber's got this power.
                    To make herself be on fire. Like   *
                    the Human Torch, only it hurts.

                              BUFFY
                    So I should get the skinny on   *
                    Amber. See if she's had any
                    colorful episodes before.

                              WILLOW
                    That means hacking illegally into
                    the school's computer system -- at
                    last something I can do.

She moves to a computer.

                              XANDER   *
                    I'll ask around about her.   *

                              BUFFY   *
                    Guys, you don't have to get   *
                    involved.   *

                              XANDER   *
                    What do you mean? We're a team!   *
                    Aren't we a team?   *

                              WILLOW   *
                    Yeah, you're the Slayer and we're   *
                    like the slayerettes.   *

                              BUFFY   *
                    I don't want you putting yourselves   *
                    in danger.   *

                              XANDER   *
                    I laugh in the face of danger.   *
                    Then I hide till it goes away.   *

                              BUFFY   *
                    Okay, well, I'm psyched for the   *
                    help.   *
                         (to Giles)   *
                    And what if we find out Amber   *
                    didn't cause this herself?   *

                                                    (CONTINUED)

5   CONTINUED: 2   5

                              GILES
                    Then we will have to determine who
                    or what did. And deal with it
                    accordingly.

                              XANDER
                         (off Buffy's worried
                          look)
                    Hey, we've fought vampires!
                    Anything else'll be a walk in the
                    park.

                              BUFFY
                    I hope so...
                                                       CUT TO:

6   INT. BUFFY'S KITCHEN - AFTERNOON   6

There are crates strewn about. Joyce is opening them with a
crowbar (and some difficulty).

Buffy enters, throws her books on the kitchen table.

                              BUFFY
                    Hey, Mom.

                                                 (CONTINUED)

6   CONTINUED: 6

                                    JOYCE
                    Hi. How was school?

                                    BUFFY
                    A reverent joy. What's all this?

                                    JOYCE
                    It's for the tribal art display.

Buffy picks up a statue, looks at it.

                                    BUFFY
                    Oh. Cool.

She sits down on the table, grabbing a donut. Watches Joyce
a minute -- Joyce hasn't looked back at her -- before
offering:

                                    BUFFY
                    We had tryouts today.

                                    JOYCE
                    Great! How'd it go?

                                    BUFFY
                    Well, I didn't get to try out yet.
                    There was an accident. Pretty fierce
                    competition, though.

                                    JOYCE
                    I know you'll do fine. Keep on
                    plugging. Just have to get back on
                    the horse.

Joyce tries to pry open the crate on the table next to
Buffy. It won't budge.

                                    BUFFY
                    Mom?

                                    JOYCE
                            (finally looking around)
                    Yeah?

                                    BUFFY
                    What was I trying out for?

                                    JOYCE
                            (stops, stumped)
                    Um... some activity? I have no
                    idea, I'm sorry.

                                                        (CONTINUED)

                       BUFFY
          That's okay. Your platitudes are
          good for all occasions.

                       JOYCE
          I'm distracted. I've got a lot of
          inventory to go through here. This
          is my gallery's first major show.

She gives up, turns to another crate.

                       JOYCE
          It might not physically kill you to
          give me a hand...

Buffy casually flips the lid off the unopenable crate with
one hand.

                       BUFFY
          It was cheerleading tryouts.

                       JOYCE
          Oh! Good. I'm glad you're taking
          that up again. Keep you out of
          trouble.

                       BUFFY
          I'm not in trouble, mom.

                       JOYCE
          No, not yet. I mean -- you stopped
          cheerleading right before the
          trouble. So it's good you're going
          back --

She pulls a statue of a man halfway out of a crate, stops.

                       JOYCE
          Oh, dear.

She puts it back.

                       BUFFY
          What is it?

                       JOYCE
          Fertility statue. You don't need
          to see it.

Buffy heads for the fridge. Looking in:

                                (CONTINUED)

6 CONTINUED: 3　　　　　　　　　　　　　　　　　　　　　　　　6

                         BUFFY
               You know, this girl Amy trains with
               her mom like three hours a day.
                    (closes the fridge)
               Sounds like her mom's really into
               it.

                         JOYCE
                    (Absently)
               Sounds like her mom doesn't have a
               whole lot to do.

She exits, carrying a couple of pieces. Buffy watches her a
moment, then looks down into the crate with the fertility
statue. Her eyes go wide.

                         BUFFY
               Jeepers.

                                              CUT TO:

7   EXT. SUNNYDALE HIGH - DAY - ESTABLISHING   7

                         SENIOR CHEERLEADER (O.S.)
               Despite the terrible thing that
               happened yesterday...

8   INT. THE GYM - DAY   8

Cheerleader tryouts. Buffy, Amy, Cordelia (wearing pink
headband) and ten or twelve others.

                         SENIOR CHEERLEADER
               ...we still have to pick new
               cheerleaders. If you make the team,
               you'll find your name posted in the
               Quad after lunch. Let's begin with
               group performance -- Cordelia,
               Buffy, Amy, Morgan, Janice and   *
               Lishanne.

LISHANNE is an attractive African American. The five girls
walk to the center of the gym. Amy glares at her hands.

                         AMY
               Why do my hands have to sweat when
               I get nervous?

                         BUFFY
               Don't worry, you'll do great.

                                              (CONTINUED)

8   CONTINUED: 8

    MUSIC UP. The girls perform a group cheer (to be   *
    choreographed.)   *

                                                    (CONTINUED)

8   CONTINUED: 2   8

It includes synchronized leaps, twirls and basketball cheer,
ala:

                         LISHANNE   *
             We're Sunnydale, Sunnydale   *

                        GROUP CHEER   *
             We Never Fail, Never Fail   *

                         LISHANNE   *
             Jump and Shoot, Swish and Score   *

                        GROUP CHEER   *
             The Other Team Is Such A Bore   *
             YEAHHH!   *

Morgan is okay. Lishanne is great. Cordelia is surprisingly
good, as is Buffy, still a little rusty but impressive.

Amy starts out well but tries too hard -- misses a couple of
synchronized moves -- and, in the big finish (each girl
doing a cartwheel and sliding to their knees one at a time)
AMY'S HANDS slip on the floor, and she careens into:

                         CORDELIA
                      (to judges)
             You saw that, right? That wasn't
             me.

                                              CUT TO:

9   INT. GYM FOYER - MOMENTS LATER   9

Amy, in cheerleader outfit, depressed, stands before a big
trophy display case (includes cheerleader trophies and photos).

Buffy, dressed for school, exits locker room, moves up.
Looks at CHEERLEADER PHOTO. Under the photo it reads:
1977 -- TRI-COUNTY BEST.

                         AMY
             That's my mom.

                         BUFFY
             No...
                      (reads name)
             Catherine Madison. Get down with
             your bad self.

                                              (CONTINUED)

9   CONTINUED: 9

                              AMY
                    Her nickname was Catherine The
                    Great: she took that team and made
                    them tri-county champions, no one's
                    ever done that before or since. She
                    and my dad were homecoming King and
                    Queen, got married right after
                    graduation

                                                     (CONTINUED)

                          BUFFY
                    That's kinda romantic.

                          AMY
                    Well... he was a big loser,
                    couldn't make any money, took off
                    with Miss Trailer Trash when I was
                    twelve.

                          BUFFY
                    Okay, that part's less romantic.
                    My folks split up, too.

                          AMY
                    Drag, huh. He left my mom with
                    nothing. She put herself through
                    cosmetology school, bought me
                    everything I ever wanted and never
                    gained a single pound...

                          BUFFY
                    She sounds great, Amy, but that
                    doesn't mean you have to, you know,
                    lock step as far as the
                    cheerleading thing —

Amy turns to Buffy, eyes filling.

                          AMY
                    It's just, she was the best, and I
                    can't get my body to move like
                    hers. I choked in there so bad.

Amy looks very sad and forlorn as Willow enters. She tries
to put on a brave face, heads for the GIRLS' LOCKER ROOM.

                          AMY
                    ...I gotta get changed...

                          WILLOW
                        (to Amy's departing back)
                    Hi Amy...
                        (to Buffy)
                    She okay?

                          BUFFY
                    She's wiggin' about her mother...
                        (re: photo)
                    ...the big cheer queen back when.

                          WILLOW
                    Yeah. Her mom's kinda...

                                                        (CONTINUED)

9   CONTINUED: 2   9

                         BUFFY
               Nazi-like?

                         WILLOW
               Heil. If she gains an ounce she
               padlocks the fridge and won't eat
               anything but broth.

                         BUFFY
               So Mommie Dearest is really...
               Mommie Dearest.

                         WILLOW
               There's a bitter streak -- but
               Amy's nice. We used to hang in
               Junior High. When her mom'd go on a
               broth kick Amy'd come to my house
               and we'd just stuff ourselves with
               brownies.

                         BUFFY
               Any word on Amber?

                         WILLOW
                  (pulls paper from
                   bookbag)
               Nothing thrilling. Average student
               -- got detention once for
               smoking -- regular smoking, with a
               cigarette. Not being smoky. All
               pretty normal.

                         BUFFY
               We'll just have to see what happens
               next. Maybe nothing will.

     They head out.

                                                          CUT TO:

10   INT. GIRLS' LOCKER ROOM - DAY   10

     MOVING CREEPY-CAM through the dimly lit room. Past the cold
     floors, the metal lockers...

     Amy, alone, changes into her school clothes. Her movements
     are slow and tired. She rubs an aching shoulder -- hears a
     NOISE, whips her head around. HER POV - The empty locker
     room. Spooky. A lone shower DRIPS.

     She instinctively does up a couple of buttons on her blouse,
     as if to protect herself, turning slowly around in a
     circle -- and suddenly

                                                     (CONTINUED)

10 CONTINUED: 10

CORDELIA IS STANDING RIGHT NEXT TO HER

Amy jumps, frightened. Cordelia is perfectly dressed and
coiffed. She holds the pink headband she wore during
auditions. She speaks very quietly and in a chillingly kind
voice, gesturing very close to Amy's face with the headband.

                    CORDELIA
          I have a dream. It's me on the
          Cheerleading Squad, adored by every
          Varsity male as far as the eye can
          see. We have to achieve our dreams,
          Amy, otherwise we wither and die.

                    AMY
          Look, I'm sorry about --

                    CORDELIA
          Shhh. If your supreme klutziness
          out there today takes me out of the
          running you are going to be so very
          beyond sorry. Have a nice day.

Cordelia hurls the headband into her own locker and SLAMS
IT! She walks out -- her locker swinging back open. Amy
takes a breath, watching Cordelia's departing back.

                                        CUT TO:

11 EXT. QUAD - DAY   11

Kids mill about after lunch. Xander and Willow walk through
them.

                    WILLOW
          I told Buffy about Amber.

                    XANDER
          Cool. was she wearing it?
               (off her look)
          The bracelet. She was wearing it,
          right? That's pretty much like
          we're going out.

                    WILLOW
          Except without the hugging or
          kissing or her knowing about it.

                    XANDER
          So now I'm a figure of fun. I
          should just ask, right?

                                        (CONTINUED)

11 CONTINUED: 11

                              WILLOW
                    Won't know till you ask.

                              XANDER
                    See, this is why you're cool.
                    You're like a guy. You're my guy
                    friend that knows about girl stuff.

                              WILLOW
                    Oh great. I'm a guy.

He sees the Senior Cheerleader moving towards the bulletin
board, list in hand. Girls begin to gather.

                              XANDER
                    Hey, they're posting the list!

He bolts for:

12 EXT. QUAD - BULLETIN BOARD - DAY   12

A sizable crowd has gathered. The Senior Cheerleader posts
the list and goes. Girls stand on tiptoe, push and poke,
trying to see. Buffy and Amy are on the periphery as   *
Xander and Willow move up. A GIRL IN TEARS breaks out of   *
the crowd, runs off. Lishanne, reading the list, jumps up   *
and down with some friends.

                              LISHANNE
                    Yess!

                              AMY   *
                    I can't take this...   *

Buffy tries to wedge into the crowd but TWO CONTENDERS step   *
right in front of her.   *

                              XANDER   *
                    Spot me, I'm goin' in.   *

Xander takes a little dive into the throng, works his way to   *
the front where he finds himself nose to nose with Cordelia   *
at the list. He lets her check it out first.   *

                              XANDER   *
                    Women and children first.   *

ANGLE - EDGE OF THRONG   *

Cordelia emerges, triumphant.   *

                                                     (CONTINUED)

12 CONTINUED: 12

                         CORDELIA   *
                       (to Amy)   *
                 You're lucky.   *

                           AMY   *
                 I made it?   *

                         CORDELIA   *
                 I made it.   *

Cordelia moves off; Xander, rubbing his arm, emerges from   *
the throng.   *

                                        (CONTINUED)

12 CONTINUED: 12

                         XANDER
              One of those girls hit me really
              hard -- we have to start testing
              for steroids --
                   (to Buffy and Amy)
              -- okay, not only did you make it,
              but you, Miss Summers, are the
              number one alternate and Amy's the
              number three!

Amy's face falls, she turns and walks off.

                         XANDER
              And what better way to celebrate
              than with a romantic drive-through
              for two at --

                         WILLOW
              Xander, alternates are the ones who
              didn't make the team. They only
              fill in if something happens to the
              ones who did.

                         BUFFY
                   (moving after Amy)
              Excuse me.

                         XANDER
              For I am Xander, King of the
              Cretins, and all lesser cretins
              must bow before me.

ANGLE - AMY, TRYING TO CONTROL HER FEELINGS

As Buffy moves up.

                         BUFFY
              At least it's over. And you know
              what I think we should do about it?
              Brownie pig-out, my house, now.

                         AMY
              How many more hours a day can I
              practice? How much more can I do?
              This would never have happened to
              my mom. Never.

Amy takes off. Buffy watches her go.

                                        CUT TO:

13 EXT. AMY'S HOUSE - DAY   13

A Sunnydale two story, a little darker and foreboding than the others on the street. WE PUSH in on the house, moving up towards the attic window.

14 INT. AMY'S ATTIC - DAY   14

Creepy, dark and strange. Walls adorned with witch and warlock paraphernalia. Burning black candles.

The floor is dominated by a large hand-painted pentagram on top of which sits the classic black iron cauldron, hideous bubbling brew cooking inside.

A HAND ENTERS FRAME drops a serpent's head into the brew. We don't see the robed WITCH'S face but we (dimly) HEAR HER CHANTING.

> WITCH
> ...Lord of Darkness, Lord of Night... accept thy supplicant's sacrifice...

The Witch moves to a ROW OF DOLLS neatly lined up on the wall. Pretty dolls, Barbie-types.

The hand picks up a brunette doll. The hand brings the doll to the cauldron. We now see CORDELIA'S PINK HEAD BAND in the Witch's other hand. The CHANTING grows more intense as the pink headband is wrapped round and round the Cordelia's doll face, tighter and tighter.

> WITCH
> ...reap thy vengeance with keen and cruel might... send thy sudden darkness out of darkest night.

And the hand drops the Cordelia doll in the brew. The pink headband soaks up the foul-colored liquid and the little doll sinks from sight.

                                        BLACK OUT.

                    END OF ACT ONE

ACT TWO

15 INT. BUFFY'S KITCHEN - MORNING   15

Buffy is getting her books together. Joyce enters carrying
an old yearbook.

                    JOYCE
          Look what I found! It's my old
          yearbook, from junior year. Oh,
          look, there I am.

Buffy looks for a second.

                    BUFFY
          Mom, I accepted that you've had
          sex. I'm not ready to know you've
          had Farrah hair.

                    JOYCE
          This is Gidget hair. Don't they
          teach you anything in history?

                    BUFFY
          That's cool. I gotta book --

                    JOYCE

          Well I was thinking, I mean I know
          the cheerleading thing didn't work
          out. Maybe you should think about
          joining the yearbook staff. I did
          it, and it was a lot of fun.

                    BUFFY
          Not really my tip, mom.

                    JOYCE
          I was photo editor. I got to be on
          every page. Made me look much more
          popular than I was.

                    BUFFY
          Have you seen the kids who do
          yearbook, mom? **Nerds** pick on
          them.

                    JOYCE
          Some of the best times I had in
          school were working on the
          yearbook.

                    BUFFY
          This just in: I'm not you. I'm
          into my own thing.

                                        (CONTINUED)

15 CONTINUED: 15

                              JOYCE
                    Your own thing, whatever it is, got
                    you kicked out of school. And we
                    had to move here to find a decent
                    school that would take you.

          Quite frankly, ouch. The sting hangs in the air before
          Buffy grabs her books and walks out.

                              JOYCE
                    Honey...

          Joyce stands there a moment, upset with herself.

                              JOYCE
                    Great parenting form. Little shaky
                    on the dismount...

                                                          CUT TO:

16 EXT. SUNNYDALE HIGH - DAY - ESTABLISHING   16

17 INT. SCHOOL HALL - DAY   17

          Cordelia, walking more slowly and regally than usual, passes   *
          Xander and Willow (pen in mouth).   *

                              XANDER   *
                         (to Cordelia)   *
                    Morning your Highness, beheadings   *
                    at noon as usual?   *
                         (to Willow, re: *
                          Cordelia's departing   *
                          back).   *
                    Okay, see how she has no clue I'm   *
                    even a mammal, much less a human   *
                    being?   *

                              WILLOW   *
                    None.   *

                              XANDER   *
                    This invisible man syndrome, a   *
                    blessing in Cordelia's case, a   *
                    curse in Buffy's.   *

                              WILLOW   *
                    You're not invisible to Buffy.   *

                                                       (CONTINUED)

                         XANDER   *
          Worse, I'm just part of the   *
          scenery, like an old shoe, or a rug   *
          you walk on every day but you never   *
          really see --   *

                         WILLOW   *
                   (trying to be helpful)   *
          -- like a pen that's all chewed up   *
          and you know you should throw it   *
          away but you don't, not 'cause you   *
          really like it that much but more   *
          'cause you're just so used to it   *
          and --   *

                         XANDER   *
          Will. That is the point and let's   *
          not drive it through my head like a   *
          railroad spike. What I have do --   *
          what I'm going to do -- is just   *
          what you said --   *

                         WILLOW   *
          Throw away the pen, forget about   *
          Buffy.   *
                   (tosses pen in trash)   *

                         XANDER
          What I have to do -- what I'm going
          to do -- is be a man and ask her
          out. No more i.d. bracelets, subtle
          innuendo, or Polaroids outside her
          bedroom window late at night --
          that last is a joke to relieve the
          tension because here she comes.

Buffy rounds a corner, heading their way.

                         WILLOW
          I know I'm relieved.

                                              (CONTINUED)

                         XANDER
            Alright. Into battle I go. Would
            you ask her out for me? No. Man.
            Me. Battle.

ANGLE - BUFFY

Passing Cordelia at her locker. Buffy sees Cordelia reach
for her combination -- her fingers miss it, find it. Buffy
moves on, is intercepted by:

                         XANDER
            Buffy, how would you like to...

                         BUFFY
                    (looking back)
            Is that even Cordelia's locker?

                         XANDER
            Huh? I don't know, what I'm saying
            here is, accompany me Friday
            night...

Buffy, not really listening, sees Cordelia give up on the
locker which won't open for her, walk off.

                         BUFFY
            Hang on, Xander, I have to... we
            can pick this up later, you don't
            mind, do you?

And she turns and goes. He watches her. A small high-pitched
sound builds slowly in the back of his throat -- the sound
of a plane going down, down, down.

                         XANDER
                    (explosion)
            Pplllewww!

                                                    CUT TO:

18 EXT. CAMPUS - DAY   18

Cordelia, still moving more slowly than usual, makes her way
across campus.

Buffy exits a building fifty yards or so behind Cordelia.
Follows her, concerned.

19 EXT. DRIVER'S ED - DAY   19

Orange cones are set up in a little course on the blacktop.
A DRIVER'S ED car, MR. POLE, the beleaguered TEACHER, two
STUDENTS. Cordelia walks up.

                    MR. POLE
          Nice of you to join us Cordelia. We
          didn't keep you waiting or anything
          did we? It's your turn to drive.
          Let's buckle up, people.

Pole and students move to the car.

                    CORDELIA
          I don't want to drive today, Mr.
          Pole.

Mr. Pole looks wildly uncomfortable for a beat, then:

                    MR. POLE
          You've flunked Driver's Ed twice -
          show me some moves or you'll be
          taking the bus to college.

Cordelia marches to the car, climbs behind the wheel.

ANGLE - BUFFY

Moving up, keeping an eye on Cordelia.

20 EXT.\INT. DRIVER'S ED CAR - DAY   20

Mr. Pole buckles up in the passenger seat.

                    MR. POLE
          Check your brake, your mirrors,
          start the engine, put the car in
          drive...

ANGLE - CORDELIA

Tight on her face, looking at the

GEAR SHIFT INDICATOR

It's a big blur. This girl is having trouble seeing.

                    MR. POLE
          ...let's move forward and through
          the cones in a gentle, even turn to
          the --

Cordelia puts the car in REVERSE, steps on the gas. The car
jerks backwards, knocking into a pole.

                                        (CONTINUED)

CONTINUED:

                         MR. POLE
              -- brakes!

Cordelia slams on the brakes, jams the car through every
gear until she finds drive, hits the gas.

The car SCREECHES forward.

                         MR. POLE
              Slow down, turn right, right,
              BRAKES, BRAKES!!

Cordelia does as she's told, yanking the wheel, stomping on
the brakes.

Cordelia's car launches into a nasty skid, right off the
blacktop, onto the grass, careening out of control now
towards the street.

Buffy starts running like hell.

Mr. Pole and KIDS IN BACK SCREAM bloody murder.

21 EXT. STREET - DAY   21

    Cordelia's car skids into the street and stops. A car
    swerves around them, tires squealing, HORN BLARING.

                         MR. POLE
              Everyone out!

    Cordelia, Pole, the students scramble out. Mr. Pole and
    the students run. Cordelia looks around, completely
    disoriented.

    CORDELIA'S POV

    Dark and murky, dimmest shape of a UPS sized **truck bearing
    down on her.** She takes a step one way, then another -- in
    about five seconds she's going to be hamburger.

    BUFFY

    Tears across the grass onto the sidewalk.

    CORDELIA

    Screams, terrified, expecting the worst.

    THE TRUCK

    Hits its breaks, heading right at Cordelia.

                                                    (CONTINUED)

21 CONTINUED: 21

BUFFY

Leaps on a parked car, using it as a booster to send her AIRBORNE.

BUFFY FLIES THROUGH THE AIR, TACKLES CORDELIA

Carrying her out of harm's way as the truck screeches past.

CORDELIA AND BUFFY

On the ground.

                    CORDELIA
          What's happening?!? I can't see
          anything!

                    BUFFY
          Cordelia, it's okay, you're gonna
          be -- Oh, God...

Buffy looks at Cordelia whose EYES GLAZE OVER TO MURKY WHITE.

                    CORDELIA
          What's happening to me!?!

                                        CUT TO:

22 INT. THE LIBRARY - DAY   22

CLOSE ON GILES.

                    GILES
          Witchcraft. Blinding your enemy to
          disable and disorient them is a
          classic.

ANGLE - Buffy, Xander, Willow. Giles holds a witchcraft text. We see AN ENGRAVING of SCARY WITCHES in SACRED CIRCLE in the woods.

                    XANDER
          First vampires, now witches... no
          wonder you can still afford a house
          in Sunnydale.

                    GILES
          Why would someone want to harm
          Cordelia?

                                        (CONTINUED)

                              WILLOW
                    Maybe because... they met her. Did
                    I say that?

                              GILES
                    Then why was Amber set ablaze?

                              XANDER
                    Yeah, those guys don't hang.

                              BUFFY
                    They're both cheerleaders.

                              GILES
                    Someone doesn't like cheerleading.

                              BUFFY
                    Or likes it too much.

                              WILLOW
                    Amy.

                              BUFFY
                    Amy.

                              XANDER
                    So you guys are leaning towards
                    Amy.

                              BUFFY
                    She's desperate to get on that
                    team... I get the feeling she'd do
                    anything to make her mom's dream
                    come true.

                              GILES
                    Now I do want to make sure I've got   *
                    this right. This witch is casting   *
                    horrible, disfiguring spells so   *
                    that she can be a cheerleader.   *

                              BUFFY   *
                    Your point being?   *

                              GILES   *
                    Priorities. Really, if I had the   *
                    power of the black mass I'd set my   *
                    sights a little higher than making   *
                    the pep squad.   *

                                                      (CONTINUED)

> BUFFY
> I think you're underestimating the
> amount of pressure a parent can lay
> on you. If you're not a picture
> perfect carbon copy they tend to
> wig.

> WILLOW
> Cheerleading was kind of her mom's
> last hurrah.

> XANDER
> We still gotta stop Amy. We should
> grab her before --

> GILES
> (flipping though text)
> Let's be certain she's the witch
> before we arouse her suspicions.
> She's capable of some fairly ugly
> things.

> BUFFY
> All right, you're a high school   *
> girl, you're desperate to make the   *
> team and please your mom, you turn   *
> to witchcraft. What's the first   *
> thing you do?   *

> WILLOW   *
> Check out the books on witchcraft!   *

Willow moves to the computer at check-out desk, scanning   *
records.   *

> XANDER
> That's the last thing you do! You   *
> don't leave a paper trail. Forget   *
> that --   *

> WILLOW   *
> It'll just take a minute --   *

> XANDER   *
> We don't have a minute.   *
> Cheerleaders' lives are in   *
> danger -- Buffy's in danger.   *
> (grabs Buffy, tries to   *
> hustle her out)   *
> You were the first alternate.   *
> (MORE)

(CONTINUED)

                    XANDER (cont'd)   *
You're on the team now that   *
Cordelia's out -- you could be   *
next, we have to get you to a safe   *
house.   *

                    WILLOW   *
    (sees something on   *
     computer)   *
Xander...   *

                    XANDER   *
    (innocent)   *
Yes?   *

                    WILLOW   *
"Witches - Historic Roots to Modern   *
Practice" checked out by Alexander   *
Harris.   *

                    BUFFY   *
    (moves to computer)   *
"The Pagan Rites", checked out by   *
Alexander --   *

                    XANDER   *
All right, all right. It's not   *
what you think.   *

                    WILLOW   *
You like to look at the semi-nude   *
engravings?   *

                    XANDER   *
Oh. Well, then it _is_ what you   *
think.   *

                    GILES   *
We'll need a conclusive test   *
anyway. There should be one - yes!   *
The ducking stool. We throw her in   *
the pond. If she floats, she's a   *
witch; if she drowns, she's   *
innocent.   *
    (off their looks)   *
... some of my texts are a bit   *
outdated.   *

                    BUFFY   *
You think?   *

                                  (CONTINUED)

            GILES   *
      (looks in another book)   *
Ah! Yes. This should work.   *
You'll need some of her hair, a   *
little quicksilver and aqua fortis. *

            WILLOW
That's just mercury and nitric
acid, we can get it in the science
lab.
                 (CONTINUED)

22 CONTINUED: 5   22

                          GILES
                    (reads)
                    "Heat ingredients and apply to
                    witch, if a spell has been cast in
                    previous forty-eight hours witch's
                    skin will turn blue." Oh, and
                    you'll need some eye of newt...

                                              SMASH CUT TO:

23 A FROG - INT. SCIENCE CLASS - DAY   23

His big ol' eye looking up at us.

PULL BACK, revealing we are seeing this in a BIG MIRROR,
mounted on the teacher's desk in front of the class. The
mirror is so the students can see what DR. GREGORY (kindly,
older) is doing. Willow, Xander, Buffy, Lishanne and Amy are
part of the class.

                          DR. GREGORY
                    Those on track one may begin their
                    dissections. Those on track two,
                    add your hydrochloric acid and
                    ammonium hydroxide to your
                    beakers...

He demonstrates, we see it in the big mirror. Smoke and gas.
He holds up the smoky beaker.

ANGLE - WILLOW AND XANDER   *

At a large table. Xander holds a scalpel poised over a   *
frog. He lowers the scalpel, then: *

                          XANDER   *
                    I can't.   *

He puts the scalpel down. Willow takes it, makes (off   *
camera) a quick neat incision.   *

                          WILLOW   *
                    One eye of newt...   *

                          XANDER   *
                    Wow, you've got a killer streak   *
                    I've never seen before. Hope I   *
                    never cross you.   *

                          WILLOW   *
                    I do too, then I'd have to carve   *
                    you up in neat little pieces.   *

                                              (CONTINUED)

23 CONTINUED:

She holds up scalpel, gives him her sweet "Willow" smile.

                    XANDER
          Ha ha.
               (takes scalpel
                respectfully)
          How's Buffy coming with the hair?

ANGLE: BUFFY

Moving past Lishanne.

                    LISHANNE
               (sarcastically)
          Isn't this exciting?

                    BUFFY
               (small laugh)
          Oh yeah.

Buffy reaches Amy at another big desk with Bunsen burner,
beakers, etc.

                    BUFFY
          Help. Which is the hydrochloric
          acid and which is the ammonium
          hydroxide?

                    AMY
          Well, the bottle that says   *
          hydrochloric acid is usually the   *
          hydrochloric acid.

                    BUFFY
          Read the bottles -- what a concept.

Buffy drops her pen, bends down to pick it up, as she does,
her hand slips INSIDE AMY'S purse, grabs some hair off Amy's
brush.

                                        (CONTINUED)

ANGLE - BUFFY STRAIGHTENS UP

Amy's looking at her -- did she see the hair grab?

Buffy moves back to her seat (in front of Willow and
Xander.) Keeping her back to them, she reaches back, drops
the hair in front of Willow who adds it to a chemical mix on
a Bunsen burner.

Amy glances at them.

                    XANDER
               (through his teeth)
          Smile and wave to the nice witch.

Willow hands the beaker to Buffy.

                    WILLOW
          All set. You have a plan?

                    BUFFY
          Spill it on her, try and make it
          look natural.

                    XANDER
          We'll be right behind you. Only
          farther away.

Buffy heads for Amy's desk with beaker. As she does,

                    DR. GREGORY
          Lishanne, can you tell me why these
          chemicals have this reaction?

Buffy casually spills a drops or two on Amy's arm. Buffy
looks at:

ANGLE: AMY'S ARM

The drops do turn blue, but we tilt up to see Amy's eyes
locked on something else:

ANGLE: LISHANNE

We see her from behind, starting to shake, to spaz out.

                    DR. GREGORY
          Lishanne? Are you -- Oh my god.

She knocks a few beakers over as she stumblingly rises and
turns, grabbing at the first thing she sees -- which is Amy.
Amy is brought face to face with Lishanne -- WHO HAS NO
MOUTH. Amy backs away, terrified by what she sees.

                                        CUT TO:

24 INT. HALL - MOMENTS LATER   24

Our three are clustered, conferring.

                    XANDER
          Did you see? Amy was as freaked
          out as the rest of us.

                    WILLOW
          So it's not her?

                    BUFFY
          The test was positive. She's our
          Sabrina. I just don't think she
          realizes what she's doing.

                    WILLOW
          Should we talk to her?

                    BUFFY
          Maybe we should talk to her
          mother. I wonder if she knows
          what she's created.

                                        CUT TO:

25 EXT. AMY'S HOUSE - DAY   25

Pushing in on the house as Amy enters frame, marches up and
through the front door.

26 INT. AMY'S HOUSE - DAY   26

Dark. Austere. Clean. Amy moves through, pissed. We haven't
seen her like this before.

                    AMY
          Where are you?!

Amy finds her mother, CATHERINE MADISON, late thirties, very
well preserved, sitting in the blue light of the T.V.
Catherine quickly flicks the T.V. off, like a kid caught
doing something wrong.

                    AMY
          Another productive day in front of
          the T.V. I got a history report due
          tomorrow. Write it.

Amy hurls her book bag on the couch next to her mother.

                                        (CONTINUED)

                          AMY
          I should be on that team by now.
          Instead, Miss Buffy and friends are
          sneaking around stealing bits of my
          hair.

CLOSE - AMY'S HAND

As she angrily dangles something from it -- the i.d.
bracelet Xander gave Buffy. We're close enough to read
"Yours Always".

                          AMY
          I'll be upstairs.

Amy wraps her fingers around Buffy's bracelet, marches out.

                                          BLACK OUT.

                      END OF ACT TWO

ACT THREE

27   INT. BUFFY'S BEDROOM - MORNING   27

We TRACK IN on Buffy sleeping.   *

ANGLE: ALARM CLOCK

It's one of the old fashioned round ones with the bell, and
it starts RINGING.

Buffy lumps around under the cover, mewling in protest
before she reaches for the clock.

She grabs it and casually CRUSHES it with her hand. Pokes
her head out from under the covers to look at what she has
wrought.

                    BUFFY
               (laughs)
          Oops.

                                                                 *

                                                                 *

                                                                 *

                                        CUT TO:

28   INT. BUFFY'S KITCHEN A BIT LATER   28

Joyce is making breakfast. Buffy comes in in a really good
mood.

                    BUFFY
               (sings to herself)
          MACHO MACHO MAN... Hey, juice.   *

She downs an entire glass in one sip.

                    BUFFY
          Quality juice. Not from
          concentrate.

                                        (CONTINUED)

                          JOYCE
                     (tentatively)
                You're in a good mood.

                          BUFFY
                I am. I'm on the squad. Which is
                great because I feel like cheering.
                And leading others to cheer. Hey,
                juice!

She downs Joyce's as well.

                          JOYCE
                Listen honey, about yesterday...

                          BUFFY
                That's totally yester. Besides,
                it's not like you were wrong. I
                did get kicked out. I'm wacky that
                way.

                          JOYCE
                Still, I want you to know that
                despite the problems you've had --

                          BUFFY
                Mom, you don't get it. Believe me,
                you don't want it. There's just
                things about being a vampire slayer
                that the older generation has a
                problem with.

                          JOYCE
                A what?

                          BUFFY
                Long story. I mean I'm kidding.

                          JOYCE
                Buffy, are you feeling well?

                          BUFFY   *
                I can't be in a good mood? That's   *
                a new house rule? Fine, I don't   *
                mind, cuz I'm a   *
                     (sings)   *
                MACHO MACHO MAN...   *

She sings her way out, leaving Joyce somewhat worried.

                                              CUT TO:

29 EXT. SUNNYDALE HIGH - DAY - ESTABLISHING   29

                         BUFFY (O.S.)
                    Turn up the music!

30 INT. THE GYM - DAY   30

The cheerleaders -- Buffy, Senior Cheerleader and the   *
rest practice. Buffy has a big, happy grin on her face,   *
she's workin' this cheer -- unfortunately she's workin' it
completely out of sync with everyone else.

                                                                *

Buffy stomps on the Senior Cheerleader's foot.

                    SENIOR CHEERLEADER
                    Ow! Get it together, Buffy, we have
                    a game in less than four hours.

ANGLE - DOOR

Willow and Xander slip in to watch.

                         BUFFY
                       (yells)
                    Hey Willow, Xander! My buds are
                    here. I love my buds.

WILLOW AND XANDER

React to Buffy.

                         XANDER
                    Is it me, or is Buffy somewhat
                    looped?

                                                                *

Each girl launches the one next to her into a spinning
cartwheel. Buffy is launched.

WILLOW AND XANDER

                         WILLOW
                    We better get her out of there.

                         XANDER
                    Yeah, before she...

                                              (CONTINUED)

30 CONTINUED: 30

    Buffy cartwheels to the Senior Cheerleader, grabs her and
    HURLS HER OUT OF FRAME like a flying sack of potatoes.

    WILLOW AND XANDER WINCE

                         XANDER
              ....hurts somebody.

    ANGLE - SENIOR CHEERLEADER

    Splatted in the corner of the gym where she landed. She gets
    up, way more angry than hurt.

                         BUFFY
              Did I do that?

                   SENIOR CHEERLEADER
              You are so out of here!

    Willow and Xander rush in, grab Buffy.

                         WILLOW
              It's not her fault --

                         XANDER
              She's on medication --

                   SENIOR CHEERLEADER
              Obviously not enough. Who's our
              next alternate -- oh.

    Amy is right there, in costume.

                   SENIOR CHEERLEADER
              Amy, you just made cheerleader.

                         BUFFY
              No no no, you don't want her, she's
              a w--

    Xander clamps a hand over Buffy's mouth as Willow and he
    hustle her out.

                         XANDER
              A wise choice indeed.

    As Amy stands, innocently joins the line,

                                                        CUT TO:

31 INT. GYM FOYER : DAY   31

    Willow and Xander drag Buffy out, shut the door.

                                                        (CONTINUED)

                              BUFFY
                    She's a witchy!!

                              WILLOW
                    Buffy --

                              BUFFY
                    I just got kicked off the team,
                    didn't I?

                              XANDER
                    I don't think it's your fault.

                              BUFFY
                    I know you don't. That's cause
                    you're my friend. You're my
                    Xander-shaped friend.
                         (wells up)
                    ...do you have any idea why I love
                    you so, Xander?

                              WILLOW
                    We gotta get you to --

                              XANDER
                    Let her speak!

                              BUFFY
                    I'll tell you. You're not like
                    other guys at all...

                              XANDER
                    Well...

                              BUFFY

                    You are completely and totally one
                    of the girls. I'm that comfy with
                    you.

Willow can't help but look a little pleased; Xander looks
like he just got cancer.

                              XANDER
                    That's great.

                              BUFFY
                    Any other guy gave me a bracelet,
                    they'd want to date me, it'd be a
                    thing, but you -- you --

She staggers a bit.

                              BUFFY
                    Oh. I don't feel so good.

                                                        (CONTINUED)

31 CONTINUED: 2   31

                                                                    *

                                                                    *

        She slumps over, pale and sweaty.

                         WILLOW
                Buffy?

                         BUFFY
                Something is really... not good...

        She collapses in their arms.

                                                    CUT TO:

32 INT. THE LIBRARY - GILES' OFFICE - DAY   32

        Buffy's laid out in two easy chairs. A cold compress on her
        head. She's conscious but very sick. Giles (ever present
        text in hand) Willow and Xander stand over her, concerned.

                         WILLOW
                We gotta get her to a hospital.

                         GILES
                They can't help her. This is a
                Bloodstone Vengeance Spell, hits
                the body hard, like drinking a
                quart of alcohol, then eradicates
                the immune system.

                         XANDER
                Vengeance spell. Like she's getting
                even with Buffy?

                         BUFFY
                    (weak)
                'Cause she knows I know she's a
                witch.

                         GILES
                The others she just wanted out of
                the running, you she intends to...

                         BUFFY
                Kill.

                         WILLOW
                How much time do we have?

                         GILES
                I'm sure we have --

                                                (CONTINUED)

                           BUFFY
Truth please.

                           GILES
Couple of hours, three at most.

                           XANDER
So how do we reverse Buffy's spell?

                           GILES
I've been researching that. We can
reverse all the spells if we can
get our hands on Amy's spell
book --

                           WILLOW
And if we can't get our hands on
it?

                           GILES
The only other way is to cut the
witch's head off.

                           XANDER
          (raising his hand)
Show of hands...

                           BUFFY
No. It's not Amy's fault. She
became a witch to survive her
mother.

                           XANDER
I don't care why, I care that you
go on breathing.

                           BUFFY
Giles, where would she be casting
these spells?

                           GILES
She needs a sacred space with a
pentagram, a large pot...

                           BUFFY
At home. Help me get up.
          (Giles helps her up)
We'll go to her house, find her
book --

                           WILLOW
We'll go with you.

                                      (CONTINUED)

32 CONTINUED: 2   32

                              BUFFY
                    No. Stay here, keep an eye on Amy.

                              GILES
                    And keep her away from the science
                    lab. We'll need it to cast our
                    counter spells.

                                                    CUT TO:

33 EXT. AMY'S HOUSE - AFTERNOON   33

Giles pulls up.

ANGLE: THE DOOR

He knocks loudly. Buffy peeks in the window by the door.

ANGLE: THROUGH THE WINDOW - AMY'S LIVING ROOM

We see Catherine start at the sound of knocking. She takes
something we can't see very well and slides it under the
coffee table. Comes anxiously to the door.

It opens, and she stands before Buffy and Giles. It's clear
from the expression on Buffy's face that this isn't what she
was expecting.

                              CATHERINE
                    What do you want? Is there
                    something wrong?

                              GILES
                    Mrs. Madison, we need to talk to
                    you about your daughter.

                              CATHERINE
                    I'm not allowed to -- you'll have
                    to come back.

She tries to shut the door -- he pushes it open rather
forcefully. He ushers Buffy in.

                                                    CUT TO:

34 INT. AMY'S LIVING ROOM - CONTINUOUS   34

Giles moves Buffy to the couch, turns to Catherine.

                                                    (CONTINUED)

> GILES
> Your daughter is up to something
> very dangerous. Are you aware of
> that?

> CATHERINE
> I don't know what you're talking
> about.

> GILES
> I think you know very well.

> CATHERINE
> You have to go. She's gonna be
> home soon.

> GILES
> This girl is very sick. You will
> shut up and you will listen to me.
> Your daughter has access to some
> very powerful magics. Somehow your
> obsession with cheerleading has
> made her --

> CATHERINE
> (near tears)
> I don't care about cheerleading!
> It's not my fault she's doing
> stuff.

Buffy is staring intently at Catherine.

> GILES
> As her mother, you should accept
> some responsibility for her
> actions.

Surprisingly, she starts laughing.

> CATHERINE
> Well, these kids today...

Buffy looks at her, then looks at what Amy hid under the table.

ANGLE: UNDER THE TABLE

is a plate of brownies.

Buffy stands, weakly.

                                              (CONTINUED)

                         CATHERINE
               She's out of her mind. Ever since
               dad -- her dad left. I can't
               control her.

                         GILES
               You're afraid of her.

She turns to look at Buffy, who approaches her slowly.
Giles turns as well.

                         BUFFY
               Amy?

Catherine takes a step back, wide eyed.

                         BUFFY
               Are you Amy?

                         GILES
               I don't understand...

                         BUFFY
               She switched, didn't she? She
               switched your bodies. She wanted
               to relive her glory days.
               Catherine the Great.

                         GILES
               Good lord...

Catherine nods, quietly.

                         CATHERINE
               She said I was wasting my youth...
               So she took it.

                                        BLACK OUT.

                    END OF ACT THREE

ACT FOUR

35 INT. AMY'S LIVING ROOM - SECONDS LATER   35

Catherine has sat down on the couch next to Buffy. She is
terrified and fighting back tears.

                    CATHERINE
          I didn't know about her... her
          power. When my dad was here they
          would fight, he called her a witch.
          I thought he meant something else.
          When he left I wanted to go with
          him but she wouldn't even let me
          call. She got crazy. She'd lock
          herself upstairs for days. And
          she'd get down on me all the time.
          She said I didn't deserve to have
          it so easy, that I didn't know how
          hard it was to be her. I guess she
          showed me, huh?

She does cry now, quietly. It takes all of Buffy's effort
to say:

                    BUFFY
          Amy, it's gonna be okay.

                    CATHERINE
          A few months ago I woke up in her
          bed, I didn't know where I was...
          and I looked in the mirror...

                    GILES
          She locked herself upstairs.
          Where?

                    CATHERINE
          She has a room in the attic.

                    GILES
          Show me.

                                        CUT TO:

36 INT. AMY'S ATTIC - A BIT LATER   36

We see the dolls lined up in the foreground as in the
background the DOOR BURSTS OPEN, Giles coming in behind it.

Catherine stays in the doorway, too afraid to enter as Giles
comes up to the dolls.

                                        (CONTINUED)

                    CATHERINE
          If she finds out I've been in here
          she'll kill me.

                    GILES
          My God...

ANGLE: TWO DOLLS

A woman and a girl. The dolls are lashed together with a
thorny vine.

                    GILES
          I believe we can reverse your
          mother's spell. All of them, in
          fact.

                    CATHERINE
          You really could?

                    GILES
          Yes, but I need her books. There
          are certain volumes she would need
          for this kind of casting.

He looks around. Tentatively, she enters, and helps. They
rummage about in the dark recesses of the place, looking on
shelves, under old blankets.

Giles discovers a small trunk. As he pulls it open he says
to Catherine:

                    GILES
          Collect those dolls, and all the
          personal --

something LEAPS at him from the trunk, SCREECHING -- a black
cat. Giles jumps back as the cat hits the floor and takes
off out of the room.

Giles takes a moment to recover himself.

                    GILES
          Nice kitty...
               (looking in the trunk)
          What were you guarding? Yes...

He pulls out the book.

                    GILES
          This is it.

                                        CUT TO:

37   INT. AMY'S LIVING ROOM - SECONDS LATER   37

    Giles comes back down with the book, Catherine with the box
    of talismans.

    Buffy is back on the couch. She looks ghastly, but she
    looks up to Giles with hope.

                         BUFFY
                Did we find?

                         GILES
                We found.

    He gently helps her to her feet. He hands the book to
    Catherine and picks Buffy up.

                         CATHERINE
                Where are you going?

                         GILES
                We're going to school. And you're
                coming with us.

                                                  CUT TO:

38   INT. THE GYM - EVENING   38

    We hear students CHEERING as the school basketball team
    takes the floor.

    The camera is in heady motion, following the team, sweeping
    across the stands, racing by the cheerleaders. The last one
    is Amy.

                                                  CUT TO:

39   INT. SCIENCE LAB - EVENING   39

    They enter, Giles placing Buffy in a chair as Catherine
    drops the box on a table. He squats before Buffy, looks her
    in the eyes.

                         GILES
                I'm going to stop this.

    ANGLE: BUFFY'S POV

    the figure of Giles is a colorful BLUR. The room seems to
    teeter and shift around him, his VOICE a bizarre and deep
    echo.

                         GILES
                I promise. Just hang on.

                                              (CONTINUED)

39 CONTINUED: 39

He stands up (we are no longer in her POV), digs in the box
for the book.

                    CATHERINE
               How is she?

                    GILES
               We only have a few minutes.

Giles pulls the book out of the box, starts looking through
it.

                    GILES
               Let's see... I'll need lead,
               sulphur, some sort of diacetate...

He goes over to the glass cabinet with the chemicals in it.
It's locked. Casually, still looking down at the book for
reference, he picks up a metal beaker and smashes the glass.
He looks in and starts picking out vials of useful
substances.

                    CATHERINE
               What should I do?

He turns to her.

                    GILES
               Find me a frog.

                                             CUT TO:

40 INT. THE GYM - CONTINUOUS   40

The game has started, the kids in the stands CHEERING. The
cheerleaders are on the sideline, doing steps.

ANGLE: AMY

Is right there with them, last on the left. She is beaming.

ANGLE: THE CROWD — AMY'S POV

They are a ROARING mass, an appreciative audience. A joyful
noise.

And she moves in SLOW MOTION, the camera circling LOW around
her, as she relives her greatest glory.

ANGLE: THE STANDS

The camera whips across the fans to find Xander and Willow
up off to the side.

                                             (CONTINUED)

40 CONTINUED: 40

     They alone are silent, their eyes never leaving Amy.

                                                        CUT TO:

41 INT. SCIENCE LAB - A BIT LATER   41

     Giles has something bubbling in a beaker, a Bunsen burner
     under it.

     Catherine is nearby, reluctantly prying out a dead frog's
     eyes.

                         GILES
                    Right.

     He throws in a powder, and begins:

                         GILES
                       (reading)
                    The center is dark.
                       (in Latin)
                    centrum est obscurus.
                       (reading)
                    The darkness breathes.
                       (in Latin)
                    tenebrae respiratis.
                       (reading)
                    The listener hears.

     He throws in another powder.   *

                         GILES
                    Hear me.

                                                        CUT TO:

42 INT. THE GYM - CONTINUOUS   42

     Amy is still strutting in step, still basking in her glory.

     ANGLE: AMY'S POV

     The appreciative crowd is before us, and then suddenly it
     becomes

     ANGLE: CATHERINE'S POV

     the lab. A table. A frog.

     It's just a flash, and then it's the audience again. Amy
     starts, wide eyed, and nearly messes up.

                                                        CUT TO:

43 INT. SCIENCE LAB - CONTINUOUS   43

Catherine is reeling just as Amy was, shaking off the
momentary change.

                         CATHERINE
                It's working...

                          GILES
                    (reading)
                Unlock the gate, let the darkness
                shine. Cover us with holy fear.
                Show me.

He barks the order again, "show me", but this time in Arabic
(waar re-nee).   *

The lights in the room blow out.

                                          CUT TO:

44 INT. THE GYM - CONTINUOUS   44

The cheerleaders are forming a pyramid, Amy at the top. She is
up there when:

ANGLE: CATHERINE'S POV

flashes before us again. This time it's clearer; we can see
Giles, and the whole room. Our gaze sweeps over to include
the dying Buffy.

Amy SCREAMS -- and falls, wrecking the whole pyramid. The
girls tumble about, the fans LAUGHING a bit.

                    SENIOR CHEERLEADER   *
                Amy, what's your problem?

Amy stands, primal fury on her face. The cheerleader backs   *
off.   *

                                                                       *

Amy RUNS out of the gym.   *

ANGLE: XANDER AND WILLOW

They see her go.

                         WILLOW
                She must be heading for Buffy!

                                          (CONTINUED)

44 CONTINUED: 44

                         XANDER
            Come on.

                                                    CUT TO:

45 INT. SCIENCE LAB - CONTINUOUS   45

ANGLE: BUFFY'S POV

Giles continues the spell, in Buffy's increasingly weird,
dark view. His voice is not even human to her anymore.

ANGLE: CATHERINE

She is still reeling from the flashes. She looks up
suddenly.

                         CATHERINE
            She's heading this way.

                                                    CUT TO:

46 INT. SCHOOL HALL - CONTINUOUS   46

Amy turns a corner and runs smack into a very casual Willow.

                    WILLOW
            Amy!

                    AMY
            Get out of my way!

                    WILLOW
            Wait! I needed to talk to you. I
            can help you.

The look Amy gives her raises one's hair.

                    AMY
            Help me? With what?

                    WILLOW
            Well, you know, all your...
            witchcraft. I know a really
            good... cauldron... do you actually
            ride a broom or --

Xander is sneaking up behind Amy. She SPINS suddenly and
glares at him. She mutters something under her breath and
he stops, suddenly unable to breathe. Drops to his knees.

                                                    (CONTINUED)

46 CONTINUED: 46

                              WILLOW
                    Xander!

Amy turns and PUNCHES Willow, knocks her to the ground.

Amy takes off.

                                                          CUT TO:

47 INT. SCIENCE LAB - CONTINUOUS   47

Things are really heating up in here. Giles holds his hands
to the heavens:

                              GILES
                    Corsheth, and Gilail, the gate is
                    closed. Receive the dark, release
                    the unworthy... Take of mine
                    energy and be sated!

He PLUNGES HIS HANDS into the brew! Huge colored cloud
shoots up.

                                                     INTERCUT WITH:

48 INT. HALL OUTSIDE LAB - CONTINUOUS   48

Amy arrives, tries the door.

Catherine sees the door rattle, starts back in terror

ANGLE: AMY

Smashes the emergency glass and pulls out an axe.

ANGLE: GILES

Pulls his dripping hands out.

                              GILES
                    Be sated! Release the unworthy!

ANGLE: THE AXE

hits the door, burying itself above the lock.

ANGLE: GILES
                              GILES
                    Release!

                                                     (CONTINUED)

48   CONTINUED: 48

ANGLE: BUFFY

Her eyes flutter shut, her head slumping over.

                          GILES
                    Release!

49   INT. SCIENCE LAB - CONTINUOUS   49

And the door BURSTS OPEN, An axe wielding Amy running in.
She takes one quick look around, heads for Buffy --

                          GILES
                    RELEASE!

Amy raises the axe -- there is a flash of light --
-- and she stops. Lowers it as

ANGLE: BUFFY

stands, completely restored. She and Amy look at each other
in wonder.

                          BUFFY
                    Amy?

And Catherine FLIES into frame, SCREAMING and tackling
Buffy. The woman has gone completely apeshit. Giles comes
at her and she just LOOKS up at him --

-- and a desk MOVES at him, knocking him down.   *

Catherine stands, comes toward the cowering Amy. Nothing
but hate in her gaze.

                          CATHERINE
                    You. You little brat.

                          AMY
                    Mom, please...

She is retreating, raising the axe more for protection than
anything else. Catherine merely cocks her head and the axe
FLIES out of Amy's hand and into her own. Amy stifles a
scream.

                          CATHERINE
                    Raise a hand to your own mother?
                    Who gave you birth, who gave up her
                    life, her LIFE so you could drag
                    your worthless carcass around and
                    call it living?

                                              (CONTINUED)

She SLAMS the axe into a table top.

Amy looks from the axe to her mother.

ANGLE: CATHERINE'S HANDS

Something is happening -- energy begins emanating from
them -- like sparks, only black. Something very powerful is
brewing in her.

                    CATHERINE
          You were never anything but
          trouble. I'll put you where you'll
          never make trouble again.

Buffy appears right behind Catherine.

                    BUFFY
          Hey, guess what?

Catherine turns.

                    BUFFY
          I feel better.

ANGLE: Catherine flies over a table, hits the ground with
all attendant smashing of glass things.

Buffy comes around the table and Catherine pops back up,
wired with fury.

                    CATHERINE
          That body was mine! Mine!

                    BUFFY
          Oh, grow up.

Catherine throws her head back in a mystical shriek —-- and
Buffy is flung back over the teacher's desk. She rises to
see Catherine shaking, about to cast the spell.

                    CATHERINE
          I shall look upon my enemy --

Her arms CRACKLE with energy -- she opens her eyes and they
are glowing darkly- she throws her arms forward with the
final phrase --

                    CATHERINE
          -- I shall look upon her and the
          dark place will have her soul!
          Corsheth! Take her!

                                        (CONTINUED)

And Buffy SWINGS her leg over the table and BREAKS the
support for the mirror above -- it comes down, hitting the
table at an angle, still supported on the other side.

It's too late for Catherine to stop. The spell shoots out
of her arms at her own reflection. It bounces right back at her.

She SCREAMS. Glows. Energy singing around her, wrapping
her up.

Then there's nothing.

Giles, no longer pinned, gets up, creeps forward with Amy.
Buffy comes from behind the desk. They all look around
them, but they are alone. After a while...

              GILES
    Well, that was interesting.

              BUFFY
    Are you guys okay?

              AMY
        (feelingly)
    I'm fine.

Buffy smiles at her.

              GILES
    I think all the spells were
    reversed. Of course, it's my first
    casting, I may have got it wrong.

              BUFFY
    You saved my life. You were a god.

              GILES
    One doesn't want to be immodest,
    but I am not unsatisfied --

              BUFFY
    Giles, stop being so proper.
    You're in America. Brag.

And they head for the door, Giles obliging:

              GILES
    Well, it was first time and some of
    those incantations are quite
    tricky. And I was somewhat
    interpretive with the
    ingredients --

                      (CONTINUED)

A FIGURE LEAPS OUT at Amy, tackles her.

It's Xander.

                    XANDER
           I got her! I got her! Cut her
           head off!

                    BUFFY
           Xander, what are you doing?

                    XANDER
           Saving you.

Buffy pulls him off Amy.

                    XANDER
           But she's evil!

                    GILES
           Well, it wasn't exactly her.

                    AMY
           I was my mom.

                    XANDER
           Oh.

It takes a moment for him to realize he has no idea what
they're talking about. Willow runs in now, carrying a
baseball bat.

                    WILLOW
           Where is she?

                    XANDER
           Willow! It's cool.

                    WILLOW
           It is?

                    XANDER
           Oh yeah. I took care of it.

                                  CUT TO:

50 INT. BUFFY'S BEDROOM - AFTERNOON   50

Buffy is throwing the pieces of her alarm clock in the trash
when Joyce enters.

                    JOYCE
           I don't get it.

                          (CONTINUED)

50 CONTINUED:

                         BUFFY
               What?

                         JOYCE
               I've been thinking a lot about
               where you're coming from, how to
               relate to you, and I've come to a
               simple conclusion. I don't get it.
               What you want, what you're
               thinking. Not a clue.

                         BUFFY
               I'm inscrutable, huh?

                         JOYCE
               You're sixteen. I think there's a
               biological imperative whereby I
               can't understand you because I'm
               not sixteen.

                         BUFFY
               Do you ever wish you could be?
               Sixteen again?

                         JOYCE
               There's a frightful notion. Go
               through all that again.
                         (shudders)
               Not even if it helped me understand
               you.

     Buffy kisses her on the cheek --

                         BUFFY
               I love you, mom.

     -- and exit, leaving Joyce thrown once more.

                         JOYCE
               I don't get it.

                                                          CUT TO:

51 INT. HALL BY THE GYM - DAY (DAYS LATER)   51

     Buffy and Amy are walking through the hall.

                         AMY
               Dad is so impossible. He doesn't
               ever want me going anywhere, wants
               to spend total quantity time
               together.
                         (MORE)

                                                          (CONTINUED)

> AMY (cont'd)
> I'm like, "Dad, I can go out, it's
> perfectly safe." He's got all this
> guilt at leaving me with mom and
> he's being a total pain.

> BUFFY
> You're loving it.

> AMY
> Every single minute.

Cordelia breezes by with the other cheerleaders as they get
out of the gym. We see Amber and Lishanne -- all recovered.

> CORDELIA
> Hey, I'm really sorry you guys got
> bumped back to alternate. Hold
> it -- wait -- no I'm not.

> AMY
> Well, I know I'll miss the
> intellectual thrill of spelling
> words out with my arms.

> CORDELIA
> Ooh, these grapes are sour.

She exits, passing Buffy, who is staring at the trophy case.
Amy looks to her, the smile leaving her face.

> AMY
> Oh, I'm sorry. I forgot you
> actually wanted to be on the squad.

> BUFFY
> No, that's okay. Cheerleading is
> just a little too hairy these days.

> AMY
> That's for sure.

For a moment they both look at Catherine's trophy.

> AMY
> Catherine the Great.

> BUFFY
> And there's been no sign of her?

> AMY
> That last spell, she said I'd never
> make trouble again. Wherever she
> is, I don't think we have to worry.

(CONTINUED)

                           BUFFY
              Twisted.

                           AMY
              I'm just happy to have my body
              back.
                   (as they walk off)
              I'm thinking of getting fat.

                           BUFFY
              Well, that look is in for spring.

As they leave, we stay on the trophy. TRACK in closer to
the cheerleading figure on top. And closer, to the
impassive bronze face.

Her eyes dart back and forth.

                                          BLACK OUT.

                    END OF SHOW

BUFFY THE VAMPIRE SLAYER

"Teacher's Pet"

Written by

David Greenwalt

Directed by

Bruce Seth Green

<u>SHOOTING SCRIPT</u>

October 8, 1996
October 9, 1996 (Blue-Pages)
October 18,1996 (Pink-Pages)

BUFFY THE VAMPIRE SLAYER

"Teacher's Pet"

<u>CAST LIST</u>

BUFFY SUMMERS......................... Sarah Michelle Gellar
XANDER HARRIS......................... Nicholas Brendon
RUPERT GILES.......................... Anthony S. Head
WILLOW ROSENBERG...................... Alyson Hannigan
CORDELIA CHASE........................ Charisma Carpenter

ANGEL................................. David Boreanaz
FLUTIE................................ *Ken Lerner
NATALIE/MANTIS........................ Musetta Vander
DR.GREGORY............................ *William Monaghan
BLAYNE................................
BUD #1................................
HOMELESS GUY/COP......................
REAL MISS FRENCH......................
CLAW..................................
TEACHER...............................

<u>BUFFY THE VAMPIRE SLAYER</u>

"Teacher's Pet"

<u>SET LIST</u>

<u>INTERIORS</u>

SUNNYDALE HIGH SCHOOL
    BIOLOGY CLASSROOM
    HALL
    LIBRARY
    *GILES' OFFICE
    CAFETERIA
    HALL OUTSIDE PRINCIPAL'S OFFICE
    COUNSELOR'S OFFICE
    HALL OUTSIDE BIOLOGY CLASSROOM
    CLOSET
THE BRONZE
NATALIE FRENCH'S HOUSE
NATALIE'S CELLAR

<u>EXTERIORS</u>

SUNNYDALE HIGH SCHOOL
    THE QUAD
THE BRONZE
WEATHERLY PARK
THE REAL MRS. FRENCH'S HOUSE
STREET

BUFFY THE VAMPIRE SLAYER

"Teacher's Pet"

<u>TEASER</u>

SCREEN IS BLACK - We hear a TERRIFIED SCREAM, PULLING BACK
we discover we were INSIDE THE SCREAMING GIRL'S MOUTH. Now
we see we're --

1   INT. THE BRONZE - NIGHT

A BLOODTHIRSTY VAMPIRE advances on BUFFY. Tables are
overturned, the BAND has stopped in mid-play, and everyone
except Buffy (in hot dress, out of breath) is scared
shitless, giving the monster a wide berth.

He lunges, she sidesteps and throws a punch, he grabs her
arm with alarming speed and slams her down on top of a
table. He's strong and scary and he's got her pinned. He
lowers his teeth for the kill as --

A HAND -- reaches in, grabs him by the hair. He looks up:

DRAMATIC ANGLE - BUFFY'S SAVIOR

Is XANDER. Calm, confident, cool.

                    XANDER
          May I cut in?

The vampire snarls and goes for Xander's throat. Xander
slams his head into the table, stands him up, and almost
casually finishes him off with a crashing blow. The vamp
careens over tables and chairs, lands in a heap on the
floor.

Xander pulls Buffy off the table to her feet.

                    XANDER
          Are you all right?

                    BUFFY
          Thanks to you.

She <u>takes his hand in hers</u>. Neither notices the Vamp
stirring.

                    BUFFY
          You hurt your hand... will you
          still be able to...?

                                        (CONTINUED)

1   CONTINUED:

                              XANDER
                    Finish my solo and then kiss you
                    like you've never been kissed
                    before?

She nods, smitten. He gives her his million dollar grin,
heads for the stage, never breaking stride as he grabs a
chair by the leg, cracks it over a table (turning the chair
leg into a stake which he flings through the vamp's heart).

He leaps on stage, grabs his guitar, assumes his GUITAR GOD
POSE and THRASHES OUT some mind-numbing, teeth-jangling
POWER CHORDS. Buffy watches in awe. The band looks on, as
Xander goes into a smoking solo.

CLOSE - BUFFY - digging him, but saying, incongruously:

                              BUFFY
                    You're drooling...

                                              SMASH CUT TO:

2   INT. BIOLOGY CLASSROOM - DAY

Xander dreams on his desk. The lights are low: the class is
being shows slides of insects.

Buffy, WILLOW and BLAYNE MALL (football star, stud) sit
nearby. Buffy shakes him.

                              BUFFY
                    Xander... you've got a little...

He bolts up from his Buffy fantasy. Buffy brushes her
mouth to indicate he should wipe his. He does,
straightening up as DR. GREGORY (kindly, older, glasses; his
name stitched on his white lab coat) turns on the lights and
moves down the aisle towards them.

                              DR. GREGORY
                    Their ancestors were here long
                    before we were - their progeny will
                    be here long after we're gone. The
                    simple and ubiquitous ant. If you
                    did the homework, you'll know the
                    two ways that ants communicate...
                    Ms. Summers?

Buffy doesn't have a clue. Glances at Willow.

                              BUFFY
                    Ways that ants communicate.

                                              (CONTINUED)

2   CONTINUED: 2

                              DR. GREGORY
                         Yes...

                              BUFFY
                    With other ants.

                              DR. GREGORY
                    No, with lemons. From the
                    homework, the ants are
                    communicating in two ways...

She watches Willow, behind Dr. Gregory's back, frantically
mime "touch" and "smell" by touching and smelling Xander --
to his discomfort.

                              BUFFY
                    ...touch... and... B.O.?

Laughter from the class.

                              BLAYNE
                         (re: Xander)
                    Thank God someone finally found the
                    courage to mention that.

                              DR. GREGORY
                    Touch and <u>smell</u>, Ms. Summers.
                         (without turning to look
                          at Willow)
                    Is there anything else Ms.
                    Rosenberg would like to tell you?

Willow hangs her head. The CLASS BELL rings. Kids grab
their stuff, shuffle out.

                              DR. GREGORY
                    Chapters six through eight by
                    Wednesday, people.
                         (to Buffy)
                    Could I see you for a moment?

Willow and Xander exchange sympathetic looks with Buffy as
they make their way out with the rest of the kids.

3   INT. SCHOOL HALL - DAY   3

Blayne shoves past, calls to GORGEOUS GIRL:

                              BLAYNE
                    Cheryl, wait up, doll.
                         (aside to Xander)
                    Isn't she something?
                              (MORE)

                                                             (CONTINUED)

3   CONTINUED: 3

                         BLAYNE (CONT'D)
              Do you know what a woman like that
              wants?
                   (Xander waits to hear:)
              No, I guess you wouldn't.

Blayne walks off. Xander calls after:

                         XANDER
                   (calls out to Blayne)
              Something really cutting!
                   (to Willow)
              Sometimes I just go with the
              generic insult.

                         WILLOW
              Why pay more for the brand name?

4   INT. BIOLOGY CLASSROOM - DAY   4

Display table in front holds an ant farm, small glass cases
with ladybugs, spiders and a praying mantis. Dr. Gregory
puts some books inside a SMALL CLOSET next to the
blackboard.

                         DR. GREGORY
              I gather you had a few problems at
              your last school.

                         BUFFY
              Well, what teenager doesn't --

                         DR. GREGORY
                   (emerging from closet)
              Cut school, get in fights, burn
              down the gymnasium?
                   (off her look)
              Principal Flutie showed me your
              permanent record.

                                                                         *

                         BUFFY
              That fire, there were major
              extenuating circumstances --
              actually it's sort of funny --

                         DR. GREGORY
              I can't wait to see what you're
              going to do here.

                                                      (CONTINUED)

4   CONTINUED: 4

                              BUFFY
                         (deflating)
                    Destructo-Girl, that's me.

                              DR. GREGORY
                    But I suspect it's going to be
                    great.

                              BUFFY
                    You mean great in a bad way?

He takes off his glasses, wipes them under:

                              DR. GREGORY
                    You've got a first rate mind. You
                    can think on your feet -- imagine
                    what you could accomplish if you
                    did...?

                              BUFFY
                    The homework thing?

                              DR. GREGORY
                    The homework thing. I understand
                    you probably have a good excuse for
                    not doing it. Amazingly enough, I
                    don't care. I know you can excel
                    in this class and so I expect no
                    less. Is that clear?

                              BUFFY
                    Okay. Sorry.

                              DR. GREGORY
                    Don't be sorry, be smart.

He holds glasses out in front of him, making sure they're
clean. We see Buffy through the glasses.

                              DR. GREGORY
                    And please don't listen to the
                    Principal or anyone else's negative
                    opinions about you. Let's make 'em
                    eat that permanent record, what do
                    you say?

                              BUFFY
                    Uh... thanks?

A moment, which he breaks, a slight smile on his lips:

                              DR. GREGORY
                    Chapters six through eight.

                                              (CONTINUED)

She exits. He folds his glasses, places them next to the praying mantis on the display table.

Humming to himself, he turns out the lights again, darkening the room. HEARS a noise. Looks over his right shoulder: nothing. He goes and starts looking over some slides on the wall.

Until, from the left, a HUGE and HORRIFYING MANTIS FORELEG jackknifes open and sinks it's SHARP SPINES into his neck. We don't see much of the creature beyond the terrible forelegs — but it's big, it's ugly, and it isn't very nice.

He's RIPPED OUT OF FRAME, banging into the display table. His glasses fall to the floor -- one lens cracks -- reflected in the glasses, we see Dr. Gregory struggling futilely in the horrible monster's grasp -- along with CRACKING and CRUNCHING SOUNDS. Something's having supper.

                                                        BLACK OUT.

                            <u>END OF TEASER</u>

                                  .

<u>ACT ONE</u>

5   INT. BRONZE - NIGHT   5

A decent crowd tonight. The band that was backing Xander up
in his fantasy is playing.

Xander is on the edge of the crowd, near the stage. He
looks about for some familiar faces. Looks up at one of the
band members, gives him a high sign and a smile like they're
best buds. The band member ignores him. Slightly
sheepishly, he moves away from the dance floor, still
searching for his buds.

ANGLE: FROM THE BALCONY

As we look down on Xander wandering, we TILT UP to find Buffy
and Willow in mid conversation at one of the tables up here.

                    BUFFY
          Dr Gregory didn't chew me out or
          anything. He was really cool. But
          Flutie showed him my permanent
          record. Apparently I fall
          somewhere between Charles Manson
          and a really <u>bad</u> person.

                    WILLOW
          And you can't tell Dr Gregory what
          really happened at your old school?

                    BUFFY
          I was fighting vampires? I'm
          thinking he might not believe me.

                    WILLOW
          Yeah, he probably gets that excuse
          all the time.

Cordelia approaches.

                    CORDELIA
          Here lies a problem. What used to
          be my table occupied by pitiful
          losers. Of course we'll have to
          burn it.

                    BUFFY
          Sad, you have so many memories
          here. You and Lawrence, you and
          Mark, you and John. You spent the
          better part of your "J" through "M"
          here.

                                        (CONTINUED)

5   CONTINUED: 5

Cordelia gives a look and moves on.

ANGLE: COUCHES NEAR COFFEE BAR

Blayne and football buds are lounging.

                    BLAYNE
          Seven. Including Cheryl. I tell
          you though, her sister was looking
          to make it eight.

                    BUD # 1
          Cheryl's sister? The one in
          college?

Xander appears at the edges of the group.

                    BLAYNE
          Home for the holidays and looking
          for love. Not my type, though.
          Girl's really gotta have something
          to go with me.

                    XANDER
          Something like a lobotomy?

                    BLAYNE
          Xander. How many times've you
          scored?

                    XANDER
          Well...

                    BLAYNE
          Just a question.

                    XANDER
          Are we talking today or the whole
          week? Uh oh, duty calls.

Xander moves to intercept Buffy and Willow, who are coming
down the stairs. He throws his arms around the two of them,
saying loudly:

                    XANDER
          Babes...

                    BUFFY
          What are you doing?

                    XANDER
          Work with me here. Blayne had the
          nerve to question my manliness.
          I'm just giving him a visual.

                                          (CONTINUED)

5   CONTINUED: 2   5

                              WILLOW
                         (clutching Xander
                          tighter)
                    We'll show him.

                              BUFFY
                         (looking off)
                    I don't believe it.

                              XANDER
                    I know. And after all my
                    conquests--

Buffy steps away, toward the door. Framed in the doorway is
ANGEL, standing half in the shadows.

Xander and Willow watch her head for him.

                              XANDER
                    Who's that?

                              WILLOW
                    That must be Angel. I think.

                              XANDER
                    That weird guy? That warned her
                    about the vampires?

                              WILLOW
                    That's him, I'll bet you.

                              XANDER
                         (a little plaintively)
                    Well, he's buff. She never said
                    anything about him being buff.

                              WILLOW
                    You think he's buff?

                              XANDER
                         (angry)
                    He's a very attractive man! How
                    come that never came up?

                                                            CUT TO:

6   EXT. RIGHT OUTSIDE THE BRONZE - CONTINUOUS   6

Buffy approaches Angel, distrust on her face.

                              BUFFY
                    Well, look who's here.

                                                        (CONTINUED)

6   CONTINUED: 5

                              ANGEL
                    Hi.

                              BUFFY
                    I'd say it's nice to see you but we
                    both know that's a big fib.

                              ANGEL
                    I won't stay long.

                              BUFFY
                    No, you'll just give me a cryptic
                    warning about some exciting new
                    catastrophe and then disappear into
                    the night. Right?

                              ANGEL
                    You're cold.

                              BUFFY
                    You can take it.

                              ANGEL
                    I mean you look cold.

Angel takes off his leather jacket.

ANGLE - XANDER AND WILLOW INSIDE

Watching Angel slip the jacket on Buffy. Xander no longer
has his arm around Willow.

                              XANDER
                    Oh right, give her your jacket.
                    It's a balmy night, nobody needs to
                    be trading clothing out there.

                              WILLOW
                    I don't think she even likes him...

ANGLE - BUFFY AND ANGEL OUTSIDE

                              BUFFY
                         (re: jacket)
                    Little big on me.

She sees a recent and unusual wound on Angel's (now bare)
arm -- three long and parallel cuts -- like a tiger's claw.
Her attitude changes to one of concern.

                              BUFFY
                    What happened?

                                                        (CONTINUED)

6   CONTINUED: 2   6

                              ANGEL
                    I didn't pay attention.

                              BUFFY
                    To somebody with a big fork?

                              ANGEL
                    He's coming.

                              BUFFY
                    The fork guy?

                              ANGEL
                    Don't let him corner you. And
                    don't give him a moment's mercy.
                    He'll rip your throat out.

                              BUFFY
                    Okay, I give you improved marks.
                    Ripping the throat out:
                    non-cryptic, it's a strong
                    visual...

He almost smiles.

                              ANGEL
                    I have to go.

He walks off, disappears around a corner. She stares after
him.

                              BUFFY
                    Sweet dreams to you, too.

After a moment she heads back into the Bronze.

                                                             DISSOLVE TO:

7   EXT. SUNNYDALE HIGH SCHOOL - DAY - ESTABLISHING   7

                              GILES (O.S.)
                    That's all he said, "Fork" guy?

8   EXT. THE QUAD - DAY   8

Kids socialize between classes. Buffy talks to Giles,
Willow reads a science book.

                              BUFFY
                    That's all. "Cryptic" guy said
                    "Fork" guy.

                                                             (CONTINUED)

8   CONTINUED: 8

                              GILES
                    I think there's too many guys in
                    your life.
                              (she gives him a look)
                    I'll see what I can find out.
                              (gazes at sky with
                               loathing)
                    God, every day here is the same.

                              BUFFY
                    Bright, sunny, beautiful. How can
                    we escape this torment?

(Alternate line, in case it's raining, foggy or dark.

                              GILES
                              (gazes at sky)
                    Reminds me of home.

                              BUFFY
                    Dark, dank, dreary. You must be so
                    happy.

He gives her a look, shoves off.

Xander saunters up as Giles exits.

                              XANDER
                    Guess what I just over-heard in the
                    office. No Dr. Gregory today.
                    Ergo those of us who blew off our
                    Science homework...
                              (shuts Willow's book)
                    ...are not as dumb as we look.

                              BUFFY
                    What happened, is he sick?

                              XANDER
                    They didn't say anything about sick
                    -- something about... missing.

                              BUFFY
                    He's missing?

                              XANDER
                    Hold on, let me think, the
                    cheerleaders were modeling the new
                    short skirts and I kinda got...
                    yeah, I think they said missing.

Xander reads Buffy's concern, turns to Willow.

                                                        (CONTINUED)

> XANDER
> Which is bad.

> BUFFY
> If something's wrong, yeah.

> WILLOW
> He's one of the only teachers who
> doesn't think Buffy is a felon.

> XANDER
> (to Buffy)
> I'm really sorry. I'm sure he'll --
> iya-hoo.

Xander sees something O.S. that chills his bacon. Buffy and
Willow follow his gaze.

THEIR POV - BEAUTY SHOT

NATALIE FRENCH, late twenties, heart-stopper. Xander and
every other boy on campus can't take their eyes off her.
She slows as she passes Xander, turns, stops.

> NATALIE
> Could you help me?

> XANDER
> Egguh -- yes.

> NATALIE
> I'm looking for Science one oh
> nine.

> XANDER
> Sure. It's, uh... I go there
> everyday --
> (to Buffy and Willow)
> -- oh god, where is it?

Blayne steps in front of Xander.

> BLAYNE
> Hi. Blayne Mall. I'm going there
> right now. It's not far from the
> Varsity Field where I took all city
> last year...

> NATALIE
> Thank you, Blayne.

She gives Xander a dazzling smile, heads off with Blayne.

(CONTINUED)

8   CONTINUED: 3   8

                          XANDER
                Funny how the earth never opens up
                and swallows you when you want it
                to.

9   INT. BIOLOGY CLASSROOM - DAY   9

A lovely hand writes "NATALIE FRENCH" on the board as
students enter, take their seats. Buffy and Willow walk
towards their desks. Something catches Buffy's eye. She
stops, turns back; Willow watches her pick Dr. Gregory's
glasses off the floor. Buffy notes the cracked lens.

                          WILLOW
                What's wrong?

                          BUFFY
                If he dropped his glasses why
                didn't he pick them up?

Buffy puts them on the display table and they take their
seats.

Natalie turns from the board as the class settles. Amongst
the students are Xander and Blayne.

                          NATALIE
                My name is Natalie French, I'll be
                substituting for Dr. Gregory.

                          BUFFY
                Do you know when he's coming back?

                          NATALIE
                No I don't...
                    (looks at seating chart)
                Buffy. They just call and tell me
                where they want me.

                          BLAYNE
                    (sotto)
                I'll tell you where I want you...

                          NATALIE
                Excuse me, Blayne?

                          BLAYNE
                I was just wondering if you were
                going to pick up where Dr. Gregory
                left off.

                                              (CONTINUED)

                         NATALIE
              Yes, his notes tell me you were
              right in the middle of insect life.

Natalie picks up the praying mantis in its little case.

                         NATALIE
              The praying mantis is a fascinating
              creature, forced to live alone.
              Who can tell me why -- Buffy?

Buffy looks at the mantis.

                         BUFFY
              Well, the words "bug ugly" kinda
              spring to mind.

Natalie's eyes suddenly go cold.

                         NATALIE
              There's nothing ugly about these
              unique creatures. The reason they
              live alone is because they're
              cannibals.

General "ee-yews" from the class.

                         NATALIE
                   (to class)
              It's hardly their fault -- it's the
              way Nature designed them: noble,
              solitary...

Buffy and Willow exchange a look -- this broad's weird --
Xander, Blayne and the boys are all transfixed -- and not by
what she's saying.

                         NATALIE
              And prolific: over eighteen
              hundred species worldwide. In
              nearly all of them the female is
              larger and more aggressive than the
              male.

                         BLAYNE
              Nothing wrong with an aggressive
              female.

Natalie picks up a text.

                         NATALIE
              The California Mantis lays her eggs
              and <u>then</u> finds a mate...

                                                    (CONTINUED)

9   CONTINUED: 2   9

She walks past Xander, giving him a warm smile on the word
"mate." He looks up at her, oh so ready to be that mate.

                    NATALIE
            ...to fertilize them. Once he's
            played his part, she covers the
            eggs in a protective sack and
            attaches them to a leaf or a twig,
            out of danger.

Natalie shows them a COLOR PHOTO of a MANTIS EGG SACK -- a
gooey cocoon-like sack 'o eggs.

                    NATALIE
            If she's done her job correctly, in
            a few months she'll have several
            hundred offspring.

Natalie pauses in front of a BULLETIN BOARD that announces:
SCIENCE FAIR PROJECTS DUE BY THE 18th.

                    NATALIE
            We should make some model egg sacks
            for the Science Fair. Who'd like
            to help me do that after school? I
            warn you, it's a delicate art, I'd
            have to work with you very closely,
            one on one...

Every male hand in the class shoots up. Natalie smiles.

10   INT. SCHOOL CAFETERIA - DAY   10

Lunch time. CAFETERIA WORKERS ladle out vile piles of
weenie casserole. Buffy, Xander, Willow are in line; on the
BULLETIN BOARD: TODAY'S SPECIAL -- HOT DOG SURPRISE.

                    BUFFY
            Hot dog surprise... be still my
            heart.

                    WILLOW
            Call me old fashioned, I don't want
            any more surprises in my hot
            dogs...

Xander admires himself in the stainless steel finish of the
food service counter.

                    XANDER
            I wonder what she sees in me...

He looks over to see if Buffy is listening. She's not.

                                                        (CONTINUED)

                              XANDER
                    Probably just the quiet good looks
                    coupled with a certain smoky
                    magnetism.

Now Buffy and Willow are looking at him.

                              XANDER
                    Miss French. You two might be a
                    little young to understand what an
                    older woman sees in a younger man.

                              BUFFY
                    Oh I understand.

                              XANDER
                    Good.

                              BUFFY
                    A younger man is too dumb to wonder
                    why an older woman can't find
                    someone her own age and too
                    desperate to care about the
                    surgical improvements.

                              XANDER
                    I'm not too dumb to... what
                    surgical improvements?

Buffy and Willow exchange a look.

                              WILLOW
                    Well, he is young.

                              BUFFY
                    And so terribly innocent.

                              XANDER
                    Those who can, do. Those who can't
                    laugh at those who... can do.

Blayne, tray piled high, moves past Xander.

                              BLAYNE
                    Gotta carb up for my one on one
                    with Miss French today. When's
                    yours? Oh right, tomorrow. You
                    came in second and I came in first.
                    I guess that's what they call
                    natural selection.

                              XANDER
                    I guess that's what they call
                    rehearsal.

                                                        (CONTINUED)

10   CONTINUED: 2   10

Blayne moves off; Xander, pleased with his comeback, turns
to Willow and Buffy, blows imaginary smoke from an imaginary
gun.

Cordelia shoves her way past them --

                    CORDELIA
               Excuse you...

-- heading for the INDUSTRIAL SIZE fridge behind the food
line.

She flashes a prescription (like a badge) at a WORKER.

                    CORDELIA
               ...medically prescribed lunch, my
               doctor ships it daily, I'll only be
               here as long as I can hold my
               breath...

She whips open the door and the HEADLESS BODY of Dr. Gregory
is wedged inside.   *

Cordelia, cafeteria workers and various kids SCREAM in
horror! Willow and Xander react -- Buffy quickly moves up,
looks down at the corpse — we won't see the gore but we do
see the name on his white lab coat: DR. GREGORY. Off Buffy,

11   INT. LIBRARY - DAY   11

Water is poured into a glass from a small pitcher. We widen
to reveal Giles, who brings the glass over to Buffy. She is
sitting with Willow, Xander pacing nearby.

                    GILES
               Here. Drink this.

                    BUFFY
               (taking it)
               No thank you.

She says it absently as she drinks the water. She's
elsewhere.

                    XANDER
               I've never seen... I mean, I've
               never seen anything like... that
               was new.

                    WILLOW
               Who would want to hurt Dr. Gregory?

                                                        (CONTINUED)

                         GILES
          He had no enemies on the staff that
          I know of. He was a civilized man.
          I liked him.

                         BUFFY
               (small voice)
          So did I.

                         WILLOW
          Well, we're gonna find out who did
          this. We'll find them and we'll
          stop them.

                         BUFFY
          Count on it.

                         GILES
          What do we know?

Buffy rises, focused now.

                         BUFFY
          Not a lot. He was killed on
          campus, I'm guessing. The same day
          we last saw him.

                         GILES
          How do you know?

                         BUFFY
          Didn't change his clothes.

                         XANDER
          This is a question nobody
          particularly wants to hear, but,
          where did they put his head?

                         WILLOW
          Good point. I didn't want to
          hear that.

                         BUFFY
          Angel. He warned me something was
          coming.

                         GILES
               (remembering)
          Yes. Yes he did and I wish I knew
          what he meant.
                         (MORE)

                                        (CONTINUED)

1

                         GILES (cont'd)
                       (grabbing a text)
             All I could locate was an oblique
             reference to a vampire who
             displeased the Master and cut off
             his hand for penance.

                         BUFFY
             Cut off his hand and replaced it
             with a fork?

                         WILLOW
             Wow, I've heard of eating
             disorders, but...

                         GILES
             I don't know what he replaced it
             with.

                         XANDER
             Why would that guy come after a
             teacher?

                         GILES
             I'm not certain he did. There was
             an incident two nights ago with a
             homeless man in Weatherly park. He
             was practically shredded. But
             nothing like Dr. Gregory.

                         XANDER
             Fork guy doesn't do heads.

                         GILES
             No.

                         BUFFY
             And Dr Gregory's blood wasn't
             drained.

                         XANDER
             So there's something else out
             there? Besides silverware man?
             This is fun. We're on Monster
             Island.

                         GILES
             We don't know it's something else.
             This fellow is still our likeliest
             suspect.

                         BUFFY
             Where was that guy killed?
             Weatherly park?

                                            (CONTINUED)

11 CONTINUED: 3   11

                            GILES
                Buffy, I know you're upset. But
                this is not the time to go hunting.
                Not until we know more. Promise me
                you won't do anything rash.

                            BUFFY
                Cross my heart.

                                              SMASH CUT TO:

12 BUFFY OUT THERE ALONE - EXT. WEATHERLY PARK - NIGHT   12

    Houses ring the park. The sidewalks are pretty deserted
    this time of night. Buffy, dressed for hunting, crosses the
    street, quickly and gracefully vaults the locked fence next
    to the sign: WEATHERLY PARK - CLOSES AT 10:00 P.M.

    She moves cautiously through the spooky trees and bushes.
    She HEARS a sound, spins into a Fu crouch as a LARGE FIGURE
    stumbles out of the bushes -- HOMELESS GUY with a bottle in
    a paper bag.

                        HOMELESS GUY
                    (drunk)
                Shouldn't be here at night l'il
                lady, s'dangerous.

    They veer off in opposite directions. She spots something
    on the ground -- a body! She runs to it, kneels down: it's
    just ANOTHER HOMELESS GUY sleeping. Buffy hunts on, passing
    some thick foliage growing up over some large rocks. She
    stops, moves back: something about the foliage bugs her.

    She pokes at it -- it's loose -- she pulls it back,
    revealing a SMALL STORM DRAIN. Someone wants to keep this
    tunnel entrance a secret.

    Buffy peers into the round hole and the blackness within.
    That's when AN ARM shoots out of the darkness -- an arm
    with three sharp claws where the hand should be. She drops
    to the ground -- the claws shredding her jacket -- and out
    of the tunnel comes one bad mother of a vampire. Long hair,
    wild eyes, we'll call him CLAW.

    He takes a big swipe at her face, she uses her feet to trip
    him. As he falls to the ground she leaps to her feet, body
    stomps him -- WHAM, WHAM, WHAM -- whips out a stake and
    dives. He rolls -- the stake sinks into the earth.

    He grabs her from behind, his claw inching towards her
    throat. She stomps on his insole, elbows him in the gut,
    turns and kicks him hard in the knee. He grabs it in pain.

                                              (CONTINUED)

12 CONTINUED: 12

                         MAN'S VOICE (O.S.)
                    Hold it! Police!

Sounds of people coming, lots of flashlights. Claw bolts
into the underbrush. Buffy, winded and hurt, crawls out of
sight as the Homeless Guy (really a cop), gun out, bursts
onto the scene followed by THREE UNIFORMED COPS.

                         HOMELESS GUY
                    I heard him -- spread out!

The homeless guy and the cops move into the foliage.

13 EXT. PARK - NIGHT   13

The opposite side from where Buffy entered. A WOMAN (we
don't see her face) carrying two grocery bags, walks down
the sidewalk. Her heels CLICK-CLACK in the night.

We can HEAR COPS SHOUTING on the other side of the park, but
it's pretty distant.

ANGLE - STALKING CAM

Shooting through the fence -- something is stalking the
woman. She's oblivious.

REVERSE ANGLE - CLAW

Sees his next meal. He scampers up the fence with
frightening speed. A beat later, Buffy appears out of the
trees, sees what's happening, bolts for the fence.

ANGLE - THE SIDEWALK

The woman walks on as Claw drops into frame RIGHT BEHIND
HER. She turns, it's sexy substitute teacher Natalie
French. Buffy, racing for the fence, sees Claw do
something unexpected -- he sniffs Natalie, pulls back in
REAL TERROR and runs (we now see -- only now -- he's
limping, thanks to Buffy's kick) into the street, diving for
the nearest sewer gutter which he slithers into,
disappearing from sight.

ANGLE - BUFFY STOPS IN THE SHADOWS

Unseen, she watches Natalie, unfazed, continue on her way.
Off Buffy wondering what kind of ju-ju this babe has,

                                             BLACK OUT.

                         END OF ACT ONE

ACT TWO

14   EXT. SUNNYDALE HIGH SCHOOL - DAY   14

Another sunny day in paradise.

                    GILES (O.S.)
          You went hunting last night.

15   INT. GILES' OFFICE - DAY   15*

Giles faces Buffy (her books and Angel's jacket nearby.)

                    BUFFY
          Yep.

                    GILES
          ...when you promised me you
          wouldn't.

                    BUFFY
          Yeah, I lied, I'm a bad person.
          Let's move on.

                    GILES
          Did you see someone with a fork?

                    BUFFY
              (nods)
          More like a jumbo claw.

                    GILES
          Oh, well, at least you weren't
          hurt.

                    BUFFY
          And I saw something else, something
          much more interesting than your
          run-of-the-mill killer vampire.

                    GILES
          What was that?

                    BUFFY
          Do you know Miss French, the
          teacher who's substituting for Dr.
          Gregory?

                    GILES
          Oh, she's lovely...
              (off Buffy's look)
          ...in a common, extremely
          well-proportioned sort of way.

                                        (CONTINUED)

15 CONTINUED: 15

> BUFFY
> I'm chasing clawguy last night,
> we're on the street...

> GILES
> Yes?

> BUFFY
> And Miss Well-Proportioned is
> heading home, I figure she's his
> next meal. He takes one look at
> her and runs screaming for cover.

> GILES
> He what? Ran away?

> BUFFY
> He was petrified.

> GILES
> Of Miss French.

> BUFFY
> Yes! So I'm an undead monster who
> can shave with his hand -- how many
> things am I afraid of?

> GILES
> Not many. And not substitute
> teachers, as a rule.

> BUFFY
> So what is her deal?

> GILES
> I think it would be a good idea to
> keep an eye on her.

> BUFFY
> Then I'd better get to class.

16 INT. HIGH SCHOOL - HALL OUTSIDE PRINCIPAL'S OFFICE - DAY 16

Buffy moves down the hall, fast. PRINCIPAL FLUTIE steps out
of his office, sees her, grabs her.

> FLUTIE
> You were there, you saw Dr.
> Gregory, didn't you?

> BUFFY
> You mean yesterday in the
> cafeteria, after he was --

(CONTINUED)

16 CONTINUED: 16

                              FLUTIE
                         (looking around)
                    Don't say "dead", or decapitated,
                    or decomposing. I would stay away
                    from "d" words all together. But
                    you witnessed the event so this way
                    please.

                              BUFFY
                    I've gotta... I'll be late for
                    biology.

                              FLUTIE
                    Extremely late. You have to see a
                    counselor. Everyone who saw the
                    body has to see a crisis counselor.

He takes her arm, leads her toward an office.

                              BUFFY
                    I really don't need --

                              FLUTIE
                    We all need help with our feelings,
                    otherwise we bottle them up and
                    before you know it powerful
                    laxatives are involved.

He parks her outside the Counselor's Office. The door is
open and we can see CORDELIA talking to an unseen counselor.

                              FLUTIE
                    I really believe if we all reach
                    out to one another we can beat this
                    thing. I'm always here if you need
                    a hug -- but not a real hug,
                    there's no touching in this school,
                    we're sensitive to wrong touching.

                              BUFFY
                    But I really feel okay.

                              FLUTIE
                    No you talk to the counselor and
                    start the healing. You have to
                    heal.

                              BUFFY
                         (starts to leave)
                    Mr Flutie, I --

                              FLUTIE
                         (as to a dog)
                    Heal.

                                              (CONTINUED)

16 CONTINUED: 2   16

    Flutie retreats. Buffy sighs, waits her turn. Buffy
    listens to Cordelia, and we:

                                                        CUT TO:

17 INT. COUNSELOR'S OFFICE - CONTINUOUS   17

    We are close on Cordelia as she unburdens herself.

                         CORDELIA
                    ...it was... let's just say I
                    haven't had been able to eat a
                    thing since yesterday... I think I
                    lost like seven and a half
                    ounces -- way swifter than the
                    so-called diet that quack put me on
                    --
                         (off counselor's unseen
                          look)
                    -- oh, I'm not saying we should
                    kill a teacher everyday just so I
                    can lose weight, I'm just saying
                    when tragedy strikes we have to
                    look on the bright side -- you
                    know, like how even a used Mercedes
                    still has leather seats.

    Off Buffy, we cut to:

18 INT. BIOLOGY CLASSROOM - DAY   18

    Xander, Willow and the rest of the class are taking a test.
    Buffy and Blayne are missing. Natalie moves down the aisle.

                         NATALIE
                    Keep your eyes straight ahead, on
                    your own test...

    She stops next to Xander, leans down, puts her GORGEOUS,
    POUTING LIPS two inches from his ear.

                         NATALIE
                    I think you meant "pollination" for
                    number fourteen.

    Xander looks up at her gratefully, changes the answer.

                         NATALIE
                    I'll see you here after school.

    She delicately puts a hand on his shoulder. His breathing
    comes a little quicker.

19 INT. HALL OUTSIDE BIOLOGY CLASSROOM - DAY   19

Buffy moves up to the door, looks through the window at the
class, bummed.

                    BUFFY
            Great, a pop quiz.

She looks at BLAYNE'S EMPTY SEAT. Then at Natalie (her back
to the door) her hand on Xander's shoulder.

As if sensing Buffy, Natalie straightens up, then slowly and
IMPOSSIBLY (SPECIAL EFFECT) cranks her head around a hundred
and eighty degrees -- a demi-second before she'd be seen,
Buffy takes a shocked step backwards, out of sight.

20 INT. LIBRARY - DAY   20

Giles pours over texts, looks up as Buffy and Willow enter.

                    BUFFY
                (to Willow)
            No, no I'm not saying she craned
            her neck, it was the full-on
            exorcist twist.

                    WILLOW
            Ouch.

                    BUFFY
            Which reminds me, how come Blayne
            who worked with her "one on one"
            yesterday, isn't here today?

                    WILLOW
            Inquiring minds want to know.

Willow moves to the computer. Buffy turns to Giles.

                    BUFFY
            Any luck?

                    GILES
            I haven't found any creature just
            yet that strikes terror in a
            vampire's heart -- I'm not sure I
            want to.

                    BUFFY
            Try looking under "Things That Can
            Turn Their Heads All The Way
            Around."

                    GILES
            Nothing human can do that.

                                        (CONTINUED)

20 CONTINUED: 20

> BUFFY
> No. Nothing human. But there's
> some insects that can.
> (beat, determined)
> Whatever she is, I'm gonna be ready
> for her.

Willow and Giles both look up as she heads for the stacks.

> GILES
> What are you going to do?

> BUFFY
> (turns back)
> My homework.

She disappears into the stack, only to return a second later.

> BUFFY
> Where's the books on bugs?

21 INT. BIOLOGY CLASSROOM - DAY   21

PAN ACROSS an OPEN TEXT. The COLOR PHOTO of the EGG SACKS.
PAN from the book to a MODEL of the egg sacks, two feet
long. Natalie traces her hand across the model, gently,
almost lovingly, then moves to a small fridge, takes out
bread, low fat mayo and a small covered tub marked "Food."

She spreads the mayo on the bread and is reaching for the
"Food" tub when Xander enters.

> NATALIE
> Oh, hi. I was just grabbing a
> snack. Can I make you something?

> XANDER
> No thanks, I never eat when I'm
> making egg sacks.
> (re: egg sack model)
> Wow, if these were real, the bugs'd
> be...

> NATALIE
> Big as you.

> XANDER
> Yeah. So where do we start?

(CONTINUED)

                         NATALIE
          Oh Xander, I've done something
          really stupid, I hope you can
          forgive me.

                         XANDER
          Forgiveness is my middle name --
          actually it's LaVelle -- I'd
          appreciate it if you'd guard that
          secret with your life.

                         NATALIE
              (smiles, then:)
          I have a teacher conference in half
          an hour and I left the paint and
          paper mache' at home. I don't
          suppose you'd want to come to my
          place tonight and work on it there.

                         XANDER
          Come to... your place?

FLASH CUT - XANDER IN HIS GUITAR GOD POSE, HITS A POWER
CHORD

BACK TO SCENE

                         NATALIE
          It'd be just the two of us. I'd
          feel more comfortable there, you
          know, about letting my hair down.

She lasers him with a steamy look.

                         XANDER
          Right, that's important, 'cause
          when your hair's not down it's...
          up.

                         NATALIE
          It's a date then. Seven-thirty.
              (hands him paper)
          Here's my address.
              (I want you)
          I'll see you tonight.

They trade a meaningful look, he turns his back, heads for
the door. She opens the tub marked "food". Inside: live
crickets. She sprinkles several on the bread.

30.

22   INT. SCHOOL HALL - DAY   22

     Xander exits, does a MIGHTY VICTORY DANCE -- this is it!

                         XANDER
                    Yessss!!

23   INT. BIOLOGY CLASSROOM - SAME TIME   23

     As Miss French bites contentedly into her sandwich,

24   INT. LIBRARY - DAY   24

     Willow's at the computer, Giles pours over texts. Buffy
     charges out of the stacks, book in hand, featuring PHOTOS of
     the praying mantis.

                         BUFFY
               Dig this -- "the praying mantis can
               rotate it's head a hundred and
               eighty degrees while waiting for a
               meal to wander by..." Hah!
                    (off their looks)
               Well, come on guys. Hah!

                         WILLOW
               Well, Miss French is sort of big.
               For a bug.

                         GILES
               She is also, by and large,
               woman-shaped.

                         BUFFY
               Factoid one: only the praying
               mantis can turn it's head like
               that. Factoid two: a pretty
               wacked-out vampire is scared to
               death of her. Factoid three: her
               fashion sense screams predator.

                         WILLOW
               It's the shoulder pads.

                         BUFFY
               Exactly.

                         GILES
               If you're right, she'd have to be a
               shapeshifter, or perception
               distorter...
                    (making a connection)
               Half a moment...
                         (MORE)

                                                          (CONTINUED)

24 CONTINUED:

                    GILES (cont'd)
I had a chum at Oxford, Carlyle,
advanced degrees in entomology and
mythology...

                    BUFFY
Whosy and whatsy?

                    GILES
Bugs and fairy tales.

                    BUFFY
I knew that.

                    GILES
If I recall correctly, poor
Carlyle, just before he went mad,
claimed there was a beast --

                    WILLOW
        (re: computer)
Buffy, nine one one. Blayne's mom
called the school, he never came
home last night.

                    GILES
The boy who worked with Miss French
yesterday?

                    WILLOW
Yeah. If Miss French is
responsible for... Xander's
supposed to be helping her right
now... he's got a crush on a giant
insect!

                    BUFFY
Let's not panic, I'll warn him. I
need you to stretch your hacker
muscles and see if you can get
something from the Coroner's
office.

                    WILLOW
What are we looking for?

                    BUFFY
Autopsy on Dr. Gregory. I've been
trying to figure out the marks I
saw on his corpse -- I'm thinking
they might have been teeth -- and
these cuddlies...

She shows Willow picture of HORRIBLE MANTIS TEETH.

                                        (CONTINUED)

                              BUFFY
                    ...should definitely be brushing
                    after every meal.
                         (to Giles)
                    You were saying something about a
                    beast?

                              GILES
                         (nods)
                    I just have to make one
                    trans-Atlantic phone call.
                         (heads for phone; stops)
                    This computer invasion Willow's
                    performing on the Coroner's
                    office -- one assumes it's entirely
                    legal?

               BUFFY   WILLOW
          Of course --   -- entirely.

                              GILES
                    So I wasn't here, didn't see it,
                    couldn't have stopped you.

                              BUFFY
                    Good idea.

          Buffy grabs her jacket (the one Angel gave her), heads out.

25 EXT. SUNNYDALE HIGH SCHOOL - DAY   25

          Late in the day. Xander, in the best mood, strolls out of
          school, humming a little tune. Buffy, wearing the jacket,
          catches up with him.

                              BUFFY
                    Hey.

                              XANDER
                    Hey.

                              BUFFY
                    So how'd it go with Miss French
                    after school?

                              XANDER
                    Well, it's a little demanding being
                    her... absolute favorite guy in the
                    universe, but I'll just have to
                    muddle through.

                              BUFFY
                    Xander, she's not what she seems.

                                             (CONTINUED)

25 CONTINUED: 25

> XANDER
> I know, she's so much more.

> BUFFY
> Look, I have to tell you some stuff
> about her and I really need you to
> listen, okay?

Xander stops, listens respectfully.

> XANDER
> Okay.

> BUFFY
> I don't think she's human. She can
> do the twisty with her head -- ever
> see the Exorcist? Plus Blayne, who
> was last seen in her class
> yesterday afternoon, is now
> missing.

> XANDER
> I see. So she's not human
> she's...?

> BUFFY
> Technically I guess you'd have to
> call her a big old bug.
>   (Xander smiles)
> I know it sounds a little weird but
> --

> XANDER
>   (laughs)
> It's not weird, it's perfectly
> understandable. I've met someone,
> you're jealous.

> BUFFY
> I'm not --

> XANDER
> Nothing I could do about it.
> There's just a certain chemical
> thing between Miss French and me.

> BUFFY
> I know, I just read about it, it's
> called, uh, a pheromone, this
> chemical attractant insects give
> off.

(CONTINUED)

                    XANDER
          SHE'S NOT AN INSECT!! -- okay?
          She's a woman. Hard as it may be
          for you to conceive, a human
          woman finds me attractive. I
          realize she's no mystery guy
          handing out leather jackets -- and
          while we're on the subject, what
          kinda girly-name is Angel anyway?

                    BUFFY
          What's that got to do with --

                    XANDER
          Nothing! It just bugs me.
               (beat)
          I really gotta...
               (he takes off)

                    BUFFY
          Xander...

26 INT. NATALIE FRENCH'S HOUSE - NIGHT   26

Candles, romantic light. She's wearing a knockout dress,
pouring martinis when there's a knock at the front door.
She opens it, revealing Xander.

                    NATALIE
          Hi, come on in.

He can't help but stare at the low-cut dress.

                    NATALIE
          Oh, should I change, is it too...?

                    XANDER
          No, no. It's the most beautiful
          chest -- dress! -- I've ever seen.

                    NATALIE
          Thank you, that's sweet. Martini?

She offers him a glass. He hesitates.

                    NATALIE
          I'm sorry, would you like something
          else? I just need to relax a
          little, I'm kind of nervous around
          you. You're probably cool as a
          cucumber.

                                        (CONTINUED)

                          XANDER
                    (mile a minute)
          I like cucumbers -- you know in
          that Greek salad thing with the
          yogurt -- you like Greek food? I'm
          exempting schwarma here, what is
          that all about, big meat hive...
                    (grabs glass, drains it)
          <u>Hehh</u>-looo.

                          NATALIE
                    (clinks his empty glass)
          Cheers.
                    (moves close)
          Can I ask you a personal question?
          Have you ever been with a woman
          before?

                          XANDER
          You mean like, in the same room --

                          NATALIE
                    (closer still)
          You know what I mean.

                          XANDER
          Oh, that. Well, let me think,
          there was... several, you know, I
          mean quite a few times that... and
          then there was... she was so
          incredibly... no.

                          NATALIE
                    (touching his hair, face)
          I know, I can tell.

                          XANDER
          You can?

                          NATALIE
          I like it. You might say I need
          it.

                          XANDER
          Well, needs are, you know, needs
          should definitely be met as long as
          they don't require ointments the
          next day or --

Dimly in the b.g., Xander HEARS someone yelling "help me!"

                          XANDER
          Do you hear --

                                             (CONTINUED)

                              NATALIE
                    No.

                              XANDER
                    Sounds like somebody crying for --

                              NATALIE
                    I don't hear anything. Your hands
                    are so...
                         (takes his hands)
                    ...hot.

Xander stares at her, then down at his hands, looking a
little woozy.

FLASHBACK - TO XANDER'S FANTASY SEQUENCE

When Buffy took his hand.

                              BUFFY
                    You hurt your hand...

BACK TO SCENE

Now he's looking very woozy, downright drugged.

                              XANDER
                    Buffy. I love Buffy... wow, so
                    that's a martini, huh?

Again the distant YELLING, "somebody help me!"

                              XANDER
                    Are you sure somebody's not --

                              NATALIE
                    Would you like to touch me with
                    those hands?

He looks down -- her HANDS stroking HIS.

                              XANDER
                    Your hands are really...

SPECIAL FX - HER FOREARM AND ONE OF HER HANDS

Suddenly ripple, turn MANTIS-LIKE.

                              XANDER
                    ...serrated? That drink must have,
                    I think I need to...

Xander passes out, hitting the floor with a THUNK. Natalie
bends down --

                                                  (CONTINUED)

26   CONTINUED: 3   26

    TWO SERRATED FORELEGS SLIDE UNDER XANDER'S FEET

    ANGLE - CELLAR DOOR

    Xander's torso is pulled out of sight.   *
                                                                   *

                                       BLACK OUT.

<u>END OF ACT TWO</u>

ACT THREE

27 INT. NATALIE'S CELLAR - DARK   27

ANGLE ON Xander, as he comes awake, looking groggily at his
surroundings.

Welcome to hell, which we will photograph tastefully as far
as the gore is concerned. The HORRIBLE SHE-MANTIS, tending   *
to some eggs, still dimly seen, shuffles about in the b.g.   *

PAN a row small barred cages. In a couple, we see bodies
-- sans heads.

In the distance he can make out the shape -- but not the
features -- of the Mantis-creature. Xander swallows hard,
tries to find his voice:

                    XANDER
          Miss... French?

To his horror, Natalie's voice (treated) emanates from the:

                    MANTIS
          Please, call me Natalie.

Off Xander,

28 EXT. SUNNYDALE HIGH SCHOOL - NIGHT   28

Dark, deserted, the only lights are coming from the library.

29 INT. LIBRARY - NIGHT   29

Giles is on the phone -- the fury of the once great English
Empire in his voice.

                    GILES
          Young lady, I don't care what time
          it is, unlock his cell, unstrap him
          and bring him to the phone this
          instant. Lives are at stake.

                    WILLOW
               (at computer)
          Got it.
               (Buffy joins her)
          Coroner's autopsy, complete with...
               (turning away)
          ...yuck, color pictures.

Buffy studies the screen (we don't see the pictures).

                                              (CONTINUED)

29 CONTINUED: 29

                              BUFFY
                    They <u>are</u> teeth marks...
                         (re: mantis in text book)
                    ...which match perfectly the one
                    insect that nips off its prey's
                    head.

                              WILLOW
                    Okay, this I do not like...

                              BUFFY
                    It's the way they feed: head first.
                    And the way they mate --
                         (re: book)
                    The female eats the male's head
                    while they're...

                              WILLOW
                         (losing it)
                    No, no, see, Xander is, I really
                    like his head, that's where you
                    find his eyes and hair, his
                    adorable smile...

                              BUFFY
                    Take it easy, Will, Xander's not in
                    any immediate danger. I saw him
                    leave school -- I'm sure he's safe
                    and sound at home right now.

30 INT. NATALIE'S CELLAR - NIGHT   30

     Xander, keeping an eye on the She-Mantis in b.g., backs into
     the farthest corner of his cage -- A HAND darts in from the
     DARK CAGE next to him.

                              XANDER
                    Yaahhhh!

     He looks in the cage, makes out:

                              XANDER
                    Blayne --

     Blayne, a blubbering mass of terror, cowers in his cage.

                              BLAYNE
                    Oh god, oh god, oh god...

                              XANDER
                    Are you --

                                                              (CONTINUED)

                              BLAYNE
               You gotta get me outta here, you
               gotta... she, she gets you and...

                              XANDER
               What? What does she do?

                              BLAYNE
               No, no, no, no...

Xander gets his hands through the cage, shakes Blayne.

                              XANDER
               Blayne! What does she do?

                              BLAYNE
               She... she takes you out of the
               cage and ties you up then she,
               like, starts throbbing and moving
               and all these eggs come shooting
               out of her -- and then...

                              XANDER
               What? Then what?

                              BLAYNE
               She mates with you!

                              XANDER
               She...?

                              BLAYNE
               That's not the worst part.

                              XANDER
                    (deadpan)
               It's not?

                              BLAYNE
               Have you seen her teeth? Right
               while she's -- right in the middle
               of -- I SAW HER DO IT!

He points to a body in a nearby cage. Xander looks from the
body to the Mantis-bitch as she delicately hangs the jellied
EGG SACK from a ceiling rafter.

                              BLAYNE
               I don't want to die like that!

                              XANDER
               Blayne... Blayne! Chill. Listen
               to me, we're gonna get out of this.

                                                       (CONTINUED)

30 CONTINUED: 2   30

                    BLAYNE
        You got a plan? What is it?

                    XANDER
              (doesn't have a clue)
        Let me just perfect it...

                    BLAYNE
              (cracking again)
        Oh god, oh god, oh god...

31 INT. LIBRARY - NIGHT   31

    Giles is on the phone.

                    GILES
        I understand, Carlyle, I'll take
        every precaution... It sounds just
        like the creature you described.
        You were right all along, about
        everything.
              (beat)
        No you weren't right about your
        mother coming back as a Dachsund,
        but... Try to rest. Ta.

    He hangs up, moves quickly to Buffy and Willow.

                    GILES
        Dr. Carlyle Ferris spent years
        transcribing a lost, pre-Germanic
        language -- what he discovered he
        kept to himself, until several
        teen-age boys were murdered in the
        Cotswalds. Then he went hunting
        for it.

                    BUFFY
        "It" being...?

                    GILES
        He calls her a She-Mantis. This
        type of creature, the Kleptes-Virgo
        or virgin-thief appears in many
        cultures: the Greek Sirens, the
        Celtic Sea-maidens who tore the
        living flesh from the bones of --

                    BUFFY
        Giles, while we're young.

                                    (CONTINUED)

31 CONTINUED: 31

                         GILES
          The She-Mantis assumes the form of
          a beautiful woman and lures
          innocent virgins back to her nest.

                         BUFFY
               (to Willow, comforting)
          Well, Xander's not a ... I mean
          he's probably --

                         WILLOW
          -- going to die!

Willow grabs a phone, dials in b.g. as Buffy stretches out
her fingers and arms, preparing for battle.

                         BUFFY   *
          This thing is breeding. We gotta
          find it and snuff it. Any tips on
          the snuffing part?

                         GILES
          Carlyle recommends cleaving all
          body parts with a sharp blade.

                         BUFFY
          Slice and dice.

                         GILES
          Whatever you do it's got to be
          sudden and swift -- this beast is
          dangerous.

                         BUFFY
          Well, your buddy Carlyle faced it,
          he's still around.

                         GILES
          Yes... in a straight jacket howling
          his innards out day and night.

                         BUFFY
          Okay Admiral, way to inspire the
          troops.

Willow slams down the phone.

                         WILLOW
          Xander's not home -- he told his
          mom he had to go to his teacher's
          house and work on a science project.
          He didn't tell her where.

                                              (CONTINUED)

31 CONTINUED: 2   31

                         BUFFY
              See if you can get her address off
              the substitute rolls.

Willow bolts to the computer.

                         BUFFY
                        (to Giles)
              You gotta record some bat sonar,
              fast.

                         GILES
              Bat sonar. Right. What?

                         BUFFY
              Bats eat them -- a praying mantis
              hears sonar, its whole nervous
              system goes kaplooie.

                         GILES
              Where am I going to find --

                         BUFFY
              -- in the vid library. I know it's
              not books but it's still dark and
              musty, you'll be right at home.

She points him toward the back of the stacks and the door
marked VIDEOS.

                         BUFFY
              I'll handle the armory.

32 INT. NATALIE'S CELLAR - NIGHT   32

She-Mantis shuffles in the b.g.. IN THE CAGES, Xander
struggles with a bar that separates his cage from Blayne's.

                         BLAYNE
              What are you -- don't do anything
              that'll make her mad.

Xander ignores Blayne, shoves and pulls until a three foot
hunk of bar comes loose.

                         BLAYNE
              Hey, all right. Now I can get out
              of my cage...
                        (realizing)
              ...into yours. What'd you do that
              for?

                                                    (CONTINUED)

32 CONTINUED: 32

> XANDER
> (hefting bar)
> A weapon.

> BLAYNE
> I think you're going to need it.

THEIR POV - THE SHE-MANTIS

is coming for them.

33 INT. LIBRARY - NIGHT   33

The printer cranks out a NAME and ADDRESS: NATALIE FRENCH,
837 WEATHERLY DRIVE, SUNNYDALE, CALIFORNIA. Buffy, dressed   *
for fighting, equipment bag in hand, runs in. Willow waits
at the printer.

> WILLOW
> Getting her address...

> BUFFY
> Giles!

Giles emerges from the video library -- hands her his micro
cassette recorder.

> GILES
> Recording bat sonar is so
> soothingly like having one's teeth
> drilled.

Willow rips the paper out of the printer.

> BUFFY
> Let's roll.

As they race for the door:

> WILLOW
> According to Miss French's
> personnel records, she was born in
> nineteen oh seven -- she's like
> ninety years old.

> GILES
> She is terribly well-preserved.

And they're gone.

34 INT. NATALIE'S CELLAR - NIGHT   34

Xander and Blayne cower in their cages as SHE steps out of
the shadows and we get our first good look at her huge,
hideous face: the triangular head with large compound eyes,
the antennae, the collection of sharp mouth parts designed
to maul and sever.

She stops in front of Blayne's cage. He screams, scrambles
for the back -- squeezes through into Xander's cage.

                    BLAYNE
          He did that, he broke the cage,
          take him not me, take him!!

She turns her insect head and gazes at Xander. He looks
back at her, trying to keep his terror down, the iron bar
gripped tightly behind his back.

35 EXT. THE REAL MRS. FRENCH'S HOUSE - NIGHT   35

The Giles-mobile, possibly an older model Citroen, roars to
a stop in front of 837 WEATHERLY, a modest, well-kempt   *
home. Giles is behind the wheel. They pile out.

ANGLE: THE FRONT DOOR

As they approach it.

                    GILES
          What now? I mean we can't just
          kick down the front door.

                    BUFFY
          Yes, that would be wrong.

She's already bracing to kick it as she speaks. Just as
she's about to kick it in, it's opened by the SWEETEST
LITTLE OLD LADY. We'll call her the REAL MISS FRENCH.

She's ninety.

                    REAL MISS FRENCH
          Hello dear, I thought I heard...
          are you selling something? Because
          I'd love to help out but you know
          I'm on a fixed income.

                    BUFFY
          I'm looking for Miss French.

                    REAL MISS FRENCH
          I'm Miss French.

                                        (CONTINUED)

35 CONTINUED: 35

                              BUFFY
              Natalie French, the substitute
              biology teacher.

                         REAL MISS FRENCH
              Goodness, that's me. I taught for
              over thirty years, then I retired
              in nineteen seventy-two...

Buffy turns to Willow.

                              BUFFY
              She used Miss French's records to
              get in the school -- bite me, she
              could be anywhere.

                         REAL MISS FRENCH
              No, I'm right here, dear.

36 INT. NATALIE'S CELLAR - NIGHT   36

The SHE-MANTIS raises a terrible, spiny foreleg -- Blayne
scurries to the farthest corner of the cage. Xander holds
his ground as she points her foreleg first at Blayne, then
at Xander, then at Blayne, etc.

                              XANDER
                         (deadpan)
              What's she doing?

                             BLAYNE
              I... think it's... eenie, meenie,
              mynie...

And, as her foreleg settles on Xander -- the chosen one.

                              XANDER
              ...moe.

Off Xander

                                                       BLACK OUT.

                         END OF ACT THREE

ACT FOUR

37   INT. NATALIE'S CELLAR - NIGHT   37

She unlocks the cage, opens the door, reaches in for him.

                    XANDER
               (to keep her from
                touching him)
          I'm coming, I'm coming.

He steps out -- and swings the iron bar at her -- hard. It
THUNKS into her body. He runs like hell. Almost makes the
stairs before he's pincered by a powerful foreleg, lifted in
the air and slammed to the ground, wind knocked out of him.

38   EXT. THE REAL MISS FRENCH'S HOUSE - NIGHT   38

Buffy heads to the street, looking at WEATHERLY PARK across
the way. Giles and Willow follow her, unsure of the next
move.

                    WILLOW
          What do we do now?

                    GILES
          Abject prayer and supplication
          spring to mind.

                    BUFFY
          I saw her walking past this park.
          Carrying grocery bags. She lives
          in this neighborhood.

They look up and down the street

THEIR POV - A LOT OF HOUSES

Willow, pretty upset, heads off in the direction of the
house next to the Real Miss French's.

                    WILLOW
          I'm gonna start banging on doors.

                    BUFFY
               (stops her)
          We don't have time for that.

                    WILLOW
          We have to do something!

                    BUFFY
          We will.

                                                   (CONTINUED)

38   CONTINUED: 38

     Buffy grabs a hefty length of rope from her equipment bag,
     heads into the street towards the rain gutter.

                              BUFFY
                    I won't be long.

     And before they can stop her, she's lowered herself into the
     gutter and disappeared from sight.

                              GILES
                    Buffy!

39   INT. NATALIE'S CELLAR   39

     Xander's hands are held fast in leather or rope shackles.
     The She-Mantis stands nearby eyeing him.

     BLAYNE IN HIS CAGE

     Quietly, insanely, watching.

                              BLAYNE
                    Oh yeah, here it comes...

                              XANDER
                    What, what's happening?!

                              BLAYNE
                    How do you like your eggs, bro,
                    over easy or sunny side up?

                              XANDER
                    Eggs? She's going to lay some...?

     Xander looks at the monster, it almost smiles.

40   EXT. STREET NEXT TO WEATHERLY PARK - NIGHT   40

     Giles and Willow wait anxiously.

                              WILLOW
                    Come on Buffy...

41   EXT. WEATHERLY PARK - NIGHT   41

     CAMERA PUSHES in on the SMALL STORM DRAIN where Buffy was
     attacked by Claw. We HEAR sounds of a struggle. The foliage
     covering the storm drain is thrust aside and Claw, SNARLING,
     is thrown out on his face, his hands tied behind his back.
     Buffy emerges from the drain, drags him to his feet (he's
     over his limp).

                                                        (CONTINUED)

41 CONTINUED: 41

                          CLAW
              You.

                          BUFFY
              Me.

She gives him a none-too-gentle shove down the path.

42 INT. NATALIE'S CELLAR - NIGHT   42

We see the She-Mantis breathing hard, PAN to the fresh BATCH
OF EGGS next to her body and find Xander. PUSH IN on
Xander.

FLASHBACK - XANDER IN BIOLOGY CLASS - DAY

                          NATALIE
              The California Mantis lays her eggs
              and then finds a mate...

She walks past Xander, giving him a warm smile on the word
"mate." He looks up at her, oh so ready to be that mate.

                                              CUT TO:

43 EXT. STREET - NIGHT - CLOSE CLAW   43

His hands bound behind him trying to close one of his razor
talons on the rope.

Buffy shoves Claw (very fast) past houses. Willow and
Giles keep their distance.

                          BUFFY
              Which house, where is she?

They pass more houses.

                          BUFFY
              You're not afraid of much, but
              you're afraid of her --

They pass more houses.

                          BUFFY
              -- and her cold blood...

                                              (CONTINUED)

43   CONTINUED: 43

    Suddenly Claw's face fills with fear, he struggles mightily
    in Buffy's grasp. Buffy follows his gaze to a small
    house, <u>white picket fence</u>.

    She drags him closer -- he growls and cringes even more.

                          BUFFY
                Better than radar...

    She sees a SMALL CELLAR window next to the driveway. The
    only light in the house is coming from here.

    ANGLE - HE'S GOT A CLAW ON ONE OF THE ROPES NOW

    Willow sees Claw cutting through the rope.

                          WILLOW
                Buffy!

                          GILES
                Run!

    Indeed, Buffy does run with Claw right on her heels. She
    dives at the white picket fence, gets her hands on the slats
    as he grabs her from behind. He closes in for the kill.
    She rips the slat loose and uses it to pierce his heart. We
    don't see the gore but we do see the surprise on his face
    before he crumbles to dust.

    Giles and Willow are staring, somewhat shocked, as Buffy
    heads up to the house.

                          BUFFY
                You guys coming?

44   INT. NATALIE'S CELLAR - NIGHT   44

    Xander, still tethered, watches in horror as the She-Mantis
    lowers her ghastly face towards him. He struggles futilely.
    It's the grossest thing that has ever happened to him,
    until, through teeth dripping with unspeakable fluids, she
    says:

                          MANTIS
                Kiss me.

    Xander struggles to keep a grasp on his sanity as that
    horrible mouth moves closer and closer.

                          XANDER
                Can I just say one thing?
                     (she seems to hesitate)
                <u>HEELLLLPPPP</u>!!

                                                        (CONTINUED)

Blayne looks away in his cage. As she engulfs Xander in her
horrible body, the SMALL GROUND FLOOR WINDOW behind her is
kicked in. Buffy drops in, equipment bag in hand.

                    BUFFY
          Let him go.

The She-Mantis HISSES, heads for Buffy who grabs two large
spray cans out of her bag.

Buffy raises the spray cans -- we SEE A PICTURE OF A DEAD
BUG -- and the words KILLS GARDEN PESTS FAST! on them.

Buffy blasts her with both barrels -- two clouds of insect
spray hit her in the face.

She HOWLS, and retreats with alarming speed into the dark
recesses of the cellar.

Giles and Willow drop in through the cellar window, run to
Xander, free him.

Blayne starts screaming from his cage:

                    BLAYNE
          Help me! Help me!!

                    BUFFY
               (to the others)
          Get him out. The bug is mine.

She advances into the darkness.

ANGLE: THE DARK PART OF THE CELLAR.

Moving very slowly, she pulls her machete from her bag and
her tape recorder from her pocket with the other. She talks
to the shadows:

                    BUFFY
          Remember Dr. Gregory -- you scarfed
          his head? He taught me if you do
          your homework you learn stuff.
          Like what happens to your nervous
          system when you hear this:

Buffy punches play.

                    GILES' VOICE
               (on recorder)
          "...extremely important to file not
          simply alphabetically by author..."

                                             (CONTINUED)

44 CONTINUED: 2   44

                         BUFFY
                Giles!

                         GILES
                That's the wrong side!

The She-Mantis comes SCREECHING from the shadows and knocks
the recorder out of Buffy's hand, sends it skittering across
the floor and under an old refrigerator.

Giles runs to the refrigerator, trying to retrieve it.

ANGLE: THE DARK PART OF THE CELLAR.

The She-Mantis swings again -- Buffy jumps -- the foreleg
slicing, just missing Buffy's legs. Buffy raises the
machete with both arms and swings it through the air --

She cuts the Mantis. The Mantis howls with rage and pain.

Xander retrieves the bug spray as Willow tries to open
Blayne's cage. Xander comes into the dark and --

-- blasts the She-Mantis with the spray. She howls, turns
on him --

                         BUFFY
                Xander, get out!

She pushes him back. The She-Mantis seizes the moment of
Buffy's distraction to SLAM Buffy to the ground with a
foreleg, the machete skittering away. She raises her
foreleg, intent on cutting Buffy's head off.

Giles retrieves the recorder, hits buttons. A HIGH-PITCHED
SOUND reverberates through the room: bat sonar. The
She-Mantis SCREECHES, howls and shakes her head -- the sonar
is driving her bat-shit.

Buffy KICKS and TRIPS the mantis up. It falls to the ground
as Buffy picks up the machete.

                         BUFFY
                Bat sonar makes your whole nervous
                system go to hell. You can go
                there with it.

She raises the machete high over her head and brings it down
-- we PAN AWAY from any gore to THE WALL where we see BUFFY
IN SILHOUETTE hack this thing to pieces.

Xander, Willow, Blayne and Giles who look down at the floor
and what's left (we don't see it) of the She-Mantis.

                                              (CONTINUED)

                         GILES
              I'd say it's deceased.

                         WILLOW
              And dissected.

                         XANDER
                    (to Buffy)
              You okay?

                         BUFFY
              Yeah.

                         XANDER
              Just for the record, you were
              right, I was an idiot and God bless
              you.

She smiles, they share the moment, then:

                         XANDER
                    (to Giles and Willow)
              And thank you guys, too.

                         BLAYNE
              Yeah. Really.

                         GILES
              Pleasure.

                         WILLOW
                    (to Xander)
              I'm really glad you're okay. It's
              so unfair how she only went after
              virgins...

                         XANDER
              What...?

                         WILLOW
              I mean here you are, doing the
              right thing -- the smart thing --
              when a lot of other boys your
              age --

                         BLAYNE
              Big flag on that play, babe. I am
              no --

                         GILES
              Cat's out of the bag, lads. It's
              part of the She-Mantis M.O.

                                        (CONTINUED)

44 CONTINUED: 4   44

                              XANDER
                    Isn't this the perfect ending to a
                    wonderful day.

                              BLAYNE
                    My dad's a lawyer -- anybody
                    repeats this to anybody, they're
                    gonna find themselves facing a
                    lawsuit.

                              XANDER
                    Blayne -- shut up.

                              WILLOW
                    I don't think it's bad at all. I
                    think it's really --

          Xander takes the machete from Buffy.

                              WILLOW
                         (big step back)
                    -- sweet. But certainly nothing
                    I'll ever bring up again --

          Xander moves <u>past</u> her and hacks at the egg sack attached
          to the rafters, destroying them.

45 INT. THE BRONZE - NIGHT   45

          Buffy is by the bar as Angel walks out of the darkness, that
          slight smile playing about his lips. For a moment, neither
          of them speaks.

                              ANGEL
                    I heard a rumor there was one less
                    vampire walking around making a
                    nuisance of himself.

                              BUFFY
                    There is. Thanks for the tip.

                              ANGEL
                    Pleasure's mine.

                              BUFFY
                    Of course, it would make things
                    easier if I knew how to get in
                    touch with you...

                              ANGEL
                    I'll be around.

                                                        (CONTINUED)

45 CONTINUED: 45

                         BUFFY
            Or who you were...

He just smiles at that one.

                         BUFFY
            Well, anyway, you can have your
            jacket back.

                         ANGEL
            Looks better on you.

He absently runs his hand along the collar for a moment.
Things get a teeny bit steamy there, but neither of them
makes a move.

He goes.

She watches him a moment.

                         BUFFY
            Oh, boy...

                                              DISSOLVE TO:

46 INT. BIOLOGY CLASSROOM - DAY   46

Several days later. Dr. Gregory's glasses lie on the
display table where he left them. Xander, Willow, Blayne,
Buffy listen to a second-rate TEACHER droning:

                         TEACHER
            All mid-term papers will be exactly
            six pages long -- no more, no less.
            One third of your grade will be
            dependent on those papers -- no
            more, no less...

PUSH IN on Buffy, missing the hell out of Dr. Gregory. The
bell rings. The kids get up, exit the class.

Buffy stops at the display table, looks down at Dr.
Gregory's glasses as the second-rate teacher neatly folds
his papers and books and marches out. Buffy picks up the
glasses, looks at them for a beat, gently wipes them off and
heads for the closet.

                                              (CONTINUED)

46 CONTINUED: 46

ANGLE: IN THE CLOSET

There is a box of Dr Gregory's personal stuff in here.
Buffy gently places the glasses in it and leaves. We hold
on the box for a moment before moving down, to the dark
bottom of the closet. Hanging from the lowest shelf, way in
the back, is a glistening egg sack. It moves. It cracks.

                                        BLACK OUT.

                        THE END

BUFFY THE VAMPIRE SLAYER

"Never Kill a Boy on the First Date"

Written by

Rob Des Hotel

&

Dean Batali

Directed by

David Semel

SHOOTING SCRIPT

October 21, 1996
October 23, 1996 (Blue-pages)
October 24, 1996 (Pink-pages)

BUFFY THE VAMPIRE SLAYER

"Never Kill a Boy on the First Date"

CAST LIST

BUFFY SUMMERS............................. Sarah Michelle Gellar
XANDER HARRIS............................. Nicholas Brendon
RUPERT GILES............................. Anthony S. Head
WILLOW ROSENBERG.......................... Alyson Hannigan
CORDELIA CHASE........................... Charisma Carpenter

MASTER.................................... *Mark Metcalf
ANGEL.................................... *David Boreanaz
OWEN..................................... *Christopher Wiehl
BOY...................................... *Andrew Ferchland
DRIVER................................... *Robert Mont
MILITIA GUY.............................. *Geoff Meed
MYSTERIOUS LOOKING GUY.................... *Paul-Felix Montez

BUFFY THE VAMPIRE SLAYER

"Never Kill a Boy on the First Date"

SET LIST

INTERIORS

SUNNYDALE HIGH SCHOOL
     CAFETERIA
     HALL
     LIBRARY
     GILES' OFFICE
BUFFY'S HOUSE
     BUFFY'S BEDROOM
     BUFFY'S FOYER
THE BRONZE
THE CHURCH
THE MASTER'S LAIR
FUNERAL HOME
     HALL
     PREP ROOM
     ENTRANCE
     OBSERVATION ROOM
VAN

EXTERIORS

SUNNYDALE HIGH SCHOOL
     CAMPUS
THE BRONZE
CEMETERY
HIGHWAY
VAN
FUNERAL HOME
GRAVEYARD BY FUNERAL HOME

<u>BUFFY THE VAMPIRE SLAYER</u>

"Never Kill a Boy on the First Date"

<u>TEASER</u>

FADE IN:

1   EXT. CEMETERY - NIGHT   1

CLOSE ON: A VAMPIRE'S FACE

Snarling in full attack mode: vicious, angry, bloodthirsty.

A CONVERSE-CLAD FOOT SMASHES squarely on the vampire's face,
knocking him back in a daze.

ANGLE: BUFFY

She leaps into the air and kicks the vampire to the ground.
He scrambles to his feet. Buffy takes a stake from her
belt.

                    BUFFY
          I don't think we've been properly
          introduced. I'm Buffy, and you
          are--

In a flash, she plunges the stake into the vampire's heart.
He falls, turning to dust. (FX)

                    BUFFY (cont'd)
          --history.

She puts her hands on her hips and surveys the carnage. She
smiles, satisfied. Her job is done. Then, from off-screen:

                    GILES (O.C.)
          Poor technique. Prioritization,
          sub-par.

Buffy's smile fades as GILES pops up from behind a
tombstone. He is holding a notebook, checking things off.

                    GILES (cont'd)
          Execution was adequate, but a bit
          too bloody for my taste.

                    BUFFY
          Oh, Giles, don't mention it. It
          was my pleasure to make the world
          safe for humanity again.

                                        (CONTINUED)

1   CONTINUED: 1

                              GILES
               I'm not saying your methods are
               without merit, but you're expending
               far too much time and energy.
                         (demonstrating)
               It should simply be 'plunge' and
               move on; 'plunge' and -- hello...

He is looking down at the pile of dust where the vampire
fell. He bends over and picks something up.

It's a ring -- old, ornate, with runic engravings around it.

                              BUFFY
               Oh, that's a great plan. I kill
               'em, you fence their stuff.
                         (he doesn't reply)
               What is it?

                              GILES
               I don't know...

                              BUFFY
               But it bothers you.

                              GILES
               Yes. I assumed this vampire was
               out on a random hunt. It may be
               something else.

                              BUFFY
               Something big.

                              GILES
               Yes. I'd best consult my books.

                                                       CUT TO:

2   INT. THE CHURCH   2

ANGLE: A DUSTY VOLUME BEING OPENED

But the hand that opens it is not Giles. It is the long,
white hand of the MASTER.

He stands at the pulpit, cradling his book in his arm.
Before him are three silent vampires, all dressed like the
first. Other shadowy figures stand farther back (i.e.
vampires we don't make up).

                                                      (CONTINUED)

2   CONTINUED:

                    MASTER
              (reads)
     There will be a time of crisis, of
     worlds hanging in the balance. And
     in this time shall come the
     Anointed, the Master's great
     warrior. The Slayer will not know
     him, will not stop him. And he
     will lead her to Hell.
              (looking up)
     As it is written, so shall it be.

He starts down, book in hand, toward the first three.

                    MASTER
              (reads)
     Five will die, and from their ashes
     the Anointed one shall rise. The
     brethren of Aurelius --

ANGLE: THE THREE VAMPIRES

Indicating that they are the brethren.

                    MASTER
     -- shall greet him, and usher him
     to his immortal destiny.
              (looks up)
     As it is written, so shall it be.

He stops by one of them, looking down at the book again.

                    MASTER
     And one of the brethren shall go
     out hunting the night before and
     get himself killed because he
     couldn't wait till his job was
     finished to eat. Oh, wait --

He lashes out and **grabs the vampire's throat.**

                    MASTER
     -- that's not written anywhere.

He lifts the vampire bodily with one hand, addressing
himself mainly to the other two, who remain silent and
contrite.

                                        (CONTINUED)

                          MASTER
                    (controlled fury)
          The Anointed will be my most
          powerful weapon against the Slayer.
          If you fail to bring him to me, if
          you allow that girl to get in your
          way...

He THROWS the third vampire across the room. The vampire
lands on a splintered old pew, a shard of wood piercing his
heart. The Master never takes his eyes off the other two.

                          MASTER
          Here endeth the lesson.

He snaps the book shut.

                                        BLACK OUT.

                    END TEASER

<u>ACT ONE</u>

3   INT. LIBRARY - DAY   3

Buffy sits cross-legged on the table, examining the ring.
Giles pours through some dusty volumes nearby.

                         GILES
              I believe this is the rune for   *
              fidelity, but that doesn't connect   *
              with any of the sects I've studied.

                         BUFFY
              What about this? On the inside. A
              sun and three stars. Haven't we
              seen that somewhere?

                         GILES
              Let me see.

She hands him the ring, picking up one of his volumes.

                         GILES
              Well I don't think this
              represents --

                         BUFFY
              Here. Sun and three stars. Check
              these guys out. I knew that looked
              familiar.

She hands him the volume.

                         GILES
              Yes, you're right...

                         BUFFY
              Ooh, two points for the Slayer,
              while the Watcher has yet to score.

The doors open and OWEN THURMAN walks in. He is good
natured, bookish. It's entirely possible he has no idea how
handsome he is.

Buffy and Giles stop what they're doing, looking at him.
Buffy's reaction to seeing him is significantly warmer than
Giles'. She in fact becomes flustered in a way we've never
seen before.

                         BUFFY
              Owen... Hi.

                         GILES
              What do you want?

                                              (CONTINUED)

                         265

3   CONTINUED:

                    OWEN
          A book.

                    GILES
          Oh.

                    BUFFY
                (to Giles)
          Yeah, see, a school has students
          and they check out books and then
          they learn things.

                    GILES
          I was beginning to suspect that was
          just a myth.

Owen comes forward, addressing himself to Buffy. It's clear
he's somewhat taken with her as well.

                    OWEN
          I lost my Emily. Dickinson. It's
          dumb but I like to have her around.
          Kind of like my security blanket.

                    BUFFY
          I have something like that. Well,
          it's an actual blanket. And I
          don't carry it around anymore --
                (floundering)
          So, Emily Dickens, huh? She's
          great.

                    OWEN
          Dickinson.

                    BUFFY
          She's good also.

He heads into the poetry section, Buffy with him.

                    OWEN
          I didn't think I'd find **you** here.

                    BUFFY
          Why not?

                    OWEN
          Oh, I didn't mean -- I mean, I
          think you can read...

                    BUFFY
          Thanks.

                                        (CONTINUED)

3   CONTINUED: 2   3

                         OWEN
              But you don't seem bookwormy. The
              type to lock yourself in a dark
              room with a lot of musty old books.

Off in another part of the room, Giles reacts, miffed.
Buffy says nothing, just looking at Owen as he pulls out the
volume he was looking for.

                         OWEN
                    (to Buffy)
              And I've offended you.

                         BUFFY
              No, I'm just... surprised you gave
              any thought to what I'm like.

                         OWEN
              You shouldn't be.

They start back down toward the table.

                         BUFFY
              Well, I love books.

                         OWEN
                    (looking at the book she
                     had, the vampire volume)
              What's this?

                         BUFFY
              Oh! Not this one.

                         GILES
                    (grabbing the book)
              No, she doesn't love this one.
                    (taking Owen's)
              Ah, Emily Dickinson.

                         BUFFY
                    (re: her and Owen)
              We're both fans.

                         GILES   *
              Yes, she's quite a good poet -- I   *
              mean, for --   *

                         BUFFY   *
              For a girl?   *

                         GILES   *
              For an American.   *
                                                   (CONTINUED)

3   CONTINUED: 3   3

Giles stamps the book, gives it back to Owen, who turns to
Buffy.

                    OWEN
          I'll see you in math... if I open
          my eyes at some point.

                    BUFFY
          Cool.

                                        (CONTINUED)

3   CONTINUED: 3

He exits. Buffy watches him go. Giles picks up right where
they left off.

                    GILES
          The order of Aurelius is a very old
          and venerated sect. If they're
          here it's for a good reason.

                    BUFFY
          That was Owen.

                    GILES
          Yes, I remember.

                    BUFFY
               (sudden inspiration)
          Do you have any more copies of
          Emily Dickinson? I need one.

                    GILES
          Buffy, while the fact of your
          wanting to check out a book is
          grounds for a national holiday, I
          do think we should focus on the
          problem at hand.

                    BUFFY
          You're right. Sorry. Vampires.
               (beat)
          Does this outfit make me look fat?

                                        CUT TO:

4   INT. SCHOOL CAFETERIA - DAY   4

Buffy and Willow are taking their trays to a table as they
speak.

                    WILLOW
          Owen Thurman was talking to you.

                    BUFFY
          It's all true.

                    WILLOW
          He hardly talks to **anyone**. He's
          solitary, mysterious... he can
          brood for forty minutes straight.
          I've clocked him.

                    BUFFY
          He was **so** nice. It was eerie.

                                        (CONTINUED)

>   WILLOW
>   What did you guys have to talk
>   about?

>   BUFFY
>   Emily Dickinson.

>   WILLOW
>   He reads Emily Dickinson.
>   (longingly)
>   He's sensitive, yet manly.
>   (on second thought)
>   But you've never even read her.

Buffy produces a copy of her poems.

>   WILLOW
>   You vixen.

Xander joins them, looking down at his tray.

>   XANDER
>   Has anyone given any thought to
>   what this green stuff is?

>   BUFFY
>   I'm avoiding the subject.

>   XANDER
>   I think it's kale. Or possibly
>   string cheese.

>   WILLOW
>   One of us is gonna have to taste
>   it.

They look at each other. Mexican stand off. Nobody tastes
it.

>   XANDER
>   So, how'd the slaying go last
>   night?

>   BUFFY
>   Xander, shhhh!

>   XANDER
>   I mean...
>   (louder)
>   How'd the **laying** go last -- no, I
>   don't mean that either.

(CONTINUED)

                              BUFFY
                    It went fine. There's some hoity
                    toity vampire sect in town.

                              WILLOW
                    That's bad.

                              XANDER
                    Hey, they bring in much needed
                    tourist dollars. Oh, check out Mr.
                    Excitement.

He points to Owen, sitting by himself, nose in a volume of
poetry. Buffy and Willow look at each other.

                              BUFFY
                    Oh, he's all alone. Someone should
                    sit with him.

                              WILLOW
                    Just to be polite.
                         (as Buffy rises)
                    Good luck.

Xander watches Buffy head over to Owen, tray in hand.

                              XANDER
                    Okay, what just happened?

Buffy approaches Owen, who looks up, pleased to see her. As
Buffy is about to sit, CORDELIA appears.

                              CORDELIA
                    Hey, look. An empty seat.

She bumps Buffy and knocks her tray to the floor. Cordelia
sits at the table and turns to Owen, but he's not there. He
is helping Buffy.

                              OWEN
                         (to Buffy)
                    Let me get that.

                              BUFFY
                    Thanks. Boy, Cordelia's hips are
                    wider than I thought.

                              OWEN
                         (picking up her tray)
                    At least now you don't have to eat
                    your Soylent Green.

Cordelia pulls Owen back down to his seat.

                                                        (CONTINUED)

4   CONTINUED: 3   4

                              CORDELIA
                    Hey, Owen, a bunch of us are
                    loitering at the Bronze tonight.
                    You there?

                              OWEN
                    Tonight? Ooh, we've got the
                    English Lit exam tomorrow. I guess
                    I can get up early. Who's all
                    going?

                              CORDELIA
                    Well, there's me.

                              OWEN
                    Oh. Who else?

                              CORDELIA
                         (genuinely confused)
                    You mean besides me?

                              OWEN
                    Buffy, what about you?

                              BUFFY
                         (caught off-guard)
                    What?

                              CORDELIA
                    No, she doesn't -- like -- fun.

                              OWEN
                         (to Buffy)
                    How about we meet there at eight?

          Cordelia glares at Buffy.

                              BUFFY
                    Yeah. Eight. There.

                                                        CUT TO:

5   INT. HALL/LIBRARY - DAY   5

          The end of the school day. Students file out.

                              BUFFY
                    Willow, it's not that big a deal.
                    It's just a bunch of people getting
                    together.

                              WILLOW
                    It's a very big deal.

                                                    (CONTINUED)

5   CONTINUED: 5

                         BUFFY
                It's not!

Giles approaches them.

                         WILLOW
                It is.
                     (to Giles)
                Tell her.

                         GILES
                I'm afraid it's very big.

                         WILLOW
                Thank you. Wait. What are you
                talking about?

                         GILES
                What are **you** talking about?

                         BUFFY
                Boys.

                         GILES
                Yes. Well, I'm talking about
                trouble. A violent and disturbing
                prophecy that's about to be
                fulfilled.

                         BUFFY
                The order of Aurelius.

                         GILES
                You were spot on about the
                connection. I looked through the
                writings of Aurelius himself. He
                prophesied that the brethren of his
                order would come to the Master, to
                bring him the Anointed.

                         BUFFY
                Who's that?

                         GILES
                I don't know exactly. A warrior.
                But it says he will rise from the
                ashes of the five on the evening of
                the 1,000th day after the advent   *
                of Septus --   *

                         BUFFY
                Well, this time we'll be ready
                whenever it --

                                            (CONTINUED)

5   CONTINUED: 2   5

                          GILES
              -- which is tonight.

                          BUFFY
              Tonight. Okay. Not okay! It
              can't be tonight!

                          GILES
              My calculations are precise.

                          BUFFY
              No, they're bad calculations! Bad!

                          WILLOW
              Buffy has a really important date.

                          BUFFY
              Owen...

                          GILES
              All right. Well, I'll get in my
              time machine, go back to the 12th
              century and ask the vampires to
              postpone their ancient prophecy by
              a few days so you can have dinner
              and a show.

                          BUFFY
              Okay, at this point, you're
              abusing sarcasm.

                          GILES
              Buffy, this is no common vampire.
              We must stop him before he reaches
              the Master.

                          BUFFY
                   (pleading)
              But... cute guy. Teenager. Post-
              pubescent fantasies.

                          GILES
              Those will have to be put on hold.
              The dark forces are aligning
              against us and we have a chance to
              beat them back. Tonight, we go
              into battle.

                                        SMASH CUT TO:

6   EXT. CEMETERY - THAT NIGHT   6

The cemetery is QUIET as Buffy and Giles sit there, bored.
Crickets chirp. Buffy finishes a huge soda with a SLURP.

                    GILES
          Perhaps I miscalculated.

                    BUFFY
          I'm thinking yes.

                    GILES
          Well, you know what they say.
          Ninety percent of the vampire
          slaying game is waiting.

                    BUFFY
          You couldn't have told me that
          ninety percent ago?

                    GILES
               (stretching)
          We certainly have been here long
          enough.

                    BUFFY
          And there's not even any fresh
          graves. Who's gonna rise?

                    GILES
          Apparently no one, tonight.

                    BUFFY
          Then I can bail? I can go to the
          Bronze and find Owen?

                    GILES
          Very well. Follow your hormones.
          But I needn't warn you about the
          hazards of becoming personally
          involved with someone who is
          unaware of your unique condition.

                    BUFFY
          Yeah, yeah. I've read the back of
          the box.

                    GILES
          If your identity as the Slayer is
          revealed, it could put you and
          those around you in grave danger.

                    BUFFY
          Oh, then in that case I won't wear
          my button that says 'I'm a
          Slayer -- Ask Me How!'

                                        (CONTINUED)

6   CONTINUED: 6

   She WALKS OFF. Giles reads from his notebook.

                         GILES
              'Five shall die and from their
              ashes the Anointed one shall rise.'
                         (then)
              I was sure it was tonight

7   EXT. VAN - NIGHT   7

   Behind him, we FOLLOW an AIRPORT SHUTTLE VAN as it passes.

                                                        CUT TO:

8   INT. VAN - NIGHT   8

   A DRIVER and FOUR PASSENGERS. We PAN ACROSS them. A
   SLEEPING MOTHER sits with her EIGHT-YEAR-OLD SON. He plays
   with a toy airplane, speaks to his neighbor:

                         BOY
              I went on an airplane.

   We END ON a MEAN-LOOKING, TATTOOED GUY who looks like he
   just stepped off the cover of 'Militia Monthly' magazine.

   CLOSE ON: HIS FACE

   He shifts his eyes, mumbling and singing incoherently.
   Calls out suddenly to the others:

                         MILITIA GUY
              You will be judged!

   And again, to himself...

                         MILITIA GUY (cont'd)
              You will be judged.

                                                        DISSOLVE TO:

9   EXT. BRONZE - NIGHT   9

   Establishing, as a soft, sexy ballad FADES IN.

                                                        CUT TO:

10   INT. BRONZE - CONTINUOUS   10

   Buffy walks in and looks around. She stops short.

                                                        (CONTINUED)

10   CONTINUED: 10

      ANGLE: OWEN AND CORDELIA

      Slow dancing. Cordelia pulls him close to her.

      ANGLE: BUFFY

      Standing there. If she had a cake, this would take it.

                                                         CUT TO:

11   INT. VAN - SAME TIME   11

      Militia Guy is walking through the aisle, preaching\
      haranguing.

                          MILITIA GUY
                  That day's gonna bring fire, yeah,
                  fire coming down. Judgment.

      He gets in the face of the now awake mother, who cowers a
      bit and clutches her boy.

                          MILITIA GUY (cont'd)
                  Don't think you're ready, ready to
                  look upon him. If sin is in there
                  it's all around, it's a liquid.

      Pacing again:

                          MILITIA GUY (cont'd)
                  On that day there won't be anyone
                  telling us what to do, or why we're
                  doing it. You can't prepare. On
                  that day...

      The driver looks in the mirror, worried.

                          DRIVER
                  Gotta sit down, okay?

                          MILITIA GUY
                      (looks at him, grinning)
                  .. will you stand with the
                  righteous?

      The driver shoots his eyes back towards the road.

      ANGLE: THROUGH THE WINDSHIELD

      A MAN stands right in the middle of the road.

                                                       (CONTINUED)

11 CONTINUED: 11

    ANGLE: THE HORRIFIED VAN DRIVER

    as he jerks the wheel.

                                                    CUT TO:

12 EXT. HIGHWAY - CONTINUOUS   12

    The van swerves to avoid the man, but to no avail. The van
    hits him and slams into a pole.

                                                    CUT TO:

13 INT. VAN - CONTINUOUS   13

    The Militia Guy is thrown down in the aisle, everyone else
    in their seats. The passengers are bloody but alive.

                         DRIVER
                Is everyone okay?

    He looks back -- they appear to be. He heads out:

                                                    CUT TO:

14 EXT. STREET - CONTINUOUS   14

    To check on the guy he hit. He leans over the prone body --

                         DRIVER
                Are you alright? Can you move?

    -- and a hand GRABS his throat.

                                                    CUT TO:

15 INT. VAN - CONTINUOUS   15

    Militia Guy raises himself from the floor.

    He puts his face to the window and tries to look out.

    ANGLE: HIS POV

    The driver appears to be struggling with the guy he hit.

    Militia Guy looks closer -- The window SMASHES IN and his
    head is pulled out.

                                                    CUT TO:

16 EXT. VAN - LONG SHOT   16

      From the distance, we SEE the van rocking and HEAR the
      sounds of vampires feasting.

      The passengers' screams FADE OFF into the night as we:

                                                    BLACK OUT.

                          END OF ACT ONE

ACT TWO

17 INT. SCHOOL HALLWAY - THE NEXT DAY   17

Buffy SLAMS her locker door, REVEALING Xander beside her.

                    XANDER
          So you just went home?

                    BUFFY
          What was I supposed to do? Say to
          Owen, 'Sorry I'm late. I was
          sitting in a cemetery with the
          librarian waiting for a vampire to
          rise so that I could prevent an
          evil prophecy from coming to pass'?

                    XANDER
               (weighing with his hands)
          Or... flat tire.

                    BUFFY
          I can't take this anymore. I feel
          like everyone's staring at me, the
          hideous dateless monster.

A STUDENT walks past. Buffy tears into him.

                    BUFFY (cont'd)
          That's right, I have no life. Move
          along pal, nothing to see here!

The student scurries on.

                    XANDER
          You're reacting a little overly,
          aren't you? I bet you could have
          any guy in the school.

                    BUFFY
          Owen's not any guy. He's more
          Oweny.

                    XANDER
          He has a certain Owenosity. But
          that's not hard to find. I mean, a
          lot of guys read... I read...

Owen comes up to them.

                    OWEN
          Hey, Buffy.

                                        (CONTINUED)

> BUFFY
> (brightening)
> Owen.

> XANDER
> Oh, look, it's Owen. Buffy and
> Owen. And Xander. That'd be me.

Xander moves aside and begins rummaging through his locker,
pretending not to listen.

> OWEN
> Where were you last night?

> BUFFY
> (rambling)
> Oh, I, uh... broke my watch, and we
> don't have any clocks in our house,
> so I didn't know what time it was,
> actually, I didn't even know what
> day it was.

> OWEN
> I thought I was the only one that
> happened to. How about we try
> again for tonight? I'll even lend
> you my watch.

Behind them, Xander listens conspicuously. Owen pulls out a
simple, beautiful, antique pocket watch, hands it to Buffy.
Xander looks insecurely at his own cheesy wristwatch: It has
Scooby Doo on it.

> BUFFY
> Tonight? You and me?

> OWEN
> We could invite the chess club but,
> you know, they drink, they start
> fights...

> BUFFY
> Well, no, it's just I kind of heard
> you and Cordelia were somewhat...
> all over each other. A little.

> OWEN
> I just danced with her a couple of
> times. She was there all alone. I
> felt sorry for her.

(CONTINUED)

>   BUFFY
>   Tonight.
>   (calculating in her head)
>   Let's see, if I rearrange, and move
>   that to next week, and then shift
>   that to -- sure. Tonight'll work.
>
>   OWEN
>   Great. How about I pick you up at
>   seven?
>
>   BUFFY
>   Seven.
>
>   OWEN
>   (pointing)
>   That's when the little hand's here.
>
>   BUFFY
>   (playing along)
>   Ah, between the six and the eight.
>
>   OWEN
>   See you then.

He walks off.

>   BUFFY
>   (to Xander)
>   Tonight! Isn't that so?
>
>   XANDER
>   (feigning ignorance)
>   What?
>
>   BUFFY
>   Me and Owen.
>
>   XANDER
>   Oh, yeah. 'So' it is.

He shuts his locker and starts away.

>   XANDER (cont'd)
>   (to himself)
>   It sure is so.

>   CUT TO:

18 INT. GILES'S OFFICE - AFTERNOON   18

Buffy walks in on Giles, talking rapid fire.

>   (CONTINUED)

18 CONTINUED: 18

                              BUFFY
                    Hey, how's it going?

                              GILES
                    All right --

                              BUFFY
                    That's great. We're working on
                    that Anointed One problem, that'll
                    probably take a few days, I mean
                    that's one obscure prophecy.

                              GILES
                    Well, yes, there's many
                    interpretations --

                              BUFFY
                    So tonight's looking pretty slow, I
                    get you, probably best to relax,
                    regroup, no big disasters coming
                    up. Great. See you tomorrow.

And she exits. Giles sits a moment.

                              GILES
                    She is the strangest girl...

                                             CUT TO:

19 INT. THE MASTER'S LAIR   19

The Master addresses the two brethren again.

                              MASTER
                    You've done well. Everything is in
                    place. When this night's work is
                    over, I'll have a mighty ally.
                    I'll be one step closer to freeing
                    myself from this mystical prison.

He reaches out and touches (FX) the mystical wall that
imprisons him.

                              MASTER
                         (almost to himself)
                    I've been trapped down here so long
                    I've nearly forgotten what the
                    surface looks like. There'll be
                    time enough to remember when I rule
                    it.

He turns back to the fellas.

                                             (CONTINUED)

19 CONTINUED: 19

                              MASTER
                    If **she** tries to stop you, kill
                    her. Give your own lives but do
                    not fail to bring the Anointed. I
                    know you won't disappoint me.

He lashes out suddenly as he did in the earlier scene. The
vampire flinches, but all the Master does is pick something
off his shoulder.

                              MASTER
                    Bug.

                                               CUT TO:

20 INT. BUFFY'S BEDROOM - NIGHT   20

Buffy is getting ready for her date. Xander and Willow are
there. Willow holds up two outfits for Buffy to choose.

                              WILLOW
                    Pick.

                              BUFFY
                    Okay. Do I want to appear shy, coy
                    and naive, or do I go unrestrained,
                    insatiable and aggressive?

                              XANDER
                    You know, Owen is a little
                    homespun. He probably doesn't like
                    that overly-assertive look.
                         (looking in her closet)
                    Hey, here's something. A nice,
                    comfy overcoat.

He pulls a drab, floor-length overcoat out of her closet.
He reaches for something else.

                              XANDER (cont'd)
                    And this ski cap. The earflaps
                    will bring out your eyes.

                              BUFFY
                         (to Willow)
                    I think I'll mix-n-match.
                         (then)
                    Xander, guy's opinion.
                         (she uncaps two
                          lipsticks)
                    Which one do you think Owen will
                    like better?

                                               (CONTINUED)

                          XANDER
             Oh, you mean for kissing you and
             then telling his friends how easy
             you are so that the whole school
             loses respect for you and talks
             behind your back? The red's good.

                          BUFFY
             Thanks. I'll go with the peach.

                          WILLOW
                    (handing Buffy some
                     clothes)
             Put this on.

They stare at Xander a beat.

                          XANDER
             You're not bothering me.

Willow turns Xander around as Buffy changes into her outfit.
As Willow and Buffy talk, Xander tries to get a glimpse of
Buffy's reflection in the doorknob.

                          WILLOW
             So, where's he taking you?

                          BUFFY
             I don't know. Where do you suppose
             the young kids are going on dates
             these days?

                          WILLOW
                    (joking)
             Well, I read somewhere that
             sometimes they go to movies.

                          BUFFY
             Movies. Interesting.

                          WILLOW
             And once on TV I saw a bunch of
             people our age at a party.

                          BUFFY
             Wow. I never knew being a teenager
             was so full of possibilities.

The DOORBELL rings.

                          BUFFY (cont'd)
             That's Owen!

                                             CUT TO:

21 INT. BUFFY'S FOYER - NIGHT   21

Buffy opens the door. Xander and Willow stand in the
hallway behind her.

                    BUFFY
          That's Giles.

ANGLE: GILES

                    GILES
          We need to talk.

                    BUFFY
          Buffy's not home.

Giles steps in anyway, holding a newspaper.

                    GILES
          I may not have been as far off in
          my calculations as I thought.

                    BUFFY
               (reading the paper)
          "5 die in van accident".

                    GILES
          From the ashes of the five shall
          rise the one. That's the prophecy.
          Now five people have died.

                    BUFFY
               (as to a child)
          In a car crash.

                    GILES
          Well, yes, that doesn't quite
          follow. But it's still worth
          investigating. Look.
               (shows a mug shot of
                Militia Guy)
          "Among the dead was Andrew Borba,
          whom the police sought for
          questioning in a double murder."
          He could be the Anointed. Now the
          bodies have been taken to the
          Sunnydale Funeral Home. We can --

                    BUFFY
          Giles, why do you want to hurt me?

                    GILES
          What do you mean?

                                        (CONTINUED)

Owen comes in.

                    OWEN
          Hey!
               (to Giles, warily)
          Uh, hi.

                    GILES
               (to Buffy)
          You have a date?

                    BUFFY
               (covering)
          Yes, but I'll return those overdue
          books by tomorrow.

                    GILES
          You're not getting off that
          easily...

                    OWEN
               (to Giles)
          Man, you really care about your
          work.

Willow and Xander, on alert, pull Owen away.

                    WILLOW
          Uh, Owen--

                    XANDER
          Yeah. A couple of things about
          tonight.

ANGLE: BUFFY AND GILES

                    GILES
          Another date. Don't you ever do
          anything else?

                    BUFFY
          This is the first date! There's
          never been a date, okay? This is
          my maiden voyage.

Buffy and Giles argue in hushed tones during the following.

                    OWEN
          What? She doesn't like to dance?

                                        (CONTINUED)

                    XANDER
Well, it's too late to do anything
about that. But you should
probably know Buffy doesn't like to
be kissed. Actually, she doesn't
even like to be touched.

                    WILLOW
Xander...

                    XANDER
As a matter of fact, don't even
look at her. Just to be safe.

                    OWEN
You know what? I think I'll let
Buffy lead.

                    XANDER
Now that she hates.

ANGLE: BUFFY AND GILES

                    BUFFY
We don't even know if this is
anything.

                    GILES
No, we don't...

                    BUFFY
And I haven't had a night off for a
while.

                    GILES
True...

                    BUFFY
And a cranky Slayer is a careless
Slayer.

He's giving ground, and it's with less than firm conviction
that he offers:

                    GILES
Buffy, maintaining a normal social
life when you're a Slayer is
problematic at best.

                    BUFFY
Come on, this is the 90's! The
1990's, in point of fact and I
can do both. Clark Kent has a
job. I just wanna go on a date.

                                        (CONTINUED)

                         GILES
          Well... I guess... this is a fairly
          slim lead.

                         BUFFY
          Thank you thank you thank you. And
          look. I won't go far. If the
          apocalypse comes --
                    (holds up a beeper)
          -- beep me.

The other three approach.

                         OWEN
          Is everything cool?

                         BUFFY
                    (sweetly)
          All set!

                         GILES
                    (trying to cover)
          Yes, you'll have a hefty fine to
          pay in the morning.

                         BUFFY
                    (to the three)
          Well, bye.
                    (dragging Owen off)
          Don't wait up.

Buffy and Owen start down the walk. Xander and Willow watch
them go, turn to Giles.

                         WILLOW
          Is something going on?

                         GILES
          Probably not. I suppose I'll go to
          the funeral home just in case, see
          if anything comes up...

He wanders off, deep in thought.

                         WILLOW
          This is bad.

                         XANDER
          I <u>wish</u> it was just bad.

                         WILLOW
          I think we better tag along.

                                        (CONTINUED)

21 CONTINUED: 4   21

                              XANDER
                    You're right. I do not trust that
                    Owen. It's the eyes. Crazy.

                              WILLOW
                    Xander, we have to go with Giles.
                    He could get in trouble.

We hear Giles' car take off.

                              XANDER
                    He's gone. And he'll be fine.
                    He's like SuperLibrarian. Everyone
                    forgets, Willow, that knowledge is
                    the ultimate weapon.

Willow gives him a look.

                              XANDER (cont'd)
                    All right, all right. You're
                    always bossing me around...

                                              DISSOLVE TO:

22 EXT. BRONZE - NIGHT   22

Establishing, as music plays.

23 INT. THE BRONZE - CONTINUOUS   23

THE CAMERA works its way through a sea of people and eventually
arrives at a table, where Owen and Buffy are sitting.

                              OWEN
                    The thing about Emily Dickinson
                    that I love is that she's just so
                    incredibly morbid. Lot of loss,
                    lot of death, it gets me. And a
                    lot about bees, for some reason.

                              BUFFY
                    Did she have a terrible and
                    romantic life? With a lot of bees?

                              OWEN
                    Quiet. Kind of sequestered, and
                    uneventful, which I can really
                    relate to. I don't get out much.

                              BUFFY
                    I don't get that.

                                              (CONTINUED)

23 CONTINUED: 23

                              OWEN
                  It's my fault. I just find most
                  girls pretty frivolous. I mean,
                  there's more important things in
                  life than dating, you know?

This stops her, as she gets a faraway look, thinking about
Giles. Looks down at her beeper.

                              OWEN
                  Did I say something wrong?

                              BUFFY
                       (shaking it off)
                  No. Come on.

She leads him onto the dance floor and they start to dance.

                              OWEN
                  It's weird.

                              BUFFY
                  What is?

                              OWEN
                  You. One minute you're right
                  there, I got you figured, the
                  next... It's like you're two
                  people.

                              BUFFY
                  Really? Which one do you like
                  better?

                              OWEN
                  I'll let you know.

They get pretty close.

ANGLE: CORDELIA

as she enters with a Cordette. She stops short.

REVEAL she is watching Buffy dance with Owen.

                              CORDELIA
                  Aren't there laws against this kind
                  of thing?

Cordelia approaches them.

                              CORDELIA (cont'd)
                  Owen. Look at you here all alone.

                                              (CONTINUED)

23   CONTINUED: 2   23

                              OWEN
                    Cordelia, I'm here with Buffy.

                              CORDELIA
                    Oh, okay. Want to dance?

                              OWEN
                    No, I'm still here with Buffy.

                              CORDELIA
                    You are so good, helping the needy.

                              BUFFY
                    Cordelia, Owen and I would like to
                    be left alone right now, and in
                    order for that to happen, you would
                    have to go somewhere that's away.

                              CORDELIA
                         (to Owen)
                    Well, let me know when you want to
                    move up to the big leagues.

Cordelia moves off.

Buffy and Owen continue dancing.

                              OWEN
                    Are you having a good time?

                              BUFFY
                    Oh yeah. I feel almost like a
                    girl.

                                             CUT TO:

24   EXT. FUNERAL HOME - NIGHT   24

A sign says 'SUNNYDALE FUNERAL HOME -- WE'LL TAKE CARE OF
THE REST.' In the background is the building, atop a grassy
hill. A chain blocks the entry to the long driveway.

A car pulls up and kills its lights. The door opens. Giles
steps out.

He makes his way through the graveyard toward the funeral
home. It's a creepy night, full of moving shadows.

A NOISE stops him. He looks around. Nothing. Keeps going.

One of the brethren suddenly steps in front of him. He
starts back, spins --

                                             (CONTINUED)

24 CONTINUED: 24

    -- another is behind him. He looks at them as they silently
approach. Genuine fear fills his face.

                      GILES
                (softly)
        Damn...

                                        BLACK OUT.

                    END OF ACT TWO

ACT THREE

25   EXT. GRAVEYARD BY FUNERAL HOME - MOMENTS LATER   25

Giles tries to back away slowly from the two brethren. They
move slowly, silently toward him.

He digs a cross from his pocket, holds it in front of him.
They hesitate, and, he maneuvers himself closer to the
funeral home. He turns and runs.

                                                        CUT TO:

26   INT. BRONZE - NIGHT   26

Buffy and Owen are leaving the dance floor. Buffy's eyes
suddenly go wide -- as if she senses Giles' peril.

                          BUFFY
                Oh, no...

ANGLE: HER POV

She sees a GIRL walk into the shadow of a doorway, followed
by a MYSTERIOUS GUY -- light skin, dark hair, dark clothing.

                          BUFFY (cont'd)
                Look out!

Buffy hurdles over a table, leaps into the doorway, and
grabs the guy. She throws him to the ground and puts her
knee on his chest, raising a fist to strike.

                          MYSTERIOUS GUY
                          (frightened)
                Go ahead! You can use it first!

He holds a quarter up to her, terrified.

REVEAL a pay phone on the wall, which the girl is using.

In the light, Buffy realizes this guy is no vampire. He's
just very pale, with a widow's peak and a fondness for the
wardrobe stylings of Johnny Cash.

                          BUFFY
                I am so begging your forgiveness.

She helps the guy up and brushes him off. Buffy turns to
make sure not many people saw her. Not many did, but Owen
is there. He looks at her, concerned.

                          OWEN
                Did you want to go somewhere else?

                                                    (CONTINUED)

26   CONTINUED: 26

                          BUFFY
              No, I'm having a great time!

                          OWEN
                       (suspicious)
              So, this is normal behavior for
              you?

Owen leads Buffy back to the bar.

                          BUFFY (cont'd)
                       (to herself)
              Buffy, reality. Reality, Buffy.
              Nothing is going to happen tonight.

                                                    CUT TO:

27   INT. FUNERAL HOME - NIGHT   27

      Giles bursts through the front door at top speed, hurls the
      door open and enters.

                                                    CUT TO:

28   INT. FUNERAL HOME HALLWAY - A MOMENT LATER   28

      Giles runs down the hall and tries a door. It's locked.

                          GILES
              Blast!

      He tries another door. It's locked. The third door opens,
      and he runs into the

                                                    CUT TO:

29   INT. FUNERAL HOME PREP ROOM - CONTINUOUS   29

      and locks the door behind him. In the room are tables for
      dressing the bodies, caskets, a table of urns, and huge
      drawers on every wall. There is a large sink with cabinets
      beneath it, and at one end of the room is a cremation oven.

      Giles leans against the door, breathing hard.

                                                    CUT TO:

30   INT. HALL - CONTINUOUS   30

     The brethren enter the front door. They look around and
     head straight for the door Giles went in.

                                                      CUT TO:

31   INT. PREP ROOM - CONTINUOUS   31

     Giles pushes a cabinet against the door, barricading it.

     The door handle moves and he backs away, eyes on it. It
     jiggles a bit, then stops.

     Giles backs close to the window -- and someone **appears
     right behind him.**

                         GILES
               Gahh!

                         WILLOW
               Giles, it's us!

                         GILES
               What are you doing here?

                         XANDER
               We saw two guys go in there after
               you. Are they --

                         GILES
               They are. You have to get to
               safety.

                         WILLOW
               Can you get out this window?

     He looks. The bars are strong.

                         GILES
               I'm afraid not.

     There is a sudden POUND at the door. They all react.

                         XANDER
               Not to state the obvious, but this
               looks like a job for Buffy.

                         GILES
               She has a beeping thing --
                    (looks around)
               No phone. Of course.

                         XANDER
               We'll get her. Just hang in there.

                                                  (CONTINUED)

31 CONTINUED: 31

     Xander and Willow run off. Another SMASH at the door.
     Giles looks at it, staying calm.

                              GILES
                    Do hurry...

                                                        CUT TO:

32 INT. THE BRONZE - NIGHT   32

     Buffy and Owen are in the lounge section.

                              OWEN
                    You want something to eat?

                              BUFFY
                    Sure. My only rule is no raisins.

                              OWEN
                    I can live with that.

     He smiles at her and goes off.

     ANGLE: CORDELIA AND A CORDETTE

     who have been watching Buffy and Owen.

                              CORDELIA
                    What a disgusting display. Is that
                    really appropriate conduct in a
                    public forum?

     The Cordette opens her mouth to speak.

                              CORDELIA (cont'd)
                    Doesn't Owen realize he's hitting a
                    major backspace by hanging out with
                    that loser?

     The Cordette tries to speak again.

                              CORDELIA (cont'd)
                    I mean, have you ever seen a girl
                    throw herself at a guy like that?
                         (then, seeing someone
                          else)
                    Hel-lo, salty goodness!

     ANGLE: ANGEL

     who has just walked in. He looks around.

                                                        (CONTINUED)

                         CORDELIA (O.C.)
              Pick up the phone. Call 9-1-1.

ANGLE: CORDELIA

as she primps a bit.

                         CORDELIA (cont'd)
              That boy's going to need some
              serious oxygen after I'm through
              with him.

She heads his way, but he goes right to Buffy. Cordelia
stops and stares in disbelief.

                         CORDELIA (cont'd)
                       (completely distraught)
              Why is this happening to me?

ANGLE: BUFFY'S TABLE

                         ANGEL
              Buffy.

Buffy turns and sees him. A smile flashes on her face.
It's quickly gone as she tries to play it cool.

                         BUFFY
              Angel.

                         ANGEL
              I was hoping I'd find you here.

                         BUFFY
                       (a little flustered)
              You were hoping--?

                         ANGEL
              There's severe stuff happening
              tonight. You need to be out there.

So it's business. Her expression hardens.

                         BUFFY
              Oh, no. Not you too.

                         ANGEL
              You already know?

                         BUFFY
              Prophecy, Anointed One, yada yada
              yada.

                                              (CONTINUED)

                          ANGEL
              So you know. Fine. I just thought
              I'd warn you.

                          BUFFY
              Warn me?
                   (indicating Owen)
              See that guy over at the bar? He
              came here to <u>be</u> with me.

                          ANGEL
              You're here on a date?

                          BUFFY
              Yeah. Why is that such a shock to
              everyone?

Owen comes back to the table and hands Buffy a delicious
buttery croissant.

                          OWEN
              Here you go.

                          BUFFY
              Owen, this is Angel. Angel, this
              is Owen. Who is my date.

                          ANGEL
              Hey.

                          OWEN
              Hey.

There is an awkward 'guy beat.'

                          OWEN (cont'd)
              So, where do you know Buffy from?

                          ANGEL
                   (a beat)
              Work.

                          OWEN
                   (to Buffy)
              You work?

Xander and Willow run up, breathless.

                          WILLOW
              Buffy--

                                              (CONTINUED)

>   OWEN
>   (suspicious)
>   Look at this. You're just showing
>   up everywhere. Interesting.

>   XANDER
>   You don't know the half of it.
>   (sees Angel)
>   What are you doing here?

>   ANGEL
>   My guess is the same thing you're
>   doing here.

>   BUFFY
>   Excuse me. What are any of you
>   doing here?

>   XANDER
>   We've got to get to--

Willow nudges him and glances over at Owen.

>   XANDER
>   Uh, we thought it'd be fun to make
>   thi a double date.

He puts his arm around Willow.

>   BUFFY
>   (suspicious)
>   With you? I didn't know you two
>   were seeing each other.

>   WILLOW
>   Oh, yeah. We knew it would happen
>   eventually and figured, hey, why
>   fight it?

>   OWEN
>   And you guys were thinking double.
>   All of a sudden.

>   XANDER
>   Cuz of... the fun.

>   OWEN
>   (to Angel)
>   And you're here because of work.

>   XANDER (cont'd)
>   Maybe we should all go somewhere
>   together.

                                                        (CONTINUED)

32 CONTINUED: 4   32

                          BUFFY
                Gee, that is so nice of you to ask.
                But Owen and I were kind of, well,
                Owen and I.

                          XANDER
                You know what would be cool? The
                Sunnydale Funeral Home.

                          WILLOW
                I've always wanted to go there.

                                              CUT TO:

33 INT. FUNERAL HOME PREP ROOM - SAME TIME   33

    Giles continues barricading the door. The pounding is
    getting worse.

                                              CUT TO:

34 INT. THE BRONZE - CONTINUOUS   34

                          BUFFY
                       (getting it)
                The funeral home?

                          OWEN
                Actually, that might be cool. Do
                you think we could sneak in?

                          XANDER
                Well, we saw some guys in there
                before.
                       (pointedly)
                And they looked like they were
                having fun.

    Buffy's suspicions are confirmed.

                          BUFFY
                Damn.

                          XANDER
                Exactly.

                          BUFFY
                Uh, Owen, I gotta go.

                          OWEN
                I thought we were gonna go to the
                funeral home.

                                              (CONTINUED)

34 CONTINUED: 34

                              BUFFY
                 No. You can't. I tell you what.
                 I'll be back. In a little while.

Owen pulls her aside.

                              OWEN
                 Buffy, what's the deal? If you
                 want to bail on me...

                              BUFFY
                 I don't. But I -- remember you
                 said I was like two people? Well
                 one of them has to go. But the
                 other one is having a great time
                 and will come back. I promise.

She walks away. We hold on Owen, looking bemused. After a
beat Buffy comes back into the frame and KISSES him.

ANGLE: XANDER, ANGEL AND CORDELIA

All watching the kiss, all with differing degrees of the
same reaction.

Buffy heads out, Xander and Willow behind. Owen is just as
bemused as before. He comes up beside Angel, looking out at
her departing figure.

                              OWEN
                 She is the strangest girl...

Angel nods agreement.

                                                    CUT TO:

35 INT. FUNERAL HOME HALLS - LATER   35

Empty. Silent.

                                                    CUT TO:

36 INT. FUNERAL HOME ENTRANCE WAY - CONTINUOUS   36

Buffy and the others enter. She looks around, tense.

                              BUFFY
                 Which way?

                              WILLOW
                 The room's around the back.

                                                    (CONTINUED)

36 CONTINUED: 36

They pick a hall, start down it.

                                                    CUT TO:

37 INT. HALL - CONTINUOUS   37

They go down, turn the corner -- a dead end.

                        BUFFY
                Dammit!

They start back -- and someone is right behind them!

It's Owen.

                        OWEN
                This is so cool.

                        BUFFY
                Owen, what are you -- you can't be
                here.

                        OWEN
                Oh, but I suppose you guys are
                allowed. What are we gonna do?
                Are we gonna see a dead body?

                        BUFFY
                Possibly several. Guys, watch him.

She takes off down another hall.

                        OWEN
                Is she pissed?

                        WILLOW
                She just wants to make sure there's
                no guards or anything. So we don't
                get in trouble.

                        OWEN
                Good thinking.

                        XANDER
                    (to Willow, sotto voce)
                Good thinking.

                                                    CUT TO:

38 INT. ANOTHER HALL - CONTINUOUS   38

Buffy looks around, moving at a good clip. She stops, very
worried, and heads for:

39   INT. FUNERAL HOME PREP ROOM - A MOMENT LATER   39

She enters and we see the cause for concern -- the barricade
has been broken apart, the door nearly off its hinges.

She enters, looking about in the dark space.

                    BUFFY
                (softly)
            Giles...

It's more a statement than a calling out -- it looks like
she's too late to save him.

WE HEAR a shard of glass fall to the floor. Buffy looks up
and sees that a window high on the opposite wall is
completely shattered, the bars bent apart.

She heads for the window, looks out and sees nothing.
Starts slowly back across the room, by the drawers in the
wall.

One of them SHOOTS OPEN right in front of her. She gasps,
sees:

ANGLE: GILES LAYS IN THE DRAWER NEXT TO A CORPSE.

                    BUFFY
            Giles!

                    GILES
            It **is** you. Good.

                    BUFFY
            What happened?

He crawls out, dusts himself off.

                    GILES
            Two more of the brethren were here.
            They came after me but I was more
            than a match for them.

                    BUFFY
            Meaning?

                    GILES
            I hid. This fellow was kind enough
            to bunk with me till they went
            away.

                    BUFFY
            So they were here after you? Or is
            it the prophecy thing.

                                        (CONTINUED)

                         GILES
          That's what we have to find out. I
          don't know what these brethren are
          meant to do exactly. Find the
          Anointed one, perhaps give him
          something -- it's all very vague.
          They may have fulfilled their
          purpose already. The Anointed one
          may be long gone.

                         BUFFY
          But he may not be.

                         GILES
          Let's find out.

                         BUFFY
          All right. I've got to get Owen
          and the others out of harm's way.

                         GILES
          Owen? You brought a date?

                         BUFFY
          I didn't bring him. He came.

                         GILES
          Buffy, when I said you could slay
          vampires and have a social life I
          didn't mean at the same time!

                         BUFFY
          I'll get rid of him!

                         GILES
          You can't send him outside alone.
          We don't know where the brethren
          are. I'll just tell him --

                         BUFFY
          If he sees you here he's gonna have
          even more questions than he does
          right now. Stay.

                                        CUT TO:

40 INT. HALL - MOMENTS LATER   40

     Buffy walks down the hall. The other three are nearby.

                         WILLOW
          Is everything okay?

                                        (CONTINUED)

                         BUFFY
              It is.

Xander and Willow look suitably relieved.

                         XANDER
              And we'll be leaving.

                         OWEN
              We haven't finished looking around!

                         BUFFY
                   (pointedly, to the
                    others)
              No, we haven't. So let's find a
              nice safe -- fun -- room to look
              around in.

                         OWEN
              We tried the office here, but it's locked.

Buffy goes to the door. She loudly COUGHS as she forces it
open, braking the lock.

                         BUFFY
              No, it's not.

41 INT. FUNERAL HOME OBSERVATION ROOM - A MOMENT LATER   41

'PRIVATE OBSERVATION ROOM' is written on the door. Buffy
enters and quickly checks out the room. There are some easy
chairs, a couch, and an end table or two.

A window looks into an adjacent viewing room.

                         BUFFY (cont'd)
              All clear.

Buffy ushers the others inside. Owen looks around.

                         OWEN
              I don't think we're going to find
              much in here.

                         BUFFY
              That's the plan.

                         OWEN
              Okay.
                   (then)
              What?

                                                    (CONTINUED)

41 CONTINUED: 41

                         BUFFY
          I'll be right back. I gotta pee.
          If you hear anything, like a
          security guard, just be real quiet.
          And barricade the door.

She heads out.

                                          CUT TO:

42 INT. FUNERAL HOME PREP ROOM - A LITTLE WHILE LATER   42

ANGLE: FROM INSIDE A DRAWER

It opens, revealing Buffy looking inside. She hesitates,
then closes it again.

We're inside another as it opens, Giles standing over it.

And another, as Buffy looks in and makes a face.

                         BUFFY
          Uuhhgglh. Parts.

                         GILES (O.C.)
          Keep looking. He's got to be
          somewhere.

She shuts the drawer, sending us back into blackness.

                                          CUT TO:

43 INT. FUNERAL HOME OBSERVATION ROOM - SAME TIME   43

Owen is poking about absently. Xander and Willow have moved
the furniture in front of the door.

                         OWEN
          What are you guys doing?

                         WILLOW
          Just in case.

Owen shrugs, wanders to the glass, opens the curtains.
Looks in the next room. He stops.

                         OWEN
          Oh, my...

                                          CUT TO:

44   INT. FUNERAL HOME PREP ROOM - SAME TIME   44

      Almost all of the drawers are open. Buffy stands over a
      drawer with a stake raised high. She pulls the drawer open
      with a jerk. It's empty.

                           BUFFY
                  Nothing.

                           GILES
                  The Anointed One must be gone.

                           BUFFY
                  I guess. I mean, they keep all the
                  bodies here, right?

                                              CUT TO:

45   INT. FUNERAL HOME OBSERVATION ROOM - SAME TIME   45

      The camera circles behind Owen to reveal A BODY laid out
      under a sheet, one tattooed arm dangling off the table.

      He stares at it through the glass. The others approach as
      he begins to speak.

                           OWEN
                  I'm reading about death all the
                  time, and I've never seen a real
                  dead body before.

      We hold on Owen's face for a good long time as his
      expression alters slightly.

                           OWEN
                  Do they usually move?

      Xander and Willow look, start back as they see:

      ANGLE: ON THE TABLE

      The arm comes up and pulls the sheet off. Militia Guy
      stands up, now a vampire. His shirt is off, and his
      prodigious muscles are covered with tattoos -- most of them
      prison work. He looks at his hands, feels his face. Smiles
      in wonder.

                           MILITIA GUY
                  I have been judged...

                                              BLACK OUT.

                           END OF ACT THREE

ACT FOUR

46   INT. FUNERAL HOME OBSERVATION ROOM - CONTINUOUS   46

The Militia Vampire moves towards the glass. Our gang in
the room moves back, staring in fear.

                         OWEN
                  What's going on?

Militia Guy smiles at them, then SMASHES his head through
the glass.

                                              CUT TO:

47   INT. PREP ROOM - CONTINUOUS   47

Buffy and Giles hear the glass, look at each other.

                         BUFFY
                  Oh, NO!

She bolts out of the room.

48   INT. FUNERAL HOME VIEWING ROOM - CONTINUOUS   48

The kids frantically move their barricade out of the way as
Militia Guy climbs through the broken window.

                      MILITIA GUY
                  He is risen in me! He fills my
                  head with song! Pork and beans,
                  pork and beans.

They move the rest of the furniture as he approaches.

                      MILITIA GUY
                  I can smell you. You're the chaff.
                  Unblessed. I'll suck the blood
                  from your hearts. He says I may.

They get the door open and run out --

                                              CUT TO:

49   INT. FUNERAL HOME HALLWAY - CONTINUOUS   49

They run right into Buffy.

                        XANDER
                  He's in there!

                                          (CONTINUED)

49 CONTINUED: 49

                              BUFFY
                    Go! Get out!

She shoves them in the direction of the front door. She
turns and runs in the opposite direction. Xander and Willow
herd Owen toward the front door.

                              XANDER
                    She'll be all right! Come on!

                                             CUT TO:

50 INT. FRONT HALLWAY - A MOMENT LATER   50

The three kids are racing for the door --

ANGLE: THE DOOR

is open, safety beckons -- and **one of the Brethren steps
out** into view just beyond it.

The kids come to a halt, Willow letting out a short sharp
shriek.

The vampire pauses, and **slams** the door in their faces.

                              XANDER
                    NO!

They hear the door being bolted from the outside. Turn
around as another sound fills the hall: singing.

                              MILITIA GUY (O.C.)
                    Shall we gather at the river... the
                    beautiful the beautiful river...

                              WILLOW
                    I think he's coming this way...

They back away into:

                                             CUT TO:

51 INT. FUNERAL HOME ADJOINING HALLWAY - CONTINUOUS   51

They turn the corner. Dead end.

                              OWEN
                    Oh, God, this is too much...

                                             CUT TO:

52   INT. FUNERAL HOME PREP ROOM - CONTINUOUS   52

Buffy runs in.

                         BUFFY
               What've you got?

                         GILES
               What?

                         BUFFY
               What did you bring? Stake,
               cross --

He hands her one of each. She starts for the door.

                         GILES
               What should I do?

                         BUFFY
                    (turns in the doorway)
               Get outside and make sure the
               others are --

Militia Guy FILLS the doorway, GRABBING Buffy. Before she
has time to react he THROWS her halfway across the room.
Giles runs to her, never taking his eyes off the vampire.

                         MILITIA GUY
               They told me about you. When I was
               sleeping.

He advances -- Giles holds up a cross and he stops, staring
at it. Confusion fills his face.

                         MILITIA GUY
               Why does he hurt me?

Buffy tightens her grip on the stake.

                                             CUT TO:

53   INT. HALL - CONTINUOUS   53

Owen looks at the others. He's scared but resolved.

                         OWEN
               Somebody's got to help Buffy.

And he bolts.

                         WILLOW
               Owen!

                                             CUT TO:

54   INT. PREP ROOM - CONTINUOUS   49

Militia Guy grabs Giles and squeezes his hand till the cross
drops. He backhands Giles -- he goes back, stumbling into a
large BUTTON.

ANGLE: THE OVEN

As soon as the button is hit, FLAMES shoot up inside.

Giles drops to the ground, dazed.

Buffy comes at Militia Guy and they spar -- he's doing
better. He knocks the stake away. He grabs her face
suddenly and begins to SQUEEZE --

ANGLE: OWEN

Appears in the doorway.

                    OWEN
              NO!

He runs in, grabbing a metal tray and slamming into Militia
Guy's head. The brute stumbles back -- then grabs Owen by
the throat, bares his fangs, and moves in.

                    OWEN
              Ahhh!

Owen hits him with the tray again and Militia Guy goes down.
Owen turns to Buffy. He's breathing hard, scared but
strangely exhilarated.

                    OWEN (cont'd)
              Did you see that? He tried to bite me.
              What a sissy.

Militia immediately pops up behind Owen, grabs him, and
slams a drawer into his head. Owen goes limp. Militia
holds the lifeless body up.

                    MILITIA VAMPIRE
              Dead.

He drops Owen to the ground.

                    MILITIA VAMPIRE (cont'd)
              He was found wanting.

Buffy looks at the body, then at Militia Vampire.

                    BUFFY
              No...

                                              (CONTINUED)

Horror and fury fill her face. She kicks the gurney into
his midsection. He doubles over, she pushes her end down,
sending his end up into his chin.

He stumbles back, smashing into lots of NOISY stuff, as
 Buffy leaps on him and proceeds to **punch him many times**.

Willow and Xander enter, racing over to Owen.

ANGLE: OWEN

His eyelids begin to flutter and he tries to sit up.

Willow and Xander see this.

> BUFFY
> You killed my date!

> WILLOW
> Buffy --

> XANDER
> Give her a sec.

> BUFFY
> **You killed my date!**

Militia Guy blocks a punch and hits her.

> MILITIA GUY
> Your turn.

She kicks him -- he flies back, lands on the gurney -- it
rolls back, **slamming** into the bottom of the oven --
Militia Guy **slides right in**, engulfed in flames.

Giles **slams** the oven door shut, trapping him. We hear an
inhuman ROAR emanating from the oven.

ANGLE: OWEN

He is coming out of his daze, not sure where he is.

> OWEN
> Does anybody have an aspirin? Or
> sixty?

> BUFFY
> Owen!

She rushes to him, helps him to his feet.

(CONTINUED)

                         OWEN (cont'd)
                        (still groggy)
                   What happened to that guy?

                         BUFFY
                   We scared him away.

                         OWEN
                   Good, because, you know, I would
                   have...

                         BUFFY
                   I know.
                        (a beat)
                   I'm sure this isn't what you
                   expected on our first date.

                         OWEN
                   Yeah, I thought maybe we'd finish
                   up at Ben & Jerry's--

                         BUFFY
                   We still could.

                         OWEN
                   No, I think I'll just walk home.

He starts out, then turns back.

                         OWEN (cont'd)
                   Um, which way is home?

                         BUFFY
                   I'll get you there.

She reaches for him. He backs away from her.

                         OWEN
                   Uh, no. I'll go it alone.

He walks off.

                         XANDER
                   We'll make sure he gets there okay.

He and Willow follow after Owen.

Buffy watches as they go. Giles moves to Buffy.

                         GILES
                   Buffy, if I might--

                                        (CONTINUED)

54   CONTINUED: 3   54

                              BUFFY
                         (putting a hand up)
                    Don't.

She turns and walks out, leaving Giles there.

                                                      DISSOLVE TO:

55   EXT. CAMPUS - THE NEXT DAY   55

Buffy is with Xander and Willow.

                              BUFFY
                    Did Owen say anything about me on
                    the way home?

                              WILLOW
                    You mean specifically about you?

                              BUFFY
                    Or generally, in the area, in the
                    ballpark, any sort of implication--

                              XANDER
                    Oh, well, in that case, no.

                              WILLOW
                    But he was pretty incoherent, so
                    maybe we missed it.

                              BUFFY
                    You think?

                              XANDER
                    No.

                              BUFFY
                    I knew it. I totally blew it.

                              XANDER
                    What you need is a guy who already
                    knows your deepest, darkest secrets
                    and still says, 'hey, I like that
                    girl.' Someone like--

                              BUFFY
                    Owen!

ANGLE: OWEN

as he comes up to them.

                                                      (CONTINUED)

                          WILLOW
                    (to Xander)
            I think this is our stop.

Willow moves off. Xander stands there. He feels a tug on
his shirt as Willow pulls him away.

                          OWEN
            Hi.

                          BUFFY
            Hi.

A long beat of silence.

                          BUFFY (cont'd)
            This is going well.

                          OWEN
            All right, I don't know how to say
            this, but, about last night--

                          BUFFY
            You don't even have to. I'm sure
            you were pretty freaked out.

                          OWEN
            Totally. And I was hoping I could
            see you again.

Buffy stands there stone-faced. She snaps out of it.

                          BUFFY
            Um, that was my hopeful ear.
                    (turning her head)
            Could you repeat that?

                          OWEN
            I think you're the coolest. You're
            so sweet, but there's something...
            dangerous about you.

                          BUFFY
                    (smiling)
            Really?

                          OWEN
            Last night was incredible. I never
            thought that nearly getting killed
            would make me feel so alive.

                          BUFFY
            That's why you want to be with me?

                                              (CONTINUED)

                         OWEN
          Absolutely. When can we do
          something like that again?

                         BUFFY
          Something like--

                         OWEN
          Like... walk downtown at three in
          the morning. Pick a fight in a
          bar. How about tonight?

                         BUFFY
          Tonight would be--

She stops herself. Something isn't right.

                         BUFFY (cont'd)
          --not a workable thing.
               (then)
          Did I say that?

                         OWEN
          Tomorrow, then? I'm free any night
          this week.

                         BUFFY
               (regretfully)
          I'm not.
               (struggling for words)
          You see, the thing is... you're a
          really nice guy. But...

She pulls out his watch, hands it to him.

                         BUFFY
          The timing's all off.

                         OWEN
          Oh. Timing.

                         BUFFY
          Don't take this personally. I
          mean, it's not you, it's me.

                         OWEN
               (nodding)
          Right. It's you.

                         BUFFY
          That doesn't mean we can't--

                                        (CONTINUED)

> OWEN
> I get it. You just want to be
> friends.

> BUFFY
> That'd be nice.

> OWEN
> (backing away)
> Friends. Yeah. Great.

Owen turns and goes. Buffy watches him disappear into the
mass of students.

> BUFFY
> Yeah. Great.

Giles approaches her.

> GILES
> I was 10 years old when my father
> told me I was destined to be a
> Watcher. He was one, and his
> mother before him. And I was to be
> next.

> BUFFY
> Were you thrilled beyond all
> measure?

> GILES
> No. I had very definite plans for
> my future. I was going to be a
> fighter pilot. Or possibly a
> grocer. But my father gave me a
> very tiresome speech about
> responsibility and sacrifice.

> BUFFY
> (watching Owen go)
> Sacrifice, huh?

> GILES
> He seems like a nice boy.

> BUFFY
> Yeah, but he wants to be Dangerman.
> You, Xander, Willow, you know the
> score. You're careful. Two days
> in my world and Owen really **would**
> get himself killed. Or I'd get
> him killed.
> (looking at Giles)
> Or someone else.

(CONTINUED)

55 CONTINUED: 4   55

A beat, as he absorbs her concern.

                    GILES
          I went to the funeral home of my
          own free will.

                    BUFFY
          And I should have been with you. I
          blew it.

                    GILES
          Buffy, I have volumes of lore, of
          prophecies and predictions. I
          don't have an instruction manual.
          We feel our way as we go along.
          I'd say as a Slayer you're doing
          pretty well.

                    BUFFY
          Giles, you just had something nice
          to say. You complimented me.

                    GILES
               (a bit embarrassed)
          Yes, let's not call attention to
          it.

                    BUFFY
          Well, I did stop that prophecy from
          coming true.

                    GILES
          You did. Handily. No more
          Anointed One to worry about. I
          imagine the Master, wherever he is,
          is having a fairly bad day himself.

                                        CUT TO:

56 INT. THE MASTER'S LAIR   56

The Master is speaking to someone who is as yet unseen. We
can't tell if he's pleased or not.

                    MASTER
          And in this time will come the
          Anointed. The Slayer will not know
          him, she will not stop him. And he
          will lead her to Hell.

He smiles. It isn't nice.

                                        (CONTINUED)

                              MASTER
                        Welcome, my friend.

It is the eight-year-old boy from the van. The brethren
stand in the background.

The boy looks up at the Master innocently. He smiles, his
mouth full with fangs.

                                        BLACK OUT.

                         THE END

BUFFY THE VAMPIRE SLAYER

"The Pack"

Written by

Matt Kiene

&

Joe Reinkemeyer

Directed by

Bruce Seth Green

<u>SHOOTING SCRIPT</u>

November 1, 1996
November 4, 1996 (Blue-Pages)
November 7, 1996 (Pink-Pages)
January 21, 1997 (Green-Pages)

BUFFY THE VAMPIRE SLAYER

"The Pack"

CAST LIST

```
BUFFY SUMMERS............................... Sarah Michelle Gellar
XANDER HARRIS............................... Nicholas Brendon
RUPERT GILES............................... Anthony S. Head
WILLOW ROSENBERG........................... Alyson Hannigan


KYLE....................................... *Eion Bailey
LANCE...................................... *Jeff Maynard
RHONDA..................................... *Michael McCraine
TOR........................................ *Brian Gross
HEIDI...................................... *Jennifer Sky
FLUTIE..................................... *Ken Lerner
ZOOKEEPER.................................. *James Stephens
COACH HERROLD.............................. *Gregory White
ADAM....................................... *Jeffrey Steven Smith
MR. ANDERSON............................... *David Brisbin
MRS. ANDERSON.............................. *Barbara Whinnery
*JOEY...................................... *Justin Jon Ross
*YOUNG WOMAN............................... *Patrese Borem
```

BUFFY THE VAMPIRE SLAYER

"The Pack"

SET LIST

INTERIORS

SUNNYDALE HIGH SCHOOL
     HALL
     GYM
     CLASSROOM
     LIBRARY
     FLUTIE'S OFFICE
THE BRONZE
ZOO
     HYENA HOUSE
     HYENA CAGE
     *ZOOKEEPER'S OFFICE
*CAR

EXTERIORS

SUNNYDALE HIGH SCHOOL
     COURTYARD
THE ZOO
     BY THE MONKEY CAGE
WOODS
DRIVEWAY

"The Pack"

1   EXT. THE ZOO - DAY   1

We see VARIOUS ANGLES of ANIMALS in their cages. Find BUFFY
in front of one of them, walking by herself. Other students
pass by, talking. Buffy looks at animals until:

                    KYLE
          Oh, look.

This is THE PACK: KYLE, RHONDA, TOR and HEIDI. They are the
kind of kids who seem to exist only to ridicule others.
They are always together, always with fairly bad intent.

                    KYLE
          It's Buffy.
               (indicating she's alone)
          And all her friends.

                    BUFFY
          That's witty.

                    TOR
          Do you ever wonder why nobody cool
          ever wants to hang out with you?

                    BUFFY
          I'm just thankful.

                    RHONDA
          So, were you this popular at your
          old school? Before you got kicked
          out?

Sore spot. Buffy glares at her, as the group drifts off.

                    TOR
               (to Rhonda)
          Careful -- she might beat you up.

She looks like she might. After a moment she turns back to
the animals.

                    XANDER
               (off screen)
          Hey!

XANDER and WILLOW run up to her, excited.

                                                        (CONTINUED)

                              ___
                              325

1   CONTINUED:

> XANDER
> Buffy!

> WILLOW
> You missed it!

> BUFFY
> Missed what?

> XANDER
> We saw the Zebras mating! Thank
> you, very exciting...

> WILLOW
> It looked like the Heimlich. With
> stripes.

> BUFFY
> And I missed it. Yet somehow I
> will find the courage to live on.

> WILLOW
> Where were you?

> BUFFY
> I was looking at the fishes.

> WILLOW
> Was it cool?

> BUFFY
> It was fishes.

> XANDER
> I'm feeling that you're not in the
> field trip spirit here.

Buffy looks briefly in the direction the pack left in.

> BUFFY
> Well, it...
>   (shrugs it off)
> It's nothing. Anyway, we did this
> every year at my old school. Zoo
> trip. Same old same old.

> XANDER
> Buffy, this is not just about
> looking at a bunch of animals.
> This is about **not being in class**.

> BUFFY
> You're right. The animals suddenly
> look shiny and new.

(CONTINUED)

> XANDER
> Perspective.

CUT TO:

2   EXT. BY THE MONKEY CAGES   2

Stands LANCE, all alone. Thin, bookish, nerdy, he looks at the monkeys and takes notes until he is approached by the pack.

> KYLE
> Lance, how's it going?

> LANCE
> (a bit nervous)
> Hey, Kyle.

> KYLE
> So is this like a family reunion?

> LANCE
> No.

> KYLE
> I think it's a family reunion.
> It's so touching. Doesn't anybody
> have a camera?

> RHONDA
> (picks at his hair)
> Does your mom still pick out your
> lice, or are you old enough to do
> it yourself?

> LANCE
> Quit it.

Tor reaches out and grabs Lance's notebook.

> LANCE
> Hey! Guys, come on.

> TOR
> (pretends to read)
> I am a total loser who will never
> have a girlfriend as long as I
> live.

> KYLE
> See, I wouldn't have put that in
> writing. I would have kept it to
> myself.

(CONTINUED)

Tor tosses the book to Heidi, who makes as if to throw it in
the cage.

                    HEIDI
          Let's see what your family thinks
          of it.

                    LANCE
          That's got all my notes!

                    MR. FLUTIE (O.S)
          What's going on here?

PRINCIPAL FLUTIE strides up to the kids. They are somewhat
cowed by him, though they glare at him sullenly.

                    MR. FLUTIE
          I have had it up to here with you
          four. What are you doing?

                    KYLE
          Nothing.

                    MR. FLUTIE
          Did I ask you to speak? Okay, I
          guess I did. But I want the truth.
          Lance?

A beat, as Lance looks around at the other kids.

                    LANCE
          They weren't doing anything.
          Really. We were just playing
          around.

A beat, as he studies the kids, who say nothing.

                    MR. FLUTIE
          All right. But this is not a place
          for horseplay. Save that sort of
          thing for class. I don't mean
          class.
                (turns to go, turns back)
          I'm watching you.

He leaves, the kids relaxing. Kyle turns to Lance with
seeming menace, points.

                    KYLE
          You. Came through big time.

                    RHONDA
          Way to go, Lance.

                                        (CONTINUED)

                              TOR
               Flutie's just looking for a reason
               to come down on us.

                              LANCE
               It's okay. Can I have my notebook
               back?

A moment -- are they going to start up again? Then:

                              HEIDI
               Sure.

                              KYLE
                    (to Lance)
               Come on. We're gonna check out the
               hyena house.

                              LANCE
               But -- I think it's off limits.

                              KYLE
               And therein lies the fun.

As they move off,

ANGLE: BUFFY, WILLOW AND XANDER

Are nearby. They see:

ANGLE: THEIR POV: LANCE AND THE PACK

Heading down a path that is marked with a sign: HYENA HOUSE.
POSITIVELY NO ADMITTANCE.

                              WILLOW
               What are Kyle and his buds doing
               with Lance?

                              XANDER
               Playing with him, as the cat plays
               with the mouse.

                              BUFFY
               What is it with those guys?

                              WILLOW
               They're obnoxious. Professionally.

                              XANDER
               Every school has 'em. Start a
               school, you get desks, some
               blackboards, and your mean kids.

                                              (CONTINUED)

                    BUFFY
          I better extract Lance before --

                    XANDER
          I'll handle it. I don't think this
          job requires actual slaying.

He heads off down the hyena path himself. Buffy and Willow
move toward it, to wait for him. Buffy looks down the path.

                    BUFFY
          You don't think we should follow?

                    WILLOW
          Kyle and those guys are jerks, but
          they're all talk.
                    (suddenly doubtful)
          Mostly.

                    BUFFY
          Why don't we --

                    WILLOW
          Yeah, why don't we --

They move for the path --

                    ZOOKEEPER
          Are you blind? Or are you just
          illiterate?

The ZOOKEEPER steps in front of them. He is 40ish,
weathered. A menacing glint in his eye.

                    ZOOKEEPER
          Because Hyenas are quick to prey on
          the weak.

                    BUFFY
          We were just --

                    ZOOKEEPER
          You're not going in there. Anyone
          that does is in a world of trouble.

The girls look down the path where Xander went.

                    WILLOW
          No, no one's going in there.

                    BUFFY
          How come it's off limits?

                                        (CONTINUED)

2   CONTINUED: 4   2

                            ZOOKEEPER
              Quarantine. They just came from
              Africa. So keep out.

The Zookeeper begins to walk away. Then turns back.

                            ZOOKEEPER
              ...Even if they call your name.

                            BUFFY
              What're you talking about?

                            ZOOKEEPER
              A Masai tribesman once told me that
              Hyenas can understand human speech.
              They follow humans by day, learning
              their names. At night, when the
              campfire has died, they call out to
              the person. And once that person
              is separated...
                      (beat; for effect)
              ...the pack devours him.

                                              CUT TO:

3   INT. HYENA HOUSE - DAY   3

It's dark and creepy in here, with cages at one end.
Nothing can be seen in them just yet. We see a door pushed
open.

The pack and Lance enter the dark space slowly, looking
around them. On the wall are lit up pictures of hyenas in
the wild. Some of them are a bit gruesome. The kids
approach the seemingly empty cage.

                            KYLE
              Cool...

                            LANCE
              I don't see any hyenas...

As if on cue, one moves ever so slightly out of the shadows.
The kids stop near the cage, watching it. Lance is made
visibly nervous.

                            LANCE
              Well, we've seen it...

                            RHONDA
              It looks cute.

                                              (CONTINUED)

3   CONTINUED: 3

                         KYLE
               It looks hungry.

He and Tor GRAB Lance from either side, the girls helping
push him toward the cage.

                         TOR
               Come on, Spot! Suppertime!

                         LANCE
               Ow! Stop it!

Lance struggles, when suddenly, XANDER pushes KYLE and pries
Lance free. Lance stumbles away from the group.

                         XANDER
               Why don't you pick on someone your
               own species?

                         KYLE
               You're gonna get in my face?

Kyle and Xander are about to fight when a shrill, horrifying
HYENA CACKLE stops everyone cold --

CAMERA PUSHES IN on the HYENA'S EYES -- they FLASH
YELLOW --, then INTERCUTS with KYLE'S EYES -- which flash
also --, the Hyena's EYES, then RHONDA'S EYES, INTERCUTTING
faster between each of them until the final exchange is
between the Hyena's and XANDER'S EYES.

HIGH ANGLE: XANDER AND THE PACK

stand inside a malevolent TOTEMIC HYENA FACE on the floor.

LANCE takes off but slips, falling and injuring his knee.

                         LANCE
               Owwwww --

They blink, then turn as one to look at Lance -- only Xander
doesn't turn his head. Then, Kyle begins a cruel laugh...
XANDER finally turns toward us. His eyes FLASH YELLOW.

                                        BLACK OUT.

                        END TEASER

ACT ONE

4 INT. BRONZE - NIGHT   4

Buffy and Willow sit in the section behind the stairs
drinking sodas. Buffy picks at a croissant, wearing Angel's
jacket. Willow cranes around for Xander.

> WILLOW
> I thought Xander would be here by
> now.

> BUFFY
> That would make him on time. We
> couldn't have that.

> WILLOW
> Did he seem upset at all on the bus
> back?

> BUFFY
> About what?

> WILLOW
> I don't know. He was quiet.

> BUFFY
> I didn't notice anything. Of
> course I'm not as hyper-aware of
> him as, oh, for example, you...

> WILLOW
> Hyper-aware?

> BUFFY
> Well, I'm not constantly monitoring
> his moods, his health, his blood
> pressure...

> WILLOW
> (wistfully)
> 130 over 80.

> BUFFY
> You got it bad, girl.

> WILLOW
> He makes my head go tingly. You
> know what I mean?

> BUFFY
> I dimly recall.

(CONTINUED)

4   CONTINUED: 4

                              WILLOW
                    But it hasn't happened to you
                    lately.

                              BUFFY
                    Not of late.

                              WILLOW
                    Not even for a dangerous and
                    mysterious older man who's leather
                    jacket you're wearing right now?

                              BUFFY
                         (dismissively)
                    It goes with the shoes.

                              WILLOW
                    Come on. You gotta admit that
                    Angel pushes some of your buttons.
                    You know he does.

                              BUFFY
                    I suppose some girls might think
                    he's good looking, if they.... have
                    eyes... All right, he's a honey.
                    But he's never around, and he only
                    wants to talk about Vampires,
                    there's nothing there that's
                    interesting in the sense of --

                              WILLOW
                    There he is!

                              BUFFY
                         (excited)
                    Angel?

                              WILLOW
                    Xander.

ANGLE: XANDER

enters and surveys the crowd. There is something different
in his step: he is more graceful, more contained. Looks
about himself warily.

He passes a good looking cheerleader type. Stares at her as
he passes -- she stares back, intrigued.

Willow frowns at that exchange. Xander reaches her and
Buffy.

                              XANDER
                    Girls.

                                                              (CONTINUED)

                         BUFFY
          Boy.

                         XANDER
                    (sitting by Buffy)
          Sorry I'm late. I forgot we were
          gonna be here.

He looks about him, his mind elsewhere. Takes Buffy's
croissant and starts eating it.

                         XANDER
          Hungry.

                         WILLOW
          Xander, you still want me to help
          you with Geometry tomorrow? We can
          work after class.

                         XANDER
                    (distracted)
          Yeah.
                    (re: croissant)
          What is this crap?

                         BUFFY
          Well it **was** my buttery croissant.

                         XANDER
          Man, I want some **food**. Birds
          live on this.

They are staring at him. He looks back, smiles winningly in
the old Xander way.

                         XANDER
          What?

                         BUFFY
          What's up with you?

                         WILLOW
          Is something wrong? Did I do
          something?

                         XANDER
          What would you ever do? That's
          crazy talk. I'm just restless.

                         WILLOW
          Well, we could go to the ice cream
          place...

                                                        (CONTINUED)

                          XANDER
                 I like it here.

He sniffs suddenly, near Buffy.

                          BUFFY
                 What is it?

                          XANDER
                 You took a bath.

                          BUFFY
                 Yeah, I often do. I'm known for
                 it.

                          XANDER
                    (shrugs)
                 That's okay.

                          BUFFY
                 And the weird behavior award goes
                 to...

But he is looking towards the door. Buffy follows his gaze,
as does Willow.

ANGLE: THE HYENA PEOPLE

enter. There is a subtle shift in their behavior, not
unlike Xander's. They stay close together, looking about
them, saying nothing. (Their dress has also begun to rhyme
with Xander's: subtle, earthy browns and grays.)

                          BUFFY
                 Oh great. It's the winged monkeys.

Then the HYENA PEOPLE lock eyes with Xander and stop. He
stares back -- but instead of the trouble we expect, they
regard Xander with an almost animal intensity, as if some
PRIMAL CONNECTION is being made.

Then, without a word exchanged, the Hyena People move on
through the parting crowd. They reach a table being manned
by a heavy kid by himself.

                          KYLE
                 I don't understand why you're
                 sitting at our table.

                          RHONDA
                 Shouldn't you be hovering over a
                 football stadium with "Goodyear"
                 written on you?

                                              (CONTINUED)

4   CONTINUED: 5   4

    The kid retreats as the pack laughs, takes the table.

    Buffy and Willow scowl -- and notice that Xander is
    chuckling to himself. He sees their looks, shrugs.

                        XANDER
                Kid's fat.

                                                        CUT TO:

A5   INT. LIBRARY - NEXT MORNING   A5*

    CLOSE ON: GILES   *

    who is holding up a fighting pad. A leg SLAMS into it.   *

    WIDER ANGLE: *

    The leg is Buffy's, and she follows the kick with an   *
    impressive fighting routine, hammering Giles with spinning   *
    kicks and jabs   *

    Buffy stops, barely even breathing hard.   *

                            GILES   *
                Well, that's enough training for   *
                one day.   *

                            BUFFY   *
                I was a little sloppy on the   *
                roundhouse. You want me to try it   *
                again?   *

                            GILES   *
                No, that's fine. You run along to   *
                class, and I'll wait for the   *
                feeling to return to my arms.   *

                                                        CUT TO: *

5   INT. SCHOOL HALLWAY - DAY   5*

    We continue the ominous feel, as CAMERA MOVES SLOWLY above
    the cold linoleum floor. We only HEAR low ANIMAL GRUNTING.
    Suddenly, a student SCREAMS. CAMERA WHIPS AROUND, RACES at

    ANGLE: TWO STUDENTS

    run for their lives. CAMERA JUKES LEFT, at

                                                        (CONTINUED)

5   CONTINUED: 5

ANGLE: PRINCIPAL FLUTIE

who screams and just leaps out of the way.

                    MR. FLUTIE
          LOOK OUT! It's gotten loose!

CAMERA ZIGZAGS down the hallway as students peer out from
classroom doorways, then jump back in shock.

                    MR. FLUTIE
          STOP THE BEAST!

A football player-type stands in front of CAMERA, defensive
tackle position, but CAMERA shoots right between his legs.

Finally, the CAMERA finds Buffy - tries to race past her,
but, she leans over fast and grabs:

ANGLE: BUFFY

holds a squirming 30-pound pink PIG, HERBERT, who has a
small plastic football helmet strapped to his head.

Attached to his snout are very fake looking paper-mache
boar's tusks. Rubber-banded to his back is an equally fake
looking ridge.

                    MR. FLUTIE
          Naughty Herbert, gave Mr. Flutie
          quite a scare, didn't he?

Students gather around Buffy.

                                              (CONTINUED)

5   CONTINUED: 5

                         MR. FLUTIE
            Students, I'd like you all to meet
            Herbert, our new mascot for the
            Sunnydale High Razorbacks!

                         BUFFY
            He's so cute!

                         MR. FLUTIE
            He's not cute. No, he's a fierce
            <u>Razorback</u>.

                         BUFFY
                 (charmed)
            He doesn't look mean...

                         MR. FLUTIE
            -- He's mean, he's ready for
            action. See, here are the tusks,
            and... a scary... razor-back...

                         BUFFY
            I'm sure he'll strike terrorinto
            the hearts of our enemies. If
            they're very tiny.

                         MR. FLUTIE
            It's all very well for you to joke,
            young lady. Where were you during
            the Buy-A-Mascot bake sale? You
            did not **bake,** nobody **baked,** we
            raised thirty eight bucks and this
            is our mascot. Middlefield High
            had one alumni fund-raiser and they
            have a Buffalo. We have Herbert.
            Deal with it.

                         BUFFY
                 (backing off)
            I'm sure he's a fine mascot and
            will engender school spirit.

                         MR. FLUTIE
            He'd better -- costs a fortune to
            feed him.
                 (to Herbert)
            Let's get you back in your cage.

Buffy moves to hand him over to Flutie -- who backs off, not
wanting to touch him. He indicates for Buffy to follow.

                         MR. FLUTIE
            This way.

                                              CUT TO:

6   EXT. SCHOOL - CONTINUOUS   6

Willow and Xander sit with their geometry books, working
together.

                    XANDER
          I'm not getting this.

There's an edge to his voice. He rubs his eyes, indicating
a headache.

                    WILLOW
          Well, it's simple, really: see,
          the bisector of a vertex is the
          line that divides the angle at that
          vertex into two equal parts.

                    XANDER
          It's like a big blur, all these
          numbers and angles...

                    WILLOW
          It's the same stuff from last week
          and you had it down then.

                    XANDER
          Why do I need to learn this?

                    WILLOW
          'Cause otherwise you'll flunk math.

                    XANDER
          Now explain the part where that's
          bad.

                    WILLOW
          You remember: you fail math, you
          flunk out of school, you end up
          being the guy at the pizza place
          that sweeps the floor and says "Hey
          kids, where's the cool parties this
          week-end?" We've been through
          this.

He is rubbing his eyes again.

                    WILLOW
          Do you have a headache?

                    XANDER
          Yeah, and I know what's causing it.

He stands, tosses his geometry book in the trash.

                                          (CONTINUED)

6   CONTINUED: 6

                         XANDER
               That's better. It goes right to
               the source of the pain.

                         WILLOW
               Xander...

                         XANDER
               Forget it, okay? I don't get it, I
               won't ever, I don't care.

He takes off. Willow calls out:

                         WILLOW
               We can finish this another time.

He doesn't respond. She watches him go, perturbed. Stands and
retrieves his book from the trash.

                         WILLOW
               Oh. Nice and wet.

                                              CUT TO:

7   INT. HALL\CLASSROOM - CONTINUOUS   7

Buffy and Flutie head for the classroom, Buffy still holding
Herbert.

                         MR. FLUTIE
               See, the problem is, you kids today
               have no school spirit. Hold on,
               let me get his outfit off.

He starts undressing Herbert as he talks, the two of them
standing near the door.

                         MR. FLUTIE
               Today it's all gangs and drugs and
               those movies on Showtime with the
               nudity.
                    (off her look)
               I don't have cable. I only heard.
                    (back to disrobing
                     Herbert)
               When I was your age, we cared about
               the school's reputation, the
               football team's record, all that
               stuff.
                         (MORE)

                                              (CONTINUED)

7   CONTINUED: 7

                                    MR. FLUTIE (cont'd)
                                (stops a moment)
                        Of course, when I was your age I
                        was surrounded by old guys telling
                        me how much better things were when
                        they were my age.

Buffy, previously bored, smiles a bit at this. Flutie heads
to the cage.

ANGLE: IN THE HALL

Xander enters, walks by the classroom.

ANGLE: BUFFY

looking down at Herbert --

                                    BUFFY
                        You're cooler than a Buffalo,
                        aren't you, Herbert?

-- and Herbert sees Xander passing by and SHRIEKS with
primal terror. Buffy barely holds onto the Pig, as Xander
walks past, unconcerned by the Pig's reaction. On her look
of concern, we hear the ominous SOUND of THUNDER, as we

                                                        CUT TO:

8   INT. HIGH SCHOOL GYM - DAY   8

We PULL BACK to see COACH HERROLD, 50's, fake Marine.

                                    COACH HERROLD
                        Alright, it's raining. Regular gym
                        activities are canceled. And you
                        know what that means...

ANGLE: COACH HERROLD HOLDS UP A DODGE BALL

right in front of his face.

                                    COACH HERROLD
                        Dodge ball. For those of you who
                        may have forgotten, the rules are
                        as follows: You dodge. Okay,
                        captains...
                                (choosing)
                        Adam... and Kyle.

                                                        CUT TO:

9   INT. SAME - A MINUTE LATER   9

The teams are shaping up. Kyle has his whole pack on his
team, ADAM has Buffy and Willow on his.

                         ADAM
               Uh... Xander.

Our girls smile, motion for Xander to join them. He looks
at them, at the other bunch.

He steps over to Kyle and his bunch instead.

                         ADAM
               Uh, okay, not Xander. Uh, Ginny.

ANGLE: BUFFY AND WILLOW

                         BUFFY
               What's that all about?

                         WILLOW
               I'm not sure...

MONTAGE of the following:

The DODGE BALLS start flying between the two teams. On one
is Buffy and Willow, on the other, Xander and the pack.

Dodge balls whiz all around Xander's team, but the Hyena
People leap over them with animal finesse. Xander easily
catches a ball, hurls it back with intensity, hitting

WILLOW in the arm. She walks to the sidelines, looking more
hurt that Xander was the one who hurled the blow.

Soon Buffy is one of the few left on her team. The Hyena
People HOLD FIRE, gather up their dodge balls.

Buffy stands alone, determined, awaiting their onslaught.
Suddenly, Xander and the Hyena People turn on LANCE, their
own teammate. They POUND Lance MERCILESSLY with DODGE
BALLS.

Lance squints, trying to protect himself until he falls,
hands over head, when

BUFFY WHIPS A DODGE BALL straight into Tor, which ricochets
into Heidi, knocking them to the ground.

ANOTHER BALL WHIPS INTO Rhonda, Kyle and Xander, knocking
the wind out of them. They're out. Buffy won. The Hyena
People glower back with a newly respectful hatred.

                                              (CONTINUED)

9   CONTINUED: 9

ANGLE: COACH HERROLD

blows his whistle.

Buffy helps up a grateful Lance but she locks eyes with
Xander -- who leaves with the Hyena People. The silence is
deafening.

ANGLE: COACH HERROLD

                    COACH HERROLD
              God, this game is brutal. I love
              it.

                                             CUT TO:

10   INT. SCHOOL HALLWAY - DAY   10

ANGLE: XANDER AND THE HYENA PEOPLE

move down the Hallway, tight now, like a Pack. Willow is
waiting, stops Xander.

                    WILLOW
              What's wrong with you, Xander?

Xander suddenly turns toward Willow -- only it's the old
Xander with the gentle eyes. He pulls her slightly away
from the Pack. Leans in, somewhat confidentially.

                    XANDER
              Guess you've noticed -- I've been
              different around you, lately --

                    WILLOW
              Yes.

Xander looks around awkwardly. Then directly into Willow.

                    XANDER
              I think... I think it's because my
              feelings... for you... have been
              changing...
                    (off Willow's look)
              We've been friends for such a long
              time... and... well... I feel like
              I need to tell you something...

Willow softens a bit.

                                          (CONTINUED)

10 CONTINUED: 10

                        XANDER
              I've... I've decided to drop
              geometry... so...

Willow just looks at Xander, confused.

                        XANDER
              I won't need your math help
              anymore... which means...
                   (for the crowd)
              I won't have to look at your pasty
              face again.

The Pack laughs hysterically. Willow looks like she's been
hit in the stomach. She internalizes the pain, walks past

ANGLE: BUFFY

who can't believe her ears. Buffy locks eyes with Xander.
He looks like he's about to say something, but --

                        BUFFY
                   (stone cold)
              Are you gonna say something to me?

Xander stares menacingly, then turns to the others.

Xander and the Hyena People turn, walk away, cackling.
Buffy turns and heads after Willow.

                                            CUT TO:

11 EXT. COURTYARD - DAY   11

Picnic tables filled with students eating lunch. In b.g. we   *
see the pack, roving.   *

ANGLE - THE PACK   *

Moving and grooving. Xander scents the air.   *

                        XANDER   *
              Dogs.   *

                        KYLE   *
              Where?   *

Kyle's head snaps in the direction Xander's looking. They   *
veer off towards the picnic tables.   *

                                            (CONTINUED)

11 CONTINUED: 11

ANGLE - A TABLE   *

Three GUYS with hot dogs. One of them bites into one as   *
another (ADAM) says: *

                          ADAM   *
               ...you're out of your mind, that's   *
               not lead guitar, that's just hunt   *
               'n peck...   *

The pack glides in, circling them. Adam spots: *

                          ADAM   *
               Hey Xander, you've seen Wretched   *
               Refuse, what do you think of the   *
               guy who plays lead?   *

Heidi grabs one of the guys' hot dogs out of his bun, Tor   *
grabs Adam's.   *

                          ADAM   *
               What are you guys...?   *

                          RHONDA   *
               Shut up.   *

                          KYLE   *
               You're sharing.   *

                          XANDER   *
               Friends <u>like</u> to share.   *

                          ADAM   *
                       (to Xander)   *
               You hanging with these guys now?   *

Heidi and Tor each take big bites of the dogs. Chew...   *
swallow. Look displeased.   *

                          XANDER   *
                    (to Heidi and Tor)   *
               Good?   *

                          TOR   *
               Too well done.   *

Heidi and Tor toss what's left of the hot dogs into the   *
dirt.   *

                          ADAM   *
               Hey, that is not cool...   *

                                                    (CONTINUED)

11   CONTINUED: 2   11

    But that's as far as Adam is willing to challenge them.   *
    Xander catches another SCENT, sniffs the air. A small smile   *
    comes to his face. He looks at the others and they move on,   *
    leaving Adam and friends staring after them.   *

    CAMERA PUSHES in on door in distance as Pack heads for it   *
    and enters.   *

                                                  CUT TO:

12   INT. CLASSROOM - DAY   12

    The empty classroom seems eerie under the HUM of its
    fluorescent lighting.

    ANGLE: THE HYENA PEOPLE AND XANDER

    enter. Heidi carefully shuts the door behind them. Their
    eyes narrow as they slowly move into the room. We HEAR a
    RUSTLING noise and their HEADS turn toward CAMERA, smiling.

                       XANDER
              Let's do lunch.

    The camera arms down to reveal HERBERT in his cage, in
    foreground.

                                    BLACK OUT.

                            END ACT ONE

<u>ACT TWO</u>

13   EXT. SCHOOL COURTYARD - AFTERNOON   13

    The Courtyard is filled with the SOUNDS of STUDENTS --
    laughing, talking, shouting.

    ANGLE: THE PACK

    walks, two in front, three behind, with the confidence of
    <u>The Wild Bunch</u>. We suddenly push into XANDER, entering
    his SENSORY WORLD.

    ANGLE: XANDER'S POV

    "HYENA VISION:" A GROUP of STUDENTS, talking. Then CAMERA
    ADJUSTS to see LANCE, walking past them, alone. As we
    follow his movement, Lance seems to move in slow-mo, until
    he almost instinctively looks back at us -- a wariness
    bordering on fear in his expression. He now walks more
    quickly, disappearing into another GROUP of STUDENTS.

    ANGLE: XANDER

    just WHIP TURNS to focus in another direction.

    ANGLE: XANDER'S POV

    We ZOOM FOCUS on TWO STUDENTS, talking together forty feet
    away. The background becomes muted as BUFFY and WILLOW'S
    movement seems to slow -- their images become more vivid,
    more saturated with COLOR. The DIN of the STUDENTS FADE,
    until we can only HEAR them talking.

    Willow has been crying.

                   WILLOW
          I've known him my whole life,
          Buffy. We haven't always been
          close, but... he's never...

                   BUFFY
          Willow, I think something is wrong
          with him.

                   WILLOW
          Or maybe something's wrong with me.

                   BUFFY
          What are you talking about?

                                   (CONTINUED)

13 CONTINUED: 13

                         WILLOW
            Come on. He's not picking on
            you. He's just sniffing you a
            lot. You know, so maybe three
            isn't company any more.

                         BUFFY
            You think this has something to do
            with me?

                         WILLOW
            Of course.

                         BUFFY
                (not getting it)
            Well that doesn't explain why he's
            hanging with the dode patrol. No,
            I think there's something going on.
            Something weird.

                         WILLOW
            What are you going to do?

                         BUFFY
            Talk to the expert on weird.

She heads off.

Xander, still watching, moves in her direction. He looks
back at the pack -- they are vaguely circling a girl eating
her lunch. Xander moves off, after Buffy.

                                     CUT TO:

14 INT. LIBRARY - DAY 14

GILES furrows his brow. Animatedly restates Buffy's
findings.

                         GILES
            Xander's taken to teasing the less
            fortunate?

                         BUFFY
            Yes.

                         GILES
             There's been a noticeable change in
            both clothing and demeanor?

                         BUFFY
            Uh-huh.

                                 (CONTINUED)

                              GILES
            And otherwise all his spare time,
            spent lounging about with
            imbeciles?

                              BUFFY
            It's bad?

                              GILES
            It's devastating. He's turned into
            a 16 year old boy!

Buffy shakes her head. Back to Square one.

                              GILES
            Of course, you'll have to kill him.

                              BUFFY
            Giles I'm serious.

                              GILES
            So am I, except for the part about
            killing him. Testosterone is the
            great equalizer; it turns all men
            into morons. He will, however, get
            over it.

                              BUFFY
            I can't believe you of all people
            are gonna Scully me. There's
            something supernatural at work.
            Get your books! Look stuff up!

                              GILES
            Look under what?

                              BUFFY
            I don't know! That's your
            department.

                              GILES
            But the evidence you present is --

                              BUFFY
                    (very excited)
            He scared the pig!

Giles is not nearly as impressed with that as Buffy hoped.
She deflates slightly.

                              BUFFY
            Well, he did...

                                                    (CONTINUED)

                         GILES
          Buffy, boys can be cruel. They
          tease, they prey on the weak, it's
          just natural teen --

                         BUFFY
          What did you say?

                         GILES
          Uh, what? They tease...

                         BUFFY
                (it's coming to her)
          They prey on the weak. Xander
          started acting wiggy after the Zoo.
          He and Kyle and those guys went
          into the hyena cage...
                (remembering)
          God, that laugh...

                         GILES
          Are you saying Xander's become a
          hyena?

                         BUFFY
          Or been, I don't know, possessed by
          one. Not just him, all of them.

                         GILES
          Well, I've certainly never heard --

ANGLE: WILLOW

bursts through the door, breathless.

                         WILLOW
          Herbert -- they found him!

                         BUFFY
          Herbert -- the Pig?

                         WILLOW
          Dead -- and also... eaten!
          Principal Flutie's freaking out.

                         GILES
          Eaten... by what?

                         WILLOW
                (ominous)
          By "whom"...

An ominous beat, as the meaning sinks in.

                                        (CONTINUED)

14 CONTINUED: 3   14

                          BUFFY
                        (to Giles)
                  Testosterone, huh?

Giles looks a bit sheepish. He starts for his office.

                          WILLOW
                  What are you gonna do?

                          GILES
                  Get my books. Look stuff up.

                                              CUT TO:

15   EXT. COURTYARD - DAY   15

Students are leaving as the LAST BELL RINGS. THE PACK is
still in the courtyard, minus Xander. They wander past a
couple of girls.

Tor brushes up against one -- she moves away -- and Heidi
HISSES at her, Tor is taken.

Flutie steps in front of them.

                          MR. FLUTIE
                  You four!

                          KYLE
                  What?

                          MR. FLUTIE
                  Oh, don't think I don't know.
                  Three kids saw you outside
                  Herbert's room. You're busted.
                  Yeah. You're going down.

                          RHONDA
                  How **is** Herbert?

                          HEIDI
                  Crunchy.

                          MR. FLUTIE
                  That's it. My office, right now.
                  Now!

They hesitate, but then Kyle obeys, leading the way. Very
calm, almost contented.

                                              (CONTINUED)

15 CONTINUED: 15

                          MR. FLUTIE
                You're gonna have so much detention
                your grandchildren'll be staying
                after school.

And he follows them to his office.

                                              CUT TO:

16 INT. THE LIBRARY - DAY   16

ANGLE: A PHOTOGRAPH

of a Pack of Hyenas, CACKLING at the Moon. CAMERA PULLS
BACK to see Buffy and Willow, surrounded by books and empty
Diet Slice cans. Buffy turns the page of the antique BOOK.

                          BUFFY   *
                Check this out -- Hyenas.   *
                     (reads as Willow skims   *
                      the text)   *
                Wow. Apparently, Noah rejected   *
                Hyenas from the Ark because he   *
                thought they were an evil, impure   *
                mixture of dogs and cats.   *

                          WILLOW
                Hyenas aren't well liked.

                          BUFFY
                They do seem to be the shmoes of
                the animal kingdom.

                          WILLOW
                Why couldn't Xander be possessed by
                a puppy? Or some ducks...

                          BUFFY
                That's assuming possession is the
                right word.

                          GILES
                     (emerging with book)
                Oh, I'd say it is. The Masai of
                the Serengeti have spoken of animal
                possession for generations. I
                should have remembered that.

                                              (CONTINUED)

                         WILLOW
              Didn't that Zookeeper mention the
              Masai? They said hyenas call your
              name and all that stuff?

                         BUFFY
              Right.
                   (to Giles)
              So, how does it work?

                         GILES
              Well, apparently there's a sect of
              animal worshipers, they're known as
              Primals. They're found mostly in
              northern Africa and they date back
              to...
                   (off their looks)
              No history lesson, sorry. They
              believe that humanity --
              consciousness, the soul -- is a
              perversion, a dilution of spirit.
              The animal state is holy to them.
              They were able, through
              trans-possession, to pull the
              spirit of certain animals into
              themselves.

                         BUFFY
              So they start acting like hyenas.

                         GILES
              Only the most predatory animals
              were of interest to the Primals.
              So that would fit.

                         BUFFY
              So what happens to the person once
              the spirit is in them?

                         GILES
              If it's left unchecked?

He hesitates, then slides his volume across the table at
them. Buffy looks down at it.

                         BUFFY
              I'm gonna find Xander.

She starts out.

                         GILES
              I would check the mascot's cage
              first. It might help you to know
              how far this has gone.

                                            (CONTINUED)

16   CONTINUED: 2   16

                              BUFFY
                    Right.

And she's out.

ANGLE: THE BOOK

bears an engraving of a group of people madly, hungrily
feeding. Off each other.

                                                    CUT TO:

17   INT. CLASSROOM - A MINUTE LATER   17

Buffy enters, quietly. It's a bit dark in here and she
doesn't bother with the light. She looks to make sure
nobody saw her enter and heads for the cage.

The bars have been bent, the lock torn right off.

                              BUFFY
                         (to herself)
                    So strong...

The cage is empty and she looks about her for evidence.
Something CRUNCHES under her foot. She looks down,
hesitantly.

Pig bones.

She straightens up -- and **Xander is right behind her.** She
gasps, moves away.

                              BUFFY
                    Xander...

                                                    CUT TO:

18   INT. FLUTIE'S OFFICE - CONTINUOUS   18

The four are standing vaguely around Flutie as he lectures
them. They don't seem terribly concerned.

                           MR. FLUTIE
                    I have seen some sick things in my
                    time, believe me, but this is
                    beyond the pale. What is it with
                    you people? Is it drugs? How
                    could you -- a poor defenseless pig
                    -- What are you doing?

They have started to circle him.

                                                    CUT TO:

19 INT. CLASSROOM - CONTINUOUS   19

Buffy stares at Xander, not sure what to do. He says
nothing, just grins at her. She makes a feint for the
door -- he does too. She's not going anywhere. She relaxes
--

                    BUFFY
          This is ridiculous. We have to
          talk --

-- and DIVES at him, takes him to the ground. It doesn't
seem to bother him much.

                    XANDER
          I've been waiting for you to jump
          my bones.

                                             CUT TO:

20 INT. FLUTIE'S OFFICE - CONTINUOUS   20

They are circling him, GROWLING. He is becoming somewhat
less sure of his authority here.

                    MR. FLUTIE
          Now, stop that, you're only gonna
          make things worse for yourselves.

Tor GROWLS, low.

                    MR. FLUTIE
          Okay, I tell you how this is going
          to work. I'm going to call your
          parents and they are going to take
          you all home.

He goes for the phone -- Tor is there ahead of him, slams
his hand down on top of it. Flutie tries to stare him down.
Tor picks the phone up and hands it to him.

                    MR. FLUTIE
          Thank you.

He moves to dial --

ANGLE: RHONDA

has the phone cord in her mouth. She jerks her head,
ripping it out of the wall. The line goes dead on Flutie.

                    RHONDA
          Sorry.

                                        (CONTINUED)

20 CONTINUED: 20

                              MR. FLUTIE
                    That is it.

He heads for the door - -and Kyle barks viciously at him.
Flutie backs up in genuine fear.

                                                          CUT TO:

21 INT. CLASSROOM - CONTINUOUS   21

Xander suddenly ROLLS, throwing Buffy down -- now he's on
top of her.

She is surprised to find his strength matches her own.

                              BUFFY
                    Get off me!

                              XANDER
                    Is that what you really want? We
                    both know what you really want.

She tries to get up -- he doesn't budge.

                              XANDER
                    You want danger, don't you -- you
                    like your men dangerous --

                              BUFFY
                    You're in trouble -- infected with
                    some Hyena thing, like a demonic
                    possession --

                              XANDER
                    -- Dangerous and mean, right?
                    Like Angel, your Mystery Guy --
                    Well, guess who just got mean --

                                                          CUT TO:

22 INT. FLUTIE'S OFFICE - CONTINUOUS   22

Flutie's really sweating now, trying to be firm -- or
nice -- or anything that will get him out of this office.

                              MR. FLUTIE
                    You're about this close to
                    expulsion, people. But I'm willing
                    to talk to the school counselor,
                    and we can discuss options --

Tor jumps up on Flutie's desk.

                                                          (CONTINUED)

22 CONTINUED: 22

                              MR. FLUTIE
                    Get down from there this instant --

Rhonda suddenly SWIPES at him with her hand. He reels, and
comes back up slowly, hand to his cheek. Four deep cuts
beginning to bleed. Real fear in his eyes.

                              MR. FLUTIE
                    Are you insane?

                                                          CUT TO:

23 INT. CLASSROOM - CONTINUOUS   23

                              BUFFY
                    You're sick, okay? That's all.

                              XANDER
                    -- You know how long I've waited?
                    Until you'd stop pretending we
                    aren't attracted --

Buffy rolls away and jumps to her feet. He follows her.

                              XANDER
                    Until Willow'd stop kidding
                    herself, that I'd settle for anyone
                    but you --

                              BUFFY
                    I don't wanna hurt you, Xander...

Xander suddenly PUSHES her against the wall, pinning her.
Sniffs the air.

                              XANDER
                    That make you wanna hurt me?
                    C'mon, Slayer -- I like it when
                    you're scared --

-- coming in close --

                              XANDER
                    -- The more I scare you, the better
                    you smell.

Xander roughly grabs Buffy's jaw. Begins kissing her,
biting her lips --

She pushes him away -- but he comes back, pinning her
again. In closer.

                                                        (CONTINUED)

23 CONTINUED: 23

                              XANDER
                             (soft)
                    Welcome to the jungle.

                                                    CUT TO:

24 INT. FLUTIE'S OFFICE - CONTINUOUS   24

As with a TERRIBLE ROAR Tor LEAPS from the desk, taking
Flutie to the ground. Flutie's SCREAMS are shrill and short
as the others descend upon him.

ANGLE: FROM BEHIND THE DESK

Four figures hunch over the floor, as we hear the SOUND of
FEEDING. Camera moves down, rack focusing to a shot of a
picture of a smiling Flutie in front of the school.

                                                    BLACK OUT.

                         END ACT TWO

<u>ACT THREE</u>

25 INT. THE LIBRARY - THAT NIGHT   25

ANGLE: COMPUTER SCREEN

We see vid footage of Hyenas in the wild, horribly ripping
apart a wildebeest.

Willow watches, frightened and riveted.

ANGLE: THE LIBRARY DOORS

slam open. Buffy enters, dragging an unconscious Xander.

                    BUFFY
          Hurry -- we've gotta lock him up
          somehow, before he comes to.

Willow turns off the video she's been studying.

                    WILLOW
          Ohmigod, Xander -- what happened?

                    BUFFY
          I hit him.

                    WILLOW
          With what?

                    BUFFY
          A desk. He was trying his hand at
          felony sexual assault.

Buffy HEAVES Xander into a steel-mesh book-return cage. She
SLAMS the door.

                    WILLOW
          Oh Buffy, the Hyena in him
          didn't --

                    BUFFY
          No, but it's safe to say that in
          his animal state, his idea of
          wooing somebody doesn't include a
          Yanni CD and a bottle of Chianti.

She locks the door and puts the keys on the table.

                    BUFFY
          That should hold him. Where's
          Giles?

                                              (CONTINUED)

                         WILLOW
          There was some teacher's meeting he
          got called to. What are we going
          to do? I mean, how do we get
          Xander back?

                         BUFFY
          Right now I'm worried about what
          the rest of the pack are up to.

                         GILES
               (entering from hall)
          The rest of the pack were spotted
          outside Herbert the mascot's cage.
          They were sent to the principal's
          office.

                         WILLOW
          Good. That'll show 'em.
               (suddenly doubtful)
          Did it show 'em?

                         BUFFY
               (sensing bad news)
          They didn't hurt him?

                         GILES
          They ate him.

The girls are genuinely shocked and horrified. After a beat:

                         BUFFY
               (small voice)
          They ate principal Flutie?

                         WILLOW
          Ate him up?

                         GILES
          The official theory is that wild
          dogs got into his office somehow.
          There was no one at the scene.

                         WILLOW
               (to Buffy)
          But Xander didn't -- I mean, he was
          with you.

Giles notices the prone form in the book cage for the first
time.

                         GILES
          Oh. Well, that's a small mercy.

                                              (CONTINUED)

                         BUFFY
          Giles, how do we stop this? How do
          you trans-possess some one?

                         GILES
          I'm afraid I still don't have all
          the pieces. Accounts of the
          Primals and their methods are
          sketchy. There's talk of a
          predatory act, but the exact ritual
          is... The Malleus Maleficarum deals
          with the particulars of **demonic**
          possession, which may apply...

He leafs through it.

                         GILES
          Yes, one should be able to transfer
          the spirits to another human --

                         BUFFY
          Oh yeah, any volunteers?

                         GILES
          Good point.

                         BUFFY
          What we need to do is put the Hyena
          back in the Hyena.

                         GILES
          But, until we know more --

                         BUFFY
          I'm betting that zookeeper can hep
          fill in the blanks. Maybe he
          didn't quarantine those hyenas
          'cause they were **sick.**

                         GILES
          All right, we should talk to him.

                         BUFFY
          Well, one of us has to watch
          Xander.

                         WILLOW
          I will.

                         BUFFY
          Are you sure? If he wakes up --

                         WILLOW
          I'll be all right. Go.

(CONTINUED)

25   CONTINUED: 3   25

                              BUFFY
                           (to Giles)
                    Come on.

They head out. Willow watches them, then looks at Xander in
the cage. She takes the keys from the table, holds them
tight.

                                                    CUT TO:

26   EXT. WOODS - NIGHT   26

A young woman, 25, walks through the Woods, whistling a
happy tune. Suddenly, she stops. Then she sees the four
sleeping hyena people lying on the ground, curled up in a
semi-circle, holding their full stomachs. The woman,
suspicious, looks closer.

ANGLE: HER POV

Rhonda has blood smeared on her mouth and clothes. Kyle
cradles a freshly gnawed femur. Kyle sniffs the air... his
eyes open...

ANGLE: KYLE'S POV -- HYENA VISION

The woman turns to vivid colors against the gray, flat
background. We HEAR her HEART POUNDING... and then, a
SECOND, smaller HEART POUNDS as she cautiously backs up.

The woman, horrified, turns suddenly away from CAMERA,
revealing a sleeping baby in her backpack.

Kyle licks his lips, slowly rolls onto his front arms.

The baby now wakes with a primitive fear. Begins to CRY.
The woman desperately "SHSHSHSH'S" her child and walks
faster.

Rhonda hears this and SNARLS as the other Hyena People begin
to wake and roll onto their front arms.

ANGLE: EHONDA'S POV -- HYENA VISION

CAMERA RISES slowly, creeping toward the Woman and her Baby.
We HEAR the HEART BEATS as CAMERA CREEPS faster, faster,   *
through the woods and toward the woman, until suddenly   *

CAMERA STOPS MOVING. The woman RACES up the trail,   *
looking back to see   *

                                                    (CONTINUED)

CONTINUED: 26

-- the pack.   Watching, losing interest.

                                                  CUT TO:

27 INT. THE LIBRARY - NIGHT   27

Willow watches another VIDEO, at once fascinated and
frightened. Then she HEARS:

                    XANDER
          Willow...

ANGLE: THE CAGE

where Xander now sits up, rubbing his head. Willow turns to
him.

                    WILLOW
          How do you feel?

                    XANDER
          Like somebody hit me with a desk.
          What am I doing in here?

                    WILLOW
          You're... resting.

                    XANDER
          You guys got me locked up now?

                    WILLOW
          'Cause you're sick. Buffy said --

                    XANDER
          Yeah, I'm sure. Buffy had her
          all-purpose solution: Punch 'em
          out, knock 'em down. Love to see
          what she'd do to someone who was
          really sick.

                    WILLOW
          That's not fair. Buffy's saved
          both our lives.

                    XANDER
          And before she showed up, our lives
          didn't need all that much saving,
          did they? Weren't things a lot
          simpler when it was just you and
          me?

He's drawing her in -- literally, as she moves hesitantly
forward, eyes locked on his.

                                                  (CONTINUED)

                         WILLOW
              Maybe...

                         XANDER
              When we were alone together...
              Willow, I know there's something
              wrong with me. I think it's
              getting worse. I don't want to
              stand around waiting for Buffy to
              decide it's time to punch me out
              again. I want **you** to help me. I
              want you.

She is nearing the cage, seemingly uncertain.

                         WILLOW
              I **am** helping you...

                         XANDER
              You're doing what you're told.

                         WILLOW
              Buffy's trying to help you too.
              you know that. Or, Xander does.

                         XANDER
              Right, she's so selfless, always
              thinking of us. If I'm so
              dangerous, how come she left you
              alone with me?

                         WILLOW
              Because I told her to.

                         XANDER
              Why?

                         WILLOW
              Because I know you better than she
              does. And I wanted to be here to
              see if you were still you.

                         XANDER
              You know I am. Look at me.

                         WILLOW
              Xander...

                         XANDER
              Look.

She is right outside the cage now. There is a moment of
tension between them as they stare at each other..

                                        (CONTINUED)

CONTINUED: 2

Xander's hand SHOOTS out the mail slot, grabbing for the keys. But Willow steps back readily, out of reach. She was expecting this.

>   WILLOW
>   Now I know.

Xander SLAMS his hand against the cage in frustration, GROWLING.

>   XANDER
>   Let me out! **Let me out!**

He bangs the cage, shakes it.

>   CUT TO:

28   INT. ZOOKEEPER'S OFFICE - NIGHT   28

Buffy and Giles urgently pace, look at their watches, as the Zookeeper sits. He looks like someone punched him in the stomach.

>   ZOOKEEPER
>   The students have been possessed by
>   the Hyenas.

>   GILES
>   Yes.

>   ZOOKEEPER
>   Are you sure?

>   BUFFY
>   We're really, really sure.

>   GILES
>   You don't seem very surprised.

>   ZOOKEEPER
>   The Zoo imported those Hyenas from
>   Africa. There was something
>   strange about them from day one, so
>   I did some homework. This
>   particular breed is very rare.
>   Totally vicious. Historically they
>   were worshipped by these guys --

>   GILES
>   The Primals.

>   (CONTINUED)

                         ZOOKEEPER
                     (nodding)
          Creepy guys. They had rituals for
          taking the hyenas spirits, but I
          don't see how that could have
          happened to your kids.

                         GILES
          We don't know how the ritual works.
          We know it involves a predatory act
          and some kind of symbol.

                         ZOOKEEPER
          A predatory act. Of course. That
          makes sense. Where did you read
          that?

                         GILES
          Do you have Sherman Jeffries work
          on cults and --

                         BUFFY
          Boys!

                         GILES
          Sorry.

                         ZOOKEEPER
          Look, I think together we may
          enough information to pull off a
          reverse trans-possession.

                         BUFFY
          How's about we make it quick?

                         ZOOKEEPER
          We'd better. By my calculations,
          in the next several hours, the
          possessed students will be totally
          transformed by the Hyena Spirits.
          Once that occurs, the students can
          never return to normal.

                         BUFFY
                     (horrified)
          No more Xander...

Buffy and Giles exchange an urgent glance.

                                                    (CONTINUED)

                         ZOOKEEPER
                    (a plan)
               You must get the possessed students
               to the Hyena Cage immediately --
               I'll meet you there and we can
               begin the ritual --
                    (off Buffy and Giles)
               Oh no -- what?

                         BUFFY
               Well, we can guarantee you one --
               but there's four more and we don't
               know where they are.

                         ZOOKEEPER
               I wouldn't worry about that. Once
               the hyenas feed and rest, they'll
               search for the missing member of
               their pack. They won't rest till
               they find him. They should come
               right to you.

          Giles and Buffy look at one another, horrified.

                         BUFFY
               Willow!

                                                           CUT TO:

29   INT. THE LIBRARY - NIGHT   29

          We HEAR the ferocious WHOO-WHOOPS, spine-chilling ROARS and
          the TEARING and SLURPING sounds of a slow, horrible death.
          CAMERA PULLS BACK to see Willow, steeling her resolve by
          watching another Nature Video of Hyenas attacking animals.

          Xander is in the cage, pacing back and forth (like an
          animal, duh).

                         XANDER
               Willow...

                         WILLOW
               I'm not listening...

          Willow looks up nervously.

          ANGLE: WILLOW'S POV

          The LIBRARY WINDOWS are still.

          Willow watches them a moment. Then her eyes return to the
          Video.

                                                           (CONTINUED)

29 CONTINUED: 29

But CAMERA DRIFTS back up to the windows behind Willow.
Then CAMERA ADJUSTS to SEE KYLE'S LEERING GRIN.

                          KYLE (O.S.)
              Wil-lowww... Wil-lowww...

                                              BLACK OUT.

                          END ACT THREE

ACT FOUR

30 INT. THE LIBRARY - NIGHT   30

Willow watches her tape.

                    KYLE (O.S.)
          Wil-lowwww... Wil-lowww...

                    WILLOW
          Xander, shut up...

She looks at him. He stares back at her as we hear:

                    KYLE (O.S.)
          Wil-lowww... Wil-lowww...

Willow realizes Xander's not the one calling her. Too late.
Horrified, she turns to see

THE PACK staring through the LIBRARY WINDOWS. Then a CRASH
behind her. She turns back to see

THE CAGE DOOR being kicked by Xander -- he's given up all
pretense now.

THE LIBRARY WINDOWS crash open as the HYENA PEOPLE suddenly
lunge through the open windows.

Willow BOLTS from the room, running out the double doors as
the Hyena people converge near the cage. Xander kicks --
the door buckles -- then Kyle and Rhonda PULL it, RIPPING it
open. Xander comes out, briefly nuzzling Rhonda.

He turns, looks where Willow went. There is no softness in
his eyes.

                                        CUT TO:

31 INT. HALL - MOMENTS LATER   31

The pack exits the library. They look at each other -- then
split up, looking quietly for Willow. Xander and Heidi go
forward, the others pairing off as well.

                                        CUT TO:

32 INT. CLASSROOM - CONTINUOUS   32

Willow crouches behind a desk, opposite the door to the
darkened classroom. She is silent, terrified.

                                        CUT TO:

33   INT. HALL - CONTINUOUS   33

Xander stops, sniffs. Turns to the door.

                                                          CUT TO:

34   INT. CLASSROOM\HALL - CONTINUOUS   34

Willow still hides, waiting .... And the door opens, Xander
and Heidi stepping in. They sniff the room, take a few
steps in, then look at each other. Turn to go, Heidi
exiting first.

ANGLE: WILLOW

Hears the DOOR SHUT after them. Tentatively starts out from
behind the desk.

Xander is leering at her, his face inches from hers.

She SCREAMS and jumps back as he swipes at her -- she runs
for the door, he's hard at her heels -- she hurls a desk in
his way, trips him up -- She flings the door open --

Heidi is standing right there.

Then a fire extinguisher comes down on Heidi's head and she
drops, Buffy right behind her.

                         BUFFY
             Come on!

Willow runs out -- and Xander is on her heels, grabbing her
hair, snarling --

Buffy grabs Xander and THROWS him to the ground.

The other hyenas arrive, racing around the corner.

Giles herds Willow into the class, Buffy behind, and they
SLAM the door shut. Buffy barricades it instantly.

The Hyena People POUND on it a couple of times, then they
can be HEARD departing.

                         BUFFY
             They're going.

                         WILLOW
             They could be faking it.

                                                     (CONTINUED)

34 CONTINUED: 34

                              BUFFY
                    No, they're hungry. They'll be
                    looking for somebody weak.
                         (to Willow)
                    I'm sorry. I didn't know they'd
                    come after Xander.

                              WILLOW
                    It's okay.

                              GILES
                    We've got to lead them back to the
                    Zoo if we're to stop this.

                              BUFFY
                    Yeah, and before their next meal.
                    That's my job.

                              GILES
                    Individually they nearly match you
                    in strength. As a group...

                              BUFFY
                    They're tough. But I think they're
                    getting stupider.

          She undoes the barricade, opens the door.

                              GILES
                    I should come with you.

                              BUFFY
                    You can't keep up.

35 EXT. DRIVEWAY - NIGHT   35

          A FAMILY CAR sits in the darkness. A FAMILY of three (the   *
          ANDERSONS) is getting in the car. The kids are eating
          twinkies.

                                               CUT TO:

36 INT. CAR - NIGHT   36*

                              MR. ANDERSON
                    I didn't say she looked better than
                    you, I said she looked better.

                                               (CONTINUED)

36 CONTINUED: 36

                              MRS. ANDERSON
                    I heard what I heard.
                              (to her son)
                    Joey, chew. You have to chew or
                    you'll choke.

                              MR. ANDERSON
                    I don't see why we have to have
                    this conversation every time we see
                    them.

                              MRS. ANDERSON
                    I didn't start it.

                              MR. ANDERSON
                    Damn. Where are the keys?

                              RHONDA (O.S.)
                    Joe-yyy... Joe-yyy...

Joey turns to see:

ANGLE: JOEY'S POV

KYLE leers at him, upside down, outside his window.

                              KYLE
                    Joey...

Suddenly, the car ROCKS violently as the horrified family
sees Tor and Heidi jump on their hood.

Then, the WINDSHIELD SHATTERS! Xander reaches in to grab
the shrieking family.

Xander grabs Joey. The NOISE is DEAFENING --

ANGLE: BUFFY

running across the parking lot and VAULTING onto the car,
KICKING Kyle to the ground, hard. Xander stops, looks up.

LOW ANGLE: XANDER'S POV

BUFFY stands on the car, amongst the Hyena People.

                              BUFFY
                    Didn't your Mom teach you? Don't
                    play with your food.

ANGLE: XANDER

doesn't have a snappy comeback. The possession of the Hyena
people has now reduced them to snarls and growls.

                                                      (CONTINUED)

36   CONTINUED: 2   36

                              BUFFY
                  Come on. You know what you want.

Xander just bears his teeth and lunges at her. But Buffy
runs, taunting them.

Without hesitation, Xander forgets the Family and moves
after Buffy. The Hyena People follow.

                                                        CUT TO:

37   EXT. THE ZOO - NIGHT   37

A DARK FORM, obscured by shadows, walks through it. A
FLASHLIGHT clicks on under a darkened face. It's WILLOW,
Giles right behind her. Her heart pounds anxiously as she
lowers the flashlight. Her eyes strain to search the empty
Zoo.

Finally, Willow sees something and nods for Giles to follow
her. CAMERA CREEPS with them...   *

ANGLE: A SIGN: <u>HYENA CAGE. POSITIVELY NO ADMITTANCE</u>.

                              WILLOW
                  The pathway to the Hyena Pit.

Giles' eyes warily study the ominous pathway that dissolves
into the blackness beyond. He swallows, summoning courage.

                              GILES
                  I'll go in and prepare the
                  Zookeeper. Willow, stay here --
                  you'll forewarn us when Buffy and
                  the others approach.

Another ANIMAL SHRIEKS. Willow watches Giles take another
deep breath and disappear down the pathway.

                                                        CUT TO:

38   EXT. NIGHT   38

HAND HELD CAMERA CHASES BUFFY through the Woods, toward the
Zoo. Surreal moonlight illuminates the rising mist as the
CAMERA gains on her...

We HEAR her HEART PUMPING frantically.

THE HYENA PEOPLE run with animal intensity. They can't
speak -- only GROWL and CACKLE, as they close in on Buffy.

                                                        CUT TO:

39 INT. HYENA HOUSE - MOMENTS LATER   39

Giles walks in, his heart pounding.

> GILES
> (whispering)
> Dr... Zookeeper -- are you here?

Giles HEARS a NOISE inside the cage and turns quickly to see

ANGLE: THE ZOOKEEPER

his face covered with ELECTRIC BLUE BODY PAINT, with inch   *
thick WHITE CIRCLES around his mouth and eyes, emerges from
the cage's splintered shadows.

ANGLE: GILES

heaves a relieved sigh. Then, one scholar to another:

> GILES
> Of course -- you're in the
> ceremonial Masai costume --
> (turning)
> Are you otherwise ready for the
> trans-possession?

> ZOOKEEPER
> Almost.

Giles looks down at the symbol painted on the floor.

> GILES
> Right. The sacred circle. You'd
> need that to
> (stops, puzzled)
> But then it must have been here
> when the children first came. Why
> would you...

He stands, slowly turning. Faces the Zookeeper.

> GILES
> It must have been terribly
> frustrating, having a bunch of
> school children accomplish what you
> could not.

> ZOOKEEPER
> (all pretense gone)
> It bothered me. But the power will
> be mine.

Giles tries to bolt to the left but the Zookeeper is
surprisingly swift --

(CONTINUED)

39 CONTINUED: 39

ANGLE: A WOODEN CLUB

SLAMS down on Giles' head. Giles falls to the ground and the Zookeeper pulls his prone body back into the mist.

CUT TO:

40 EXT. HYENA CAGE - LATER 40

Willow's eyes anxiously scan the surrounding area. Then she HEARS the SOUNDS of CACKLING and GROWLING -- getting nearer. She turns and runs up the pathway, toward the Hyena Cage.

CUT TO:

41 INT. HYENA CAGE - MOMENTS LATER 41

Willow runs into the walkway, through the swirling fog.

> WILLOW
> They're almost here!
> (then)
> Giles... Giles?...

Only the silence. As she walks toward the cage, she sees

ANGLE: AN ORANGE GLOW

flickering, eerie. CAMERA CREEPS, LOW ANGLE, toward the orange glow... CAMERA CONTINUES through the open cage door... into the cage, where the two Hyena had been in the Teaser... the GLOW intensifies... until we see it's a cluster of candles -- a flickering altar arranged around

ANGLE: THE ZOOKEEPER

CHANTS, back to CAMERA. He turns around.

Willow SCREAMS.

> ZOOKEEPER
> Don't scream.
> (re: body paint)
> It's all part of the Masai
> tradition.

Willow looks around the empty cage.

> WILLOW
> Where are the Hyenas for the
> trans-possession?

(CONTINUED)

41 CONTINUED: 41

                        ZOOKEEPER
              Over there, in the feeding area.

Willow turns to see

ANGLE: A LOW WALL

just outside the glowing altar. We can HEAR HYENAS pacing
and growling.

She moves to the wall, but the Zookeeper suddenly pulls her
back.

                        ZOOKEEPER
              Stay clear. They haven't been fed.

                        WILLOW
                   (looking around)
              Where's Giles?

                        ZOOKEEPER
              He's lying in wait.

Outside in the distance, we HEAR the CACKLING and GROWLING
of the Hyena People, chasing Buffy... getting nearer.

                        WILLOW
              They're almost here... shouldn't
              you bring the Hyenas out?

                        ZOOKEEPER
              When the time is right.

He kneels down at a ring in the floor, attaches a leather
strap to it.

                        ZOOKEEPER
              I'm gonna need your help.

CAMERA RISES and we realize they are standing in the

HIGH ANGLE: TOTEMIC PRIMITIVE HYENA FACE

we saw in the Teaser. Suddenly, we HEAR the ferocious
WHO-WOOPING and CACKLING of angry animals scratching their
way along the pathway, toward the cage.

                        BUFFY (O.S.)
              THEY'RE RIGHT... BEHIND ME!

                        WILLOW
              That's Buffy! Get ready!

                                              (CONTINUED)

                          ZOOKEEPER
                Here.

The Zookeeper positions Willow. He loops a leather strap
around her wrists, pulls it taut. She stands, shackled.

                          WILLOW
                What is this?

                          ZOOKEEPER
                The predatory act, remember?

He produces a huge knife.

                          WILLOW
                    (uncertain)
                Oh, right -- you'll pretend to
                slash my throat and put The Evil
                in the Hyenas behind the wall --

                          ZOOKEEPER
                Something like that.

The Zookeeper presses the knife to her throat. Willow's
dreadful realization sinks in.

ANGLE: BUFFY

enters the caged area, exhausted.

                          WILLOW
                BUFFY! IT'S A TRAP!

Buffy sees Willow held at knife point. Jumps up to help her
just as XANDER dives on top of Buffy, knocking her to the
ground.

ANGLE: XANDER'S FACE

at its most Hyena-like, lunges downward --

ANGLE: THE HYENA PEOPLE

race into the Hyena Cage and lunge for Buffy -- their MOUTHS
and HANDS begin tearing greedily.

ANGLE: THE ZOOKEEPER

holds a horrified Willow, knife denting the skin of her
throat.

                          ZOOKEEPER
                    (incanting)
                NYUMBA YA SANAA!

                                                    (CONTINUED)

ANGLE: THE HYENA PEOPLE

STOP. Look up from Buffy's body to meet the Zookeeper's
electric eyes.

CAMERA PUSHES in on KYLE'S EYES, then the ZOOKEEPER'S EYES,
then RHONDA'S EYES, then the ZOOKEEPER'S, CROSS-CUTTING
between ALL THE HYENA PEOPLE'S EYES, finally XANDER'S ...
until the Zookeeper suddenly CACKLES wildly.

ANGLE: THE ZOOKEEPER'S GLOWING YELLOW EYES (CGI)

infused with six demonic hyena spirits, lets the knife
clatter to the ground and GRABS Willow's hair with one hand,
her arm with his other, just about to rip into her when

ANGLE: XANDER

eyes alive with protective fury.

                    XANDER
          WILLOW!

He leaps up from the ground and DIVES on the Zookeeper,
jarring Willow loose. Willow struggles to free herself as
the Zookeeper quickly regroups, picks up Xander and SLAMS
him hard on the ground. He moves into Xander for the final
blow, when

BUFFY CHARGES and JUMPS to deliver a two-footed flying
drop-kick.

ANGLE: THE ZOOKEEPER

CATCHES Buffy's feet in mid-air and THROWS her backwards.

ANGLE: BUFFY

lands in a heap, the wind knocked out of her, directly in
front of the INTERNAL WALL which contains the Hyenas. We
can HEAR their hungry GROWLING behind the wall.

ANGLE: THE PACK OF KIDS

Are dazed and confused, cowering uselessly by the far wall.

ANGLE: THE ZOOKEEPER

HOWLING with the ferocity of an angry animal, CHARGES at
Buffy --

                                              (CONTINUED)

41   CONTINUED: 4   41

    ANGLE: ZOOKEEPER'S POV - HYENA VISION

    CAMERA RUSHES BUFFY as we HEAR her amplified HEART BEATS.
    She desperately looks around, her back to the wall.

    Suddenly, Buffy drops from FRAME.

    ANGLE: BUFFY

    grabs both of the Zookeeper's legs at the knees, then lifts
    and HEAVES him up and over the INSIDE WALL containing the
    real Hyenas. We HEAR the real HYENAS CACKLING and WHOOPING
    behind the wall, clawing on the Zookeeper's legs.

    ANGLE: THE ZOOKEEPER'S HORRIFIED FACE

    appears just above the wall -- barely pulling himself up.

    Buffy instinctively reaches out to help him, when we HEAR a
    spine-chilling ROAR and the Zookeeper's YANKED, WHIP-FAST
    below the wall, out of sight.

    ANGLE: BUFFY, XANDER and WILLOW

    react as they listen to the horrible chewing, crunching,
    slurping SOUNDS of the Hyena at feeding time. Then they
    HEAR another NOISE.

    ANGLE: THEIR POV

    Giles, rubbing his head as he approaches from the walkway.

                    GILES
            Did I miss anything?

                                                        CUT TO:

42   EXT. SCHOOL - NEXT DAY   42

    Our three are walking together.

                    WILLOW
            I heard the Vice Principal is
            taking over until they can find a
            replacement.

                    BUFFY
            It's shouldn't be hard to find a
            new principal -- unless they ask
            what happened to the last one.

                                                    (CONTINUED)

                          XANDER
               Okay, but I had nothing to do with
               that, right?

                          BUFFY
               Right.

                          WILLOW
               You only ate the pig.

                          XANDER
               I ate a Pig? Was he cooked and
               called bacon, or...

They shake their heads.

                          XANDER
               Oh my god. Ate a pig. I mean, the
               whole trichinosis issue aside,
               yuck.

                          BUFFY
               Well, it wasn't really you.

                          XANDER
               I remember the field trip, going
               down in the hyena cage... next
               thing this guy's holding Willow
               and he's got a knife.

                          WILLOW
               You saved my life.

                          XANDER
                    (puts his arm around her)
               Hey. Nobody messes with my Willow.

She smiles, a mess of emotion unspoken.

                          BUFFY
               This is definitely the superior
               Xander. Accept no substitutes.

                          XANDER
               I didn't do anything else, did I?
               Around you guys? Anything
               embarrassing?

The girls look at each other.

                          BUFFY
               Nahh.

(CONTINUED)

                         WILLOW
              Nothing at all.

                         BUFFY
                    (to Willow)
              Come on. We're gonna be late.

                         WILLOW
              See you at lunch.

                         XANDER
              Cool. Going Vegetarian.

The girls leave as Giles approaches Xander.

                         GILES
              I've been reading up on my animal
              possession. Doesn't say anything
              anywhere about memory loss
              afterward.

                         XANDER
                    (dropping the facade)
              Did you tell them that?

                         GILES
              Your secret dies with me.

                         XANDER
                    (totally mortified)
              Shoot me, stuff me, mount me.

                                   BLACK OUT.

                    END ACT FOUR